Good Dogs Don't Make It to the South Pole

Good Dogs Don't Make It to the South Pole

A Novel

Hans-Olav Thyvold

Translated from the Norwegian by Marie Ostby

HarperVia

An Imprint of HarperCollinsPublishers

Laurie Anderson: *Heart of a Dog*, Canal Street Communications, 2015. Used with kind permission. All rights reserved. Excerpt on pages 181–182 from *The South Pole* by Roald Amundsen. Letter to the editor from Irene McIntyre Kristensen on page 242, published by *Dagsavisen*.

HarperCollins books may be purchased for educational, business, or sales promotional use. For information, please email the Special Markets Department at SPsales@harpercollins.com.

Originally published as *Snille hunder kommer ikke til Sydpolen* in Norway in 2017 by Aschehoug.

FIRST HARPERCOLLINS PAPERBACK EDITION PUBLISHED IN 2021

Designed by SBI Book Arts, LLC

Library of Congress Cataloging-in-Publication Data is available upon request.

ISBN 978-0-06-298166-0

21 22 23 24 25 LSC 10 9 8 7 6 5 4 3 2 1

Pour Jacqueline

What are days for?
To wake us up.
To put between the endless nights.
What are nights for?
To fall through time
into another world.

—LAURIE ANDERSON

First Bite

1

So **THIS IS DEATH**. The last day of Major Thorkildsen's life. I know that as soon as I set paw into the sickroom. How do I know? The Major is a shadow of himself, he lies wheezing in the sickbed. But that's how he looked yesterday, too, and the day before, and the day before. I don't remember the day before that, or the day before that.

Mrs. Thorkildsen lifts me onto his bed, the way she's done every day for way too long now. The Major likes having me on his bed. That may be why I exist. One time an Afghan hound called me an overgrown lapdog, and that's fine with me. I'd like to know what a shaky daddy longlegs of an Afghan hound has to contribute to the bed of a dying man. Now that the time has come for tenderness and love, being an overgrown lapdog with fur and empathy is the best thing in the world.

I give the Major just the kind of lick from head to toe he's started to love in his old age, but there is no joy left in him, just a foul odor. The smell of the pain that grows inside the Major has been there since long before he got what they call "sick" and they came to get him, but now the room is filled with the smell in all its nuances. The bitterness of death. The sweetness of death.

> Always the same, always the same, your bum's behind you
> whichever way you aim.

The Major taught me that rhyme, but I had to test it out in practice before accepting it as truth. I chased down my tail with great power and endurance, and was always *so* close to catching that bastard, but at last I resigned myself to the truth:

Your bum *is* behind you whichever way you aim.

Mrs. Thorkildsen is asleep. I was afraid she'd be the first one to go if she didn't get some rest, but she has to wake up now if she's going to catch the Major's last hours on Earth, which I don't want her to miss.

The simplest thing would have been to wake her by barking, but I don't want to make noise here. I've had a genteel upbringing and can't shake the fear of being thrown out. No idea where that fear comes from, since I can't remember ever being thrown out of any place, but that's the way anxiety works—it doesn't need proof in order to blossom.

I stride across the Major's feet, sneak down from the bed, and pitter-patter across the floor to Mrs. Thorkildsen's chair. I nudge her leg, carefully, so she won't be startled, but of course she is. She's befuddled as she always is when suddenly awoken, but still jumps to her feet in what would be a tiger's leap if she had the strength. It's still quick enough that it startles me.

Mrs. Thorkildsen lays a hand on the Major's forehead. Cranes her neck and rests her ear against his mouth. Holds her breath. For a long time. Mrs. Thorkildsen looks at me. For a long time.

"Do you have to go out?" she asks.

Really? I'd be pushing my paws against the door, scratching and whimpering. Doesn't she know me better after all these years? She's both smart and well-read, the missus, but sometimes she's just so slow to get what I mean. Maybe it's because of my nature. I'm a one-man dog, and I've never tried to hide it. On the contrary. Mrs. Thorkildsen has fed and bathed me, groomed and walked me ever since the day the Major picked me up—no, even before that—but I am and will always be the Major's dog until the day he dies. It occurs to me that I haven't given a second thought to the question of what happens to Mrs. Thorkildsen and me when the day of death has passed and I'm a widower dog. Cross that bridge when you come to it. That's a good rule. Set mealtimes, however, that's a dumb rule.

Mrs. Thorkildsen softly mumbles to her husband as she moistens his mouth with a little sponge, speaks in low tones with her mild, singsongy voice, the one that contrasted with the Major's gruff words so well as they sat at home in the dark, each with their own dragon water, and hummed songs to which they'd forgotten the words. And then talked about all the weird things they'd done together. About treacherous great-aunts and Nubian kings. About the war there was and the war to come. Sometimes they talked about things they should have done. And then there were many things, done and undone, that they never talked about.

When she's done dabbing, Mrs. Thorkildsen stands still, gazing at her husband, who looks to be sleeping peacefully, but on the inside is fighting with all his last strength to die. It's not as easy as it once was.

Something must have sparked a decision in Mrs. Thorkildsen's little white head. With a clumsy heaving effort, she climbs onto the Major's giant metal bed. She almost has to squeeze herself in between the bed frame and his still-giant body, and then she falls to rest on his arm, just like I usually do.

The room grows quiet again, and I don't know what to do with myself. The bed is a little too high, I can't get up there without Mrs. Thorkildsen's help, and seeing as she has already struggled her way onto the bed, I suppose I can't really hope that she'll climb back off to lift me up and then finagle herself back into position. I remain standing on the floor and weigh my options:

> *Option A: Whining* is out of the question due to my
> aforementioned ejection phobia.
> *Option B: Restless pacing* back and forth across the floor. It can't
> hurt; then again, it probably won't help either.
> *Option C: Sit stiffly at attention*, like one of those sweet spaniels
> grieving at the grave of their long-since-deceased owner. "Fido
> sat by the gravestone for nine years." So? Couldn't Fido have
> shot himself instead and joined Dad in the great beyond?
> But then there was that damned opposable thumbs problem.
> Someone needs to build a handgun for dogs. There's a market
> there.

Mrs. Thorkildsen must know that the Major is leaving us tonight, too, but she talks to him as if this is just another day on his journey back home. When he gets there, they'll sit together with a nice glass and watch day glide into night. Light a few candles. Play a little Haydn. Build a fire in the fireplace. Talk softly and tenderly. That'll be nice.

Mrs. Thorkildsen can say whatever she wants, but I'm afraid it's too late. That part of the body she's pressing herself against tonight is about to shut off. The Major's in there somewhere, a mechanic systematically strolling around, flipping off one switch after the other, closing pipes and turning off lights. The little mechanic smells like liquor and wretchedness, and that's exactly how he wants to smell.

"I hope I don't have to tell you that I love you . . ."

Mrs. Thorkildsen's words are so obvious that they almost cover the shock that she's uttering them at all. I've never heard Mrs. Thorkildsen say anything of the sort!

The Major lets out three loud sobs. He's here, and although Mrs. Thorkildsen can't hear it, I can hear him calling me. Only the mothers of wolves know where I'm summoning my strength from, but with a giant leap I'm back on the bed. I slink in between the wall and the Major and find *my* spot with my nose nudged into his hand, which, through sickness and death, still smells of ocean and phosphorus. I'm not afraid anymore.

He stops breathing right before his heart stops beating. A dead heat. The last thing he does is emit a sound he's never made before. The sound of his voice trying to sneak out before the mechanic grabs it, too.

• • •

He's gone.

It takes a little while before Mrs. Thorkildsen realizes it's happened. I don't know if she'd dozed off, but she's wide awake now. She says his name. Hand on his forehead, ear against his mouth, holding her breath.

The central heating whistles. Then Mrs. Thorkildsen starts sobbing softly, and I'm back at it with the nose again. It takes a little while and three nudges before she senses me. She sniffles and puts her bony hand on my neck. She's a decent scratcher; she lacks the Major's perfectly measured solid grip, but she has nails to make up for it. That takes her far. She looks at me awhile before saying: "Well, Tassen, I guess it's just you and me now."

Then we go to sleep, all three of us.

2

I WAS BORN IN THE COUNTRYSIDE. The barn smell has disappeared over the years, but I'm a farm dog at heart. Six in my litter. Late in the spring. I never knew my father, but I don't think we should put too much stock in that. I'm a little suspicious of psychology. At least for dogs.

The siblings I grew up with disappeared one by one, and I would have, too, if I hadn't been born this way.

The wrong color.

My life turned out the way it did because my face is a different color than what's considered "right." And it doesn't take much. In my case, the top of my snout is the only part of me covered with white instead of black fur. One white spot on my nose, and I became a second-rate animal, useless as a show dog, less than. The one left over when the rest of the litter is sold.

An outcast.

Of course, I didn't understand any of this then. Like most puppies, I was happy every time a competitor disappeared from the trough. Those were good days, and they only got better through a summer so long and full of impressions for all the senses that when the first snow fell, it felt like the first time.

With the new snow came a new life, or several new lives, in the form of new siblings. Don't ask me who the father of this batch was, but from the day they were born, they were the bane of my existence. Mother, who had grown more and more distant over the past few months, now became directly hostile toward me. You don't know how it feels to be growled and snapped at by your own mother until you experience it yourself.

I went from a blessed only-child existence to being the pariah in my litter overnight. "Pariah" is too mild. I wasn't even part of the litter. My brother and sisters were nice enough, and they smelled good, but my relationship with Mother was never the same again. I think that's taken its toll on me, but, like I said, we'll steer clear of Freud. Pavlov, too, for that matter.

From morning to night, people of all ages, shapes, and sizes came stomping through the house, all with the same goal: to see the puppies! It was that time again, and it gave me hope that we might get back to a state of peace and quiet, if only we could get rid of the little brats. I could always forgive or, worst case, avoid Mother's growling and barking.

Despite the wide range of types and ages, the people who came by almost all reacted in the exact same way. Their voices grew soft, their heartbeats calmed down, their blood smelled sweeter. They all sang variations on the same tune, and they were all there to find a favorite. To pick a dog. The only comparison is walking into an orphanage and buying the kid who strikes your fancy.

People who compare having dogs to having kids have it all wrong. Only a few people see their dog at birth (sadly!), and even fewer take their own offspring to be put to sleep as the endpoint of a loving life together. And while your child will hopefully grow apart from you after a few years and get the hell away from you and your personal crazy, a dog stays with you their whole life, a life in which you at last become God almighty himself:

Should I let my dog live, or should I let my dog die?

It was during this second tasteless beauty pageant that I really became aware of my flaws. For no one even glanced at me until they'd had their fill gazing at the little puppy faces, and when they spotted me, they all asked the same question:

Why is that one so big? they asked, and then came the same bigoted reply about the white spot on my nose. The jig was up, but even without a white spot on my snout, I would have been no match for the four tiny creatures who hadn't yet figured out that their tails *were* behind them and that life was full of scary twists and turns.

is what most people said when they saw the puppies, and I never could figure out what they really meant by that. They pinched and they petted and they scratched until it was impossible to say who was dizzier, them or the puppies. Kids and adults, women and men, they let themselves be hypnotized one by one. I got scratched and complimented, too. When it rains it pours on all dogs, as they say, but I, a dog in the prime of my youth, still felt like an old elephant.

When I pictured a life in the hands of the nasty kids who stopped by, a chill ran down my spine and all the way to the tip of my tail. You can't give a dog to an untrained child. There were a few little girls who didn't even want a dog, they wanted a rabbit (!), but Mother and Father had decided that they *would* be getting a dog. A wise choice, but what would it do to a poor dog to grow up as a rabbit substitute?

Still, I'm glad I got to see this meat-and-fur market, and even gladder to escape it thanks to my white spot and my advanced age. I had no idea what a "dog show" was, but the words were a punch in the gut whenever I heard them. To me it wasn't just okay, it was liberating to know that I wasn't made for dog shows, although I was curious about what they actually entailed. I cultivated some unhealthy fantasies around that term, yes.

When it was my litter being shown at auction, I'd been too young and dumb to see just how cynically the selection and sale of puppies was organized. I had to grin—sarcastically—at the fortune in my misfortune. I had, it turns out, a perfectly wonderful dog's life, thanks to the fact that, despite tens of thousands of years of living with dogs, people still hadn't understood the meaning of the first commandment, point 1.1 in the user's manual: "A dog's bark is worse than its bite."

• • •

He stood out from all the others who had stopped by to rejoice over the furballs as soon as he entered the room. He was the only one who came alone. And he was the oldest. And the largest. When he stepped across the threshold, the room became his, his rules were the ones that mattered now. An old alpha who roamed around alone, hard to know what to make of that, but in my situation any news felt like bad news.

He was the only one who showed no sentimentality when he met our little flock. Without a single

he pointed straight at me and asked:

"What's wrong with that one?"

Once again, I was forced to hear my own inferiority stated and explained. I had no desire to leave, but I didn't want to be humiliated either. The big alpha didn't finish listening to the answer, but interrupted:

"Half price. Cash." And that's how the Major became my owner.

It all happened so fast that I had no idea what was happening until I, for the first time in my life, found myself in a car. At first, I thought it was not the car, but the landscape around us that was moving, which turned the trip into a nightmare. No matter where I positioned myself, I was being pulled in all directions by invisible forces until I couldn't tell up from down. Neither did my stomach. It all came up. Normally I would have wolfed down such a delicacy, but I just felt awful and lay there in my own vomit until we arrived and, without realizing it, I was home.

· · ·

Sickly and weak as I was, I didn't absorb a lot that first evening, or it might just be the familiar erasing the memory of the unfamiliar. But I've heard the story told many times of how one day, with no agreement or warning, the Major came home with a stinky puppy to a Mrs. Thorkildsen, who had already started dreading the Major's death, long before he got sick. Of how I was hosed down in the tub, wrapped in an old bathrobe, and photographed. Mrs. Thorkildsen delights in showing off that mortifying picture, even to complete strangers.

The reason I still enjoy listening to the story is that Mrs. Thorkildsen, after explaining how *she* didn't want a dog at all, always rounds it off by declaring:

"The Major knew what he was doing when he brought us Tassen!"

And when she says that, I feel like my dignity is close to being regained. Dignity is important to us dogs, although it may be hard to spot when we're rooting through the garbage or scratching our ass with the carpet.

As everyone knows, dog training is no exact science. The Major didn't believe in the old stick-and-carrot idea. More like a stick and little chunks of meat. Not to say that he beat me. That wasn't required. His grip on the scruff of my neck told me everything I needed to know about his strength. And his strength was my strength. No one messed with Major Thorkildsen's dog.

· · ·

The Major had been home a lot since he got so weak he had to go to the sick house, where they didn't allow dogs, but he rarely spent the night with us. The last time that happened, they came to get him in the middle of the night. So, in a way, we've had plenty of time to get used to the thought of it being just the two of us, Mrs. Thorkildsen and me. Still, something is different now. Mrs. Thorkildsen sits in her usual chair by the window, while I, since it's no longer forbidden, curl up in the Major's cowhide chair, a *major no-no* while he still lived with us. We've sat like this so many nights, just the two of us, that we thought we'd gotten the hang of it, but as it turns out the finish line has become a starting line. There was life after death, after all.

The Major's breath was always more like mustard gas than roses, but one day, there was a tiny, distant hint of something else, too. It grew into a nearly invisible yellow aroma that seeped into the room not only through his mouth, but through the pores in his skin as he sat there reading a book about the war. The Major, you see, read all the books about the war. Mrs. Thorkildsen read all the other books; that was the division of labor.

Mrs. Thorkildsen didn't become a librarian until she was an adult, but it seemed to be an inborn disorder. The signs were there early on. As a child, she owned two large books covered in deerskin (which I've later verified by independent sniffing), full of fantastical stories she never tired of listening to. And she had to listen, because she didn't know how to read.

With a book under one arm and a short stool under the other, she went out into the world. She asked every single person she met on the street: "Will you read to me?"

"People were poor," Mrs. Thorkildsen says whenever she tells that story, and she sometimes does, since it was one of the Major's favorite stories. At least according to Mrs. Thorkildsen. I'm not so sure of that; I would have liked to consult with the Major on that issue before drawing any conclusions.

"People were poor," Mrs. Thorkildsen says, "but everyone knew how to read."

I don't think we were poor, but we sure did read, the Major, Mrs. Thorkildsen, and I. I'm saying "I," although technically speaking I didn't read. Dogs can't read, you see. But sometimes, in short paragraphs and turns of phrase, while curled up in the corner of the couch in a haze of meatballs and sauce, I could dimly sense the Major's war books as they silently seeped into his head. Once inside, they turned into noise, clamor, images, smells, fear, and chaos. He sat perfectly still for hours in that cowhide chair, and you couldn't tell by looking at him what was happening. While Mrs. Thorkildsen both laughs and cries while she reads, the Major's reading was silent and deep, with the same steady heartbeat, the same even sigh from his nostrils, page after page, book after book. He read with such intensity that I doubt there was much left over for the next reader in the books he devoured. Sometimes he'd stop reading to mention or read aloud something from the book he was holding. This is how Mrs. Thorkildsen had some sense of where in the war he currently was. It was a big war he was dealing with, you see, not a simple dogfight.

• • •

We hunted together, the three of us. We drove to the hunting grounds, where I always stayed back and protected the car while the two of them handled the actual hunting. It was hell. A French friend of Mrs. Thorkildsen's once said hell was other people. I'd say that depends on the people. Hell is waiting alone in a car. Standing guard over a car while people are walking by in all directions is a near-impossible task for one dog, so there was a lot of barking to be on the safe side. And I was worried about how the hunt would go. You see, it wasn't small prey the Major and Mrs. Thorkildsen were up against. They returned to the car weighed down with oxen and birds, deer and swine, and on top of it all they'd also gathered everything they might need in terms of fruit, mushrooms, herbs, and vegetables. They could have that to themselves. They had good luck as fishermen, too, which was good, since dogs can't fish, and I love fish. If I were human, I'd sit on the dock and pull in stockfish all day long.

I can't remember us ever coming back from a hunt empty-handed. Never an empty bowl of food. At night, after they'd eaten a long dinner where you never knew what might fall on the floor, the Major and Mrs. Thorkildsen sat in front of the big windows in the dark and sipped dragon water as they talked late into the night.

There won't be any more of those long, comforting nights, but we'll have to get food somehow. The thought concerns me, I have to admit. Mrs. Thorkildsen had usually accompanied the Major when he went hunting, and for all I know, she is just as good a hunter as he was, but after seeing her come across a rat in the cellar, I genuinely doubt whether she'll be able to feed us. It's true that the Major, as he liked to point out, had filled the cellar with a year's supply of food and drink, but what will happen at the end of the year if Mrs. Thorkildsen can't bring herself to go hunting alone? I am worried, and a worried dog can easily become a sad dog. And what use is a sad dog?

So the surprise is even bigger and happier when Mrs. Thorkildsen, after her very first solo hunting trip, returns to the car (where I am overjoyed just to see her again) with fish and birds and the dog treats that come in a yellow bag with a picture of a sufficiently smarmy-looking Jack Russell terrier, but still taste heavenly and have just the right consistency.

The last stop of the day is the best one, since I get to go, too. It is so unexpected that I hesitate slightly when Mrs. Thorkildsen, after climbing out of the car, says: "Come on."

Those two words can be so beautiful.

I'm smart enough to realize when it's best to go on foot, and this is one of those instances. Mrs. Thorkildsen leads me through the crowd of people with a steady hand, and her sturdiness makes me feel safe.

A smell that is both familiar and strange tickles my nostrils. Mrs. Thorkildsen leads us in the direction of that smell, to the innermost corner of the room. There is a cavern into which I follow Mrs. Thorkildsen, and it isn't long before I realize where we are: in the dragon's cave.

"We should probably get a cart," Mrs. Thorkildsen says.

And that's how it is. With me shuffling along behind her on the leash, Mrs. Thorkildsen moves slowly but deliberately through the premises while pulling one bottle after another off the shelves. She puts some of them back, but most of them end up in the cart. When the cart is full, she heads for the exit, and I am excited to get back to the car and go home, where there will probably be a treat in store after such an expedition. But it isn't that easy.

First, Mrs. Thorkildsen has to remove everything from the cart and give it to the man behind the counter. He strokes the bottles one by one while Mrs. Thorkildsen explains that she is having guests over since her husband is dead and there is going to be a memorial. That seems to be reason enough. The man behind the counter says he is sorry to hear that, and Mrs. Thorkildsen gets all her bottles back. Now for the next problem. It arises after Mrs. Thorkildsen puts her bottles into plastic bags. There are simply too many bags for her to carry alone.

"How on earth am I going to get all this to the car?" she says. And I want to say that she could forget about it, she doesn't have a chance in hell, she should just grab whatever she can carry and we'll hightail it out of there, but then a burly, bearded young man offers to help. Mrs. Thorkildsen doesn't have to carry anything at all—the man takes all her bags and we walk to the car while she tells as much of her life story as time allows, and a little bit about me. Mrs. Thorkildsen can't thank him enough—she would have loved to keep talking, but the man surely has a life to get back to.

3

MRS. THORKILDSEN'S NOT EATING. Instead of cooking for herself after serving me a late breakfast, she pours herself a glass of dragon water, something I don't think I've ever seen her do this early in the day. But what do I know? That might be normal when your husband dies. She doesn't drink it. Not yet. Just stays there sitting on the kitchen stool, turning the glass around in circles.

Mrs. Thorkildsen looks at me, and I look at Mrs. Thorkildsen, and maybe we're thinking the same thing:

Which one of us will go first?

I'm six years old.

Mrs. Thorkildsen is seventy-five.

Most dogs don't have a very good understanding of numbers; almost don't have any idea about numbers at all, I'd say. Numbers don't have much use for dogs other than for counting, and here's all the counting the average dog needs:

Me.

Me and you.

Pack.

A pack can be "small" or "big," of course. It's all relative, as we know. I can see how a number could be "small" or "big." But that's as far as I get. There's nothing about "sixty-five" that tells me whether it's a "small" or "big" number. Sure, I know that five mosquitoes is more than four elephants. So: "sixty-five" is probably more than "sixty-four." Okay, I'm pretty sure. Even if we convert from elephants to chickens, multiply by herrings, and divide by polar bears. But just because I know that much, one shouldn't assume that most dogs do. Ask a Gordon setter, for example—that is, if you can get him to stop licking his balls for a moment—whether one plus one is two, and the answer you'll get is starling, starling, and more starling. I'm not being prejudiced. Gordon setters just aren't smart. It's a simple fact.

As for me, I'm an above-average smart dog. *Playful, intelligent, and eager to learn,* as a matter of fact, I've seen it in print. And I have to agree. Intelligent. At least according to human criteria. Sure, it doesn't take a whole lot for a dog to seem intelligent to human eyes. If you master both *Sit!* and *Shake!* you're well on your way to being declared a genius. I can't deny that I like low expectations. I exploit them shamelessly.

So my human friends see me as top dog. But as a dog among dogs, my ranking is slightly lower. Significantly lower, in fact. One hundred and eighty-six, maybe. Or fifteen. Or maybe a little of both. A kind of cross between one hundred and eighty-six and fifteen.

As a dog, I come up short in almost every way. Strength, size, instinct, sense of smell, aggressiveness: I score so low in all these categories that in a world run by dogs I probably wouldn't even be coupled—that is, if I were to survive the puppy stage against all odds. There's a reason most animals give birth to multiple kids at a time, and that's the fact that they sometimes end up with the likes of me. We traditionally end up as fox feed long before our testicles have descended.

In short, it's purely thanks to human intervention that I get food, a roof over my head, belly rubs, warmth, and love. Yes, love. I need a lot of love, I have no problem admitting that. I give a lot of love, too. Especially when you need it. I'm a companion dog. An oversized lapdog who could stand to lose a few pounds, but how is that supposed to happen when the treats come as close together as they do in Mrs. Thorkildsen's home?

Still, like every other dog on Earth, I'm a wolf. Somewhere deep inside, I'm still carrying all the information I need as a wolf, hidden behind memories of every single genetic link from there to here.

A wolf on paper.

At least that's something.

Simply put, a dog's memory has about the same shape as the universe. That is, something like an hourglass, or the opposite. All dogs are like this. Whether you open up the memory bank of a Chihuahua or a Bernese mountain dog, you'll see about the same thing on a different scale, though of course memories smell different for each individual.

Many of the recollections we carry around are inherited, along with the mystical instincts that aren't so mystical when it comes down to it. At the risk of sounding like a briard who's sniffed a few too many socks:

It's all one continuous stream of consciousness. In its most basic shape, it takes the form of the border collie, a dog who needs no training to do as humans wish. All you have to do is insert the batteries, and he's up and running. And running. And running. But is he happy? You can philosophize over that next time you run into an example of the species with a tennis ball in his mouth and super-alert eyes. A wolf who herds sheep instead of eating them—is that a wolf you can trust in the long run?

Many, even most, of the words of wisdom I was given as a child have turned out to be truths with sometimes *major* modifications, unless they were completely false. "Eat shit to avoid stomach issues!" for instance. Probably great advice for another time and another place, but in densely populated areas, you just can't get away with it anymore. They bust you based on your breath, if you don't cheerfully come home with poop in your mustache, that is. And they have an incredibly strong reaction. The same dog poop they pick up off the street in black plastic bags, which they carefully tie closed and deposit in the nearest dog poop receptacle, suddenly becomes reason for loud, agitated disgust.

"Oh, for fuck's sake!" they yell. Some of them hit you, and that's another subject, but what's even worse is that afterward, after you've been humiliated under the garden hose and slowly wag your way back toward the company, you find out you've dropped down a rung on the ladder. There aren't any new individuals in the pack who have challenged you and pushed you down, you just aren't quite as high up as you were before. It's a kick in the balls to your aspirations. You're at the bottom of the ladder, but perfectly content and full of ambition about climbing, who knows, maybe all the way to the top, until one day, through one unlucky event or another, with or without poop in your mustache, it becomes crystal clear that just above you on the ladder is a leap that seems impossibly large. A gap between you and the rest of the pack that will never close. "Eat shit!" are wise words that have lost their wisdom around these parts, leaving just the words. And, as we all know, words can't always be trusted.

4

THEY APPEAR AT THE DOOR after the Major's death, three humans I can't recall having met before, but it takes me just a few sniffs to ascertain who we are dealing with.

The man is Mrs. Thorkildsen's puppy, the woman is his bitch, and the boy puppy is their shared offspring.

The visit is obviously a surprise, and it puts Mrs. Thorkildsen in a mood whose scent I have never caught before. You don't even need a sense of smell to perceive it. Her soft voice gets stiff and her movements are jerky.

They are there to help, the Bitch says, and Mrs. Thorkildsen gives her a hug that makes her uncomfortable and makes me suspicious as a result.

I don't think Mrs. Thorkildsen appreciates the visit very much. Like I said, there is something in her voice. That, and the fact she suddenly develops the bad habit of going to bed early.

Unlike the Major and Mrs. Thorkildsen, the Puppy and the Bitch mostly talk about things in the future. Things that need to be done, as they call them. Life can't just be lived, it has to be planned and managed. "When?" When do we have to be at the funeral home? When are we going to empty out the garage? When are we going to church? When are you coming to visit? When is dinner?

It is unsettling to watch the interaction between the Bitch and Mrs. Thorkildsen. The Bitch is both friendly and eager, maybe a little too much of both. She wants Mrs. Thorkildsen to like her so badly, but Mrs. Thorkildsen, whom I'd describe as a thoroughly friendly and approachable woman up to this point, is having none of it. Like an old Labrador sick of food, she ignores the Bitch. The comparison isn't really a metaphor. Mrs. Thorkildsen's disciplining techniques are by and large the same ones an older bitch would use on a younger one. And the result is the same: the Bitch grows more and more uncertain and clumsy in her eagerness.

· · ·

The funeral is a disappointment as far as I am concerned, but I only have my own expectations to blame for that. It might just be the word "funeral" that fools me. Keeping in mind that we dogs are known for burying things, mostly dead things, I suppose I imagined I'd have a role in the proceedings, but that isn't to be. Mrs. Thorkildsen obviously intends to dig on her own.

"You'll stay here," she says without a trace of emotion as she shuts the front door and leaves for the Major's funeral. And that's that.

A few days later, the little pack vanishes again. I remember the exact day because of a person who would come to play a not insignificant role in our future, an important man in Mrs. Thorkildsen's life after her husband passed:

"Remember, the cable guy will be here on Thursday," is the last thing the Puppy tells his mother as he leaves.

"I don't want no cable guy," Mrs. Thorkildsen says.

. . .

I don't have any desire for a cable guy either, but the cable guy comes, and just as the Puppy predicted, he comes on Thursday. He is a pleasant man, too. Young and hairy and not without a certain penchant for dogs. A skilled neck scratcher, and that'll do it. Mrs. Thorkildsen serves up coffee and cinnamon rolls, although the young man politely declines. He drinks the coffee anyway, and as he bites into the first cinnamon roll—just to be polite, mostly to stop the old lady's nagging—he is sold. Of course, Mrs. Thorkildsen knew he would be, not that I think she had any ulterior motives. At any rate, the cable guy ends up in a deep cinnamon roll haze, and despite Mrs. Thorkildsen's mild protestations that she needs only one TV channel, he sets her up with dozens. The cable guy is sent off with a bag of cinnamon rolls, and the whole thing is lovely, but after he leaves, Mrs. Thorkildsen asks me:

"What on earth am I going to do with all these channels?" and I have to admit I have no answer.

. . .

The big change comes in small steps. Mrs. Thorkildsen discovers that she prefers to watch TV in the late morning, and that becomes the norm.

And just like she'd had a regular time when she sat down to watch the news with the Major, she now has a set time before lunch when she sits down to watch a program I can't make much sense of, which obviously gives her great pleasure. The program mostly consists of people talking and saying things I can't understand. Old people, young people, men and women, they meet every day to talk and scream and cry over one another while Mrs. Thorkildsen watches.

Neither Dr. Pill nor his patients speak a language known to me. Like all dogs, I only speak Norwegian, so I don't understand a peep of what's going on. Mrs. Thorkildsen is kind enough to always translate what the program is about that day. And it's hefty stuff. Actually, a pretty appalling parade of uniquely human problems:

> *"Was it child abuse or was it an accident?"*
> *"Why is my mother pretending she has cancer?"*
> *"My twenty-one-year-old daughter is infatuated with her*
> *   controlling, jealous, heroin addict boyfriend."*
> *"Should I divorce my sick wife?"*
> *"My husband hit me with a wooden spoon—and now he wants me*
> *   to apologize!"*

Closely followed by:

> *"I hit my wife with a wooden spoon—and she should be sorry!"*

Each day brings new calamities, and new humans crying and moaning, people acting in ways I've never seen anyone behave in Mrs. Thorkildsen's home, and which I can't imagine Mrs. Thorkildsen accepting. Still, it seems to be doing Mrs. Thorkildsen good.

"Come on, Tassen, let's go watch Dr. Pill," Mrs. Thorkildsen says. I trundle out after her to the living room, where she arranges herself in front of the TV. The music chimes in. Mrs. Thorkildsen tells me what today's program is about, and then I don't hear from her again until it's over and the TV is turned off.

"Oh, dear," she usually says when it's over. Usually no more than that, but sometimes she delivers longer, head-shaking commentaries, with the same conclusion as her comments on the news. It's all going to hell.

· · ·

Mrs. Thorkildsen's own family and emotional life is probably much less dramatic than what we see unfold on Dr. Pill's show. The people she talks to on the phone have their problems, too, but those problems mostly revolve around getting old. Hearts that don't want to beat, hip bones that break, and kids who don't come to visit. No violence, no ruinous passions, no drug abuse, just boring problems of the type you watch TV to forget. But it's good to be able to complain a little, even when you don't have much to complain about, so Mrs. Thorkildsen stretches the truth and says no one ever comes to visit her either. Which isn't true, first of all, and, second, I think she's mostly saying it to make the other person feel better.

The Puppy actually comes by quite often; he mostly talks numbers and then he leaves. He might grab a cup of coffee if he has time, but he rarely does. One day he suddenly appears in the living room and wants to take me in the car with him. To my surprise, Mrs. Thorkildsen has no problem with that.

I was confused, and honestly a little frightened when we drove off. The Puppy and me. It was a little scary that Mrs. Thorkildsen wasn't coming along on the trip. It was the only time I'd been away from her since the Major died. And it didn't make me any calmer that I could clearly pick up the scent of guns.

A weapon in the car changes, if not everything, a lot of things. Were we going to war now? Hunting? Or were we out on some other errand? I was nervous, had an unsettling sense of impending catastrophe, but as we kept driving, I understood that something literally huge was about to happen. The Puppy had the window on his side of the car open, and a whole world of smells poured in, all at once. There was no use trying to pick up one scent; all I could do was open my nostrils and let it seep through.

When it dawned on me that, for the first time in my life, I wasn't going to stay in the car but would be participating in the hunt itself, I'm ashamed to say that I went a little off the rails. Mrs. Thorkildsen has brought me to many places I, with my simple mind, assumed were the woods. I mean: grass. Trees. It's the same concept, but this was something else altogether. An infinity of trees and plants and smells and sounds. There was life everywhere—a scampering, crunching, aromatic orchestra of small animals, and I was the only dog there. My woods.

I'd never heard a weapon fired before, although the Major kept an arsenal of weapons at home his whole life, hidden in the strangest places around the house, from the pistol in the sock drawer in the hall to the double-barrel pump-action shotgun under the bed he slept in. I never saw him use any of them.

When the first shot went off, I almost pissed myself in sheer terror.

I'd never heard anything like it. I jumped and cowered in the moss, but before the echo had finished resonating through the woods, the bang was imprinted on me like our tribe's invincible roar, and by the second shot I was looking forward to the third.

So I went hunting in the woods and Mrs. Thorkildsen's puppy went hunting in the woods; we both pissed here and there to mark our territory, and it was a great day, until I bounded up a hill with the Puppy hopelessly far behind me. I was over the crest of the hill before he even saw what was happening. The Puppy started screaming and shouting in a voice that may have been powerful within four walls, but sounded feeble and weak out here among the trees. There was no way to hear his cries through the smell that saturated the air more and more. I'm usually almost impossible to control when I meet a new, exciting smell, and this was a smell more exciting and complex than anything I had ever smelled in my whole life.

Then the alarm bells went off in my tiny dog brain. The exciting, euphoric mood was shot through with an arrow of anxiety. An arrow of smell. The scent came from a spot in the moss right in front of me, but the impulse to follow it was quickly choked off. I hesitated to put my snout up to it; suddenly it seemed more appropriate to pull back a little, since the message was more than clear enough from where I stood:

Fear!

A smell that left an impression, the smell of a being that barely knows what fear is, and claims its space accordingly. That's what most of us try to assert every time we lift a paw, but most of us aren't even fooling ourselves. When, after sniffing the puddle a grumpy AmStaff has left behind in the park, I lift my leg and micturate contemptibly, I have no illusions of being able to defend the territory later in an open battle with said AmStaff.

So, yes, I've sniffed up the message of fear over a long life with many lampposts along the way, but none of the smells have ever truly scared me. Fear is what I fear most of all, but I didn't know that fear was a feeling that, boiled down to its innermost essence, smells of wolf.

I've heard of the wolf, but never really absorbed the fact that he exists. There are a lot of dogs in the city who think the wolf is just an urban legend, and barely even that. I can see where they're coming from, especially if they're hunting dogs. I was eager to believe that the wolf existed, I just wasn't prepared for what I'd feel the day I really sensed his presence. That was the day I understood what lay behind an expression that had been meaningless in my life so far: "ignorance is bliss."

The scent rose up from a giant stone, still wet. I approached it slowly, and as with each step I drew closer, the smell changed and the world changed with it. Here were battle cries and mysteries and stories that won't die. The bloodthirsty will to defend one's territory to the last breath and the indomitable will to survive. The meaning behind the moon. How to kill a snake. Forests of wisdom. Forests of fear.

I could have spent the rest of my life smelling that stone, and I probably would have, had the Puppy not suddenly appeared and grabbed my collar with an invective I won't repeat here, before giving me a smack on the nose so hard, stars and moons danced in front of my eyes. The hunt was over.

That was the end of perhaps the best dog experience in my not particularly sinful dog's life, with my tail raised high and a powerful new scent seared in my memory. I vomited in the car for the first time since

I was a young dog, and got another smack on the mouth for that, too, but it didn't matter. When we got home, the temptations were rinsed off with the garden hose until I smelled pretty boring again, but the scent of wolf was lodged inside me for good. The scent of wolf is simultaneously the most inspiring and the most humiliating thing I've ever experienced.

• • •

The Puppy was disappointed that we returned from the hunt with no bounty, and he didn't try to hide it. Mrs. Thorkildsen consoled him with a few cinnamon rolls and a cup of coffee. The Puppy called me a useless hunter, but I knew better. I know I have it in me, but I also can't stop thinking about a new, frightening suspicion:

Maybe Mrs. Thorkildsen isn't a killing machine after all.

It strikes me as odd that the Puppy, a strong, relatively young man with a weapon, can't manage to whack the slightest little treat, while old, unarmed Mrs. Thorkildsen can fell more large game than she can carry home on her own. The more I mull it over, the more restless I become: perhaps Mrs. Thorkildsen is feeding us not by her own hunting and killing, but by gathering what's left after the real predators have had their fill. Mrs. Thorkildsen, I fear, might be nothing but a simple scavenger.

So, truth be told, my respect for Mrs. Thorkildsen should have ended there once and for all. If it had ever occurred to me to challenge Mrs. Thorkildsen's role as leader of our little pack, maybe I would have succeeded. I may not be large, but I can bare my teeth and growl from the bottom of my throat when I need to (and size is irrelevant anyway, since Mrs. Thorkildsen's fear of rats speaks for itself). One leap onto Mrs. Thorkildsen's breakfast table—standing there alert, growling in her face and baring my teeth—I don't think Mrs. Thorkildsen would have taken up the fight, not without a weapon.

On the other hand, I can say with a fair amount of confidence that I'll do no such thing. It's a nice creature comfort, of course, to have your food served on a plate every day and not have to worry about a somewhat safe place to sleep. It not only satiates and nourishes you, but gives you a peace of mind that frees your thoughts to ponder other questions. Simply put, you have time to philosophize. To be fair, philosophizing isn't good for all dogs. You can see some of them in the park, plodding along without jerking the leash even the slightest bit tighter, weighed down by the mournful history and fate of all dogs, though they seem to have absented themselves from their own kind.

5

MRS. THORKILDSEN HAS STOPPED DRIVING. I don't know why, or the reason she chose this particular moment, now that we are finally finding a rhythm and shape to our new existence. Maybe she remembered her own words from the time she tried to convince the Major that *he* had grown too old and decrepit to drive a car. I remember it well, anyway, not for the words that were said but for the reaction they provoked in the Major. In fact, I had barely bothered to listen to the conversation before becoming aware of a sharp odor that emanated from the Major as soon as Mrs. Thorkildsen mentioned the word "driving" one night as they sat there talking as usual.

She started the way she usually does when she has something important to say, by referring to an actual event that occurred among their family or friends. There were plenty of those to choose from. There was always a recently widowed cousin, a nephew with jungle fever, or a second cousin's spouse who slumped dead over the steering wheel after two straight days of shoveling snow with his tractor.

The story, which she pretended was about an old fogy who fell down some stairs and almost met his untimely end, laid the groundwork for Mrs. Thorkildsen's expression of concern for the Major and *his* health. She knew him well enough to know that this would have no effect on him whatsoever, but she also knew these arguments were just a step along the way to her real mission: to make him terrified every time we were out driving a car.

• • •

Even a pug with a poor sense of smell would have sensed Mrs. Thorkildsen's growing unrest as our next hunting trip drew nearer. The second she slid into the passenger seat and buckled herself securely in with straps (while I had to hang on to the best of my ability), her voice turned dry and sharp. Her breath grew uneven and the tempo of her heartbeat shot up and down. Every time we approached an intersection, she held her breath until we had cleared it, or she let go of a tiny, barely audible whimper.

Finally, the Major stopped driving his car. Not by calling it quits and handing over his keys once and for all, but more and more often it was Mrs. Thorkildsen who sat behind the wheel when we went out hunting, and as these things usually go, it didn't take long before it felt like it had always been this way. When the Major sat behind the wheel, it was Mrs. Thorkildsen who dominated the conversation and gave directions. The Major's responses grew short when he drove, and Mrs. Thorkildsen filled the space. Now the roles were reversed.

The car has been replaced by a wheelie bag Mrs. Thorkildsen brought up from the basement, a scary blue wheelie bag she pulls behind her with one hand when we go out for a walk. She holds my leash in her other hand, and unfortunately, Mrs. Thorkildsen only has two hands. She's found a poor solution to the problem by sometimes tying my leash to the wheelie bag. I don't like this, as it looks like Mrs. Thorkildsen is walking the wheelie bag while the wheelie bag walks me. A sled dog team in reverse, with the human in front and the dog in the back. This is not how it's supposed to be. It's a matter of dignity.

• • •

The wheelie bag is just big enough for Mrs. Thorkildsen. We no longer need help from strangers when we go pick up dragon water. After explaining to the man behind the counter what she needs this time, she fills the wheelie bag with more bottles than she ever would have been able to carry, and we plod along home. Sure, it takes time, but time isn't a problem. Not for Mrs. Thorkildsen and me. And Mrs. Thorkildsen has also bought herself a pair of magic shoes. Huge and white, much bigger than any of her other shoes, but also lighter. Antelope skin. Somewhere an antelope was grazing on a savanna, and could have kept doing so, had it not occurred to an old woman up north that she was going to get rid of her car. It's hard to wrap your head around. But the shoes are beautiful. They'll really be something to sink my teeth into when the time comes. Patience.

The loss of our car has been a blessing for the passionate walker in me, although it also means a sudden encounter with a reality full of new demands and challenges, some of the type us medium-size dogs are less enthusiastic about. The suburbanites, for example. Little did I know, before we started making the journey on foot, that the hunting grounds were located in another city. The Center, as it turned out, was deep in the heart of suburbia. In the car, I had never registered the existence of the city limits; it had never occurred to me that the Center might be elsewhere, or how far away it was. But traveling on foot, it's like crossing an invisible line, and you're suddenly in suburbia.

In the city, they don't live like Mrs. Thorkildsen and me, in a single-family home behind a white-painted fence. In the city there are no fences. The houses aren't separate and alone, they're stacked vertically, so high that I get a little nauseated if I don't keep my eyes glued to the ground as we maneuver toward the Center.

With no fences, you'd think suburbia would be an El Dorado for dogs—who also wouldn't need to guard the houses, since they're big enough to guard themselves—but there aren't many dogs around, and the few we meet are well-behaved walkers on a leash. There's plenty of room to run around between the houses, but there's no one running around. Still, there's no doubt there are plenty of dogs in suburbia, and I think even Mrs. Thorkildsen would smell that if she could just be bothered to get down on all fours and stick her nose up against the lampposts. I can smell them, but I can't see them, so I'm full of questions:

Can they see me? Are they sitting up there behind the curtains in their tall houses, following my every move? Should I be worried?

The answer to the last question is yes. As a dog, you should generally always be a little worried. It's part of the job, I think. The problem is that new problems and worries come up all the time. For example, I had never before been exposed to the terrifying trial, the lonely humiliation it is to be tied up and left on the street, until Mrs. Thorkildsen stopped driving her car.

The first time it happened, I'm ashamed to admit, I went a little bananas. Totally bananas, to be completely honest. Maybe because it happened so fast and without warning. One moment we were strolling peacefully in the street together in the crisp, cool autumn air, the next I was left there, tied up and abandoned.

"Stay here, Tassen," was all she said before she left. A horrible message, so brutally curt and confusing that I had to collect myself before I could even start to register the situation around me. I was supposed to stay there, alone, tied up in a totally foreign place, without Mrs. Thorkildsen, possibly for the foreseeable future. Life turned upside down. Maybe I should have expected this, I thought to myself. When the Major came to get me, my life was suddenly transformed as if by a magic wand, and now that life—and Mrs. Thorkildsen along with it—had vanished again. I was in shock, too paralyzed to howl out my sorrow and fear. I had never felt so afraid and lonely, even before I sensed the stench that wafted up from the ground all around me, a cacophony of smells from dog after dog after dog with one common message:

"Alone!"

I wasn't the first lonely dog who had been tied up here. Ironically, in the loneliest moment of my life so far, I wasn't alone. I was just one snout among a giant pack of dogs tied up in frantic worry, and I could hear the whining, the whimpering, the anxious barking.

Somewhere deep inside this impotent herd, I found my footing again. Four paws on the ground. My seat behind me. That's all there was to it. I knew then and there that Mrs. Thorkildsen hadn't done this to punish me, and that calmed me down a little, but I was far from confident that she'd be coming back to get me. "Back" is a tricky word, truth be told.

When she finally did come back, I was naturally overjoyed, happier than I can ever remember being, and I did everything in my power to make her see it. Jumping and dancing and leaping and grinning. I smiled my friendliest smile as I ran in circles as wide as my leash would allow, then I jumped up on my hind legs and planted my front paws on Mrs. Thorkildsen's thigh the way I'd sometimes dared to do with the Major. But instead of saying "Good boy," like the Major would have done, to my surprise and disappointment Mrs. Thorkildsen shouted *"Bad boy!"* and pushed me so hard I nearly fell over. I was confused—how else was I supposed to react? And there is a point where people and dogs are frighteningly alike; a confused dog can easily become a dangerous dog.

The Major was a man who didn't permit confusion. He understood how body language worked. Let me give an example from right after I moved in with the two of them, when I was still what you might generously call a puppy. It was the first time we had a human child visit the house, the three of us. The Major and Mrs. Thorkildsen seemed totally unaffected by the event, but this peculiar being I didn't know how to relate to made me a little nervous. There was something in the combination of the shit smell and its jerky, sudden movements that confused me, so I thought I should give it a little growl, just to be safe. I'm not talking snarling and teeth-baring, but a low, barely audible, yes, I'd even go so far as to say *tentative* growl—but before I'd said my peace, I was on my back on the living room floor with the Major above me and it was all over. It was right before he sank his teeth into my exposed throat to silence me once and for all, but as you can tell, he didn't. Since then, I haven't growled at a single human child, no matter how tempting and appropriate it may have been. That's what I call good communication.

Mrs. Thorkildsen, on the other hand, gave me a scolding that was downright embarrassing. Not for me, but for her. It would have been more than enough to say *"Bad boy!"* Her tone told me everything I needed to know, but she wouldn't let it go. The whole long way back to the house, she kept coming back to the fact that I was a "bad" boy, which I found quite hurtful considering that Mrs. Thorkildsen should be very well aware than I'm not a bad boy in the least. We have a communication barrier, Mrs. Thorkildsen and me.

When the Major was alive, Mrs. Thorkildsen occasionally went to church on Sundays. At least she said she was going to church, but I was never allowed to come, so I can't guarantee that's where she went. Perhaps she was going somewhere else altogether. All I know is that I could never identify any special church smell on her clothes when she came home, possibly because I have no idea how a church smells. I stayed at home instead, reading war books with Major Thorkildsen, and as usual when he and I had a rare moment at home alone, he raided the fridge with military precision and power, and it dripped all over me. Those were the good old days.

Now Mrs. Thorkildsen and I are the ones home alone, and the days aren't so good anymore. After the grotesque scolding and yelling all the way home, I was deeply wounded and discouraged. I was disappointed that Mrs. Thorkildsen hadn't lived up to her potential as a friend to dog- or humankind, but most of all, I was disappointed in myself for my obvious inability to give her the same feeling of calm and balance the Major had obviously done, even from his sickbed.

. . .

Mrs. Thorkildsen wouldn't have behaved that way toward me if she hadn't been so dreadfully unhappy. She's been unhappy for a long time. The evenings, which furnished almost every day with a concluding high point, now sometimes end in disaster. This is how it happens: Mrs. Thorkildsen drinks dragon water until she's unsteady while she talks too long on the phone, then she sits in silence staring out the windows facing west and beyond while she drinks until she's even more unsteady. Sometimes she trips, sometimes she even falls, and occasionally she sleeps on the bathroom floor for a long time before waking up with a start and crawling to her bed on all fours.

After evenings like these, Mrs. Thorkildsen sleeps for a long time.

6

WHAT'S THE MATTER WITH MRS. THORKILDSEN? If I were a cat, that worry wouldn't faze me. Mrs. Thorkildsen fills my bowl with food; I don't have to turn to the infamous toilet bowl for water; I get hugs and scratches and kind words and two walks a day. I have nothing to complain about. Mrs. Thorkildsen clearly does, but she doesn't actually complain. Sure, she mentions her loneliness, her arthritic hands, and her reduced hearing to her cousins on the phone, but she doesn't *complain*. At least not with her words. If she feels herself nearing a complaint, she soon turns the conversation to someone who's worse off, according to her.

And so, as Mrs. Thorkildsen would say, the days pass. They pass at a relatively steady pace out there, but often with wobblier steps at home. They pass in the same tempo as the clock on the kitchen wall, the one with the hand that never stands still and never shuts up, but can still make itself invisible and inaudible for a long, long time, only to suddenly assault you with first one tick, then the next tock, then tick, tock, tick, tock until you think the ticking might drive you crazy.

Otherwise, the house has grown far too quiet, and there's not much I can do about that, other than the little I can contribute. As a guard dog, I'm simply going to have to expand my repertoire. Guard more. So I've started to experiment with barking in new situations.

I've always barked at the doorbell, but now I've decided to bark at the phone, too. And truth be told, there's not much else to bark at if I'm not going to turn into one of those loudmouth dogs I've always despised, who stand on their hind legs and jump at the window toward everything that moves outside.

Mrs. Thorkildsen does not appreciate my efforts. The first time I did it, she was quick to snap "bad boy" at me again, but it seemed half-hearted, and besides, she had to focus on answering. As she lifted the receiver, I growled a little to indicate to whomever was on the other end that Mrs. Thorkildsen was under my protection.

Tonight Mrs. Thorkildsen had time to get quite unsteady before she dozed off in the chair by the windows. The phone rings, and I jump to my feet to bark as loud as I can. She stands up, wobbly and confused. She remains still at her chair for a moment, blinking her eyes like a newborn puppy. Then she suddenly realizes what is going on, comes to her senses, and heads for the phone in the hall, while I bark and bark and bark some more. It isn't a hysterical bark, far from it, but an insistent one. An alarm. Mrs. Thorkildsen staggers over to the phone, lifts the receiver, and answers as she always does: "Twenty-eight oh-six oh-seven," whatever that means, and then she says: "Hello?" and falls silent. Meanwhile, I have switched from enthusiastic barking to light, sporadic woofing. "Hello?" she says again, and I should have reacted to the sudden sharpness in her voice. Had I heard it, I might have seen the newspaper coming too, but before I can react Mrs. Thorkildsen smacks me with the morning edition.

I stop the woofing at once, disappointed that gentle, kind Mrs. Thorkildsen has once again turned to violence without warning. It is impossible to sniff out what kind of feelings are rushing through Mrs. Thorkildsen, who is normally so easy to read. The blow is too hard to be playful, but it lacks the rage required to make it truly painful. It is the confusion that makes the whole experience so scary. I stare at her. She stares back. I stare even more intently. I bark. She starts to cry. She slides down the wall in the hall, with her back against the front door, and sobs away as the tears stream down her face, and now I can clearly smell the fear. I can't say I am glad to see her unhappy, but I must say I am relieved. Crying and sobbing, I know what to do with those.

"There, there," I say as I nuzzle my nose into her soft neck to assure her that everything is going to be fine, just fine.

Mrs. Thorkildsen looks at me with red eyes:

"Do you really think so, Tassen? That everything's going to be all right?"

It takes me a few seconds to realize it is me she is talking to, because she is using another tone of voice. Not the sharp tone that told me I was a bad boy, and not the friendly voice she uses when she is chatting to me as we run errands together. It is the voice I have missed since Major Thorkildsen went away, a voice used only within our little pack.

"Yes," I say. "I think it's going to be all right."

I say it because I believe it, but I have to admit I'm not sure what "it" is. I'm still not sure.

7

WHEN WE COME STROLLING HOME this afternoon, exhausted from our adventures and ready for the couch, Mrs. Thorkildsen's puppy, the Bitch, and the Boy Puppy are there waiting for us. Naturally I do everything I can to make them feel welcome; it is the least I can do. I wag my tail and creep toward them on the carpet, but the Puppy and the Bitch ignore me. The Boy Puppy ignores us all. They've been waiting a long time, the Puppy says, and the Bitch follows up, with a smile:

"Did you forget about us?"

The question hangs in midair, long enough for Mrs. Thorkildsen, who is already surprised, to get restless. I can hear it in her breath. She strides in the direction of the kitchen to put the coffee on, but the Puppy stops her by saying:

"They called from the bank today."

Mrs. Thorkildsen stands still for just a moment, then she continues toward the kitchen. Of course she does. What else is she supposed to do? For my part, I have no idea what to do with myself, whether to offer

Mrs. Thorkildsen a comforting nuzzle, or whether to try to relieve the uncomfortable tension in the living room that threatens to infest the whole house. Maybe I should get the ball, it could use a renaissance anyway.

I barely have to stick my snout into the kitchen to assure myself that Mrs. Thorkildsen is doing well, or at least well enough. And I should have known. Mrs. Thorkildsen is at her best in the kitchen. That's where she kneads and cooks and chops and fries happiness out of sorrow and simple ingredients. Or at least she used to. So I cheerfully plod back to the living room, determined to seize the family's attention and turn the dark mood of the room upside down, be it for a party or a scandal.

"You have to tell her!" the Bitch is hissing as I come into the living room. *"Now!"* And there's something about the way she says it that makes me invisible.

The Puppy is standing with his back to her, pretending to study the books on the shelf by the fireplace. The Boy Puppy sits on the couch with the machine in his hands and wouldn't look up if a tiger entered the room.

"We know what she's going to say," the Puppy responds, sounding a little tired. "She's going to say that she plans to live here until her dying breath."

"We should have done this while your father was alive. She would have listened to him. Now it's just a giant godforsaken mausoleum here. Over two thousand square feet for an old lady and her dog—it's just meaningless."

She pauses before snarling through clenched teeth:

"Three-door garage!"

I balk at the notion that a three-door garage should be so much worse than a one-door, but once again the magic of numbers escapes me. The Bitch lets the silence fall again. Still the Puppy says nothing, so she adds:

"This house is going to be ours." The last word.

And then nothing more is said until Mrs. Thorkildsen comes rolling in from the kitchen with her lovely tea trolley.

"Rather die than go back and forth!" Mrs. Thorkildsen says each time she uses that tea trolley. "The good waiter's motto!" She says it this time, too. And when she gets to wait on people, Mrs. Thorkildsen finds fulfillment in her own strange way.

In one swift motion, she clears off the coffee table and gets plates, cups, saucers, spoons, and napkins from the magical tea trolley. Sugar and milk are served, along with what I've smelled from a mile away, chocolate with nuts, and cookies as well. And cinnamon rolls. I want to woof with happiness and have to honestly admit that I might have done so had Mrs. Thorkildsen's puppy not been there. Because here we are, and we're all here together, and there's food. There are cinnamon rolls! What more could you possibly wish for?

The Puppy stuffs a cinnamon roll into his mouth, and while he's still chewing, says:

"Mom, we wanted to talk to you about a couple of practical things."

"Well, go ahead," Mrs. Thorkildsen says. The Bitch takes a deep breath, but as she's about to take the floor, Mrs. Thorkildsen says with timing worthy of a jazz drummer:

"But let's drink the coffee first."

This sentence is Mrs. Thorkildsen's proffered line of defense. It's not *coffee* they're going to drink, but *the coffee*. And it's going to happen now. It's a merciless one-man bureaucracy balancing on a Japanese porcelain saucer. And so, as the last cup is poured, comes the death blow, with a little nod toward the boy:

"How is everything with . . . ? Is he better? Is he still . . . at night?" Silence. The Bitch looks at the Puppy. The Puppy stares out into the room.

Mrs. Thorkildsen takes a tiny sip of her coffee.

"Oh, well, it's a good thing they have these computer games to comfort them."

For the first time, all eyes land on the Boy Puppy. They examine the motionless boy with his rapid thumbs—*thumbs!*—in silence. Mrs. Thorkildsen is an enigma now; it's impossible to sniff out her intentions, until she opens her mouth and her voice betrays her. It's the calm, controlled voice, the one that tells me she's taken a detour or two via the linen closet while tinkering around in the kitchen.

"Are you good at that? Hmmm?" The Boy Puppy does not acknowledge he's being spoken to. Then Mrs. Thorkildsen speaks directly to the Bitch:

"He's always on that thing, isn't he? In his own little world. But I guess they all are these days, aren't they?" Mrs. Thorkildsen chuckles. "Let's have a cognac in honor of your visit," she says.

"We're driving!" the Puppy and the Bitch say in unison.

Mrs. Thorkildsen is unfazed. She gets the bottle and pours a glass for each of them.

"You can decide between yourselves which one of you is driving," she says with her cruelest smile.

The Bitch has obviously given up waiting for Mrs. Thorkildsen's puppy to *Say it. Now!* so as Mrs. Thorkildsen pours her glass, she clears her throat and says it herself:

"You know we've always supported you in your wish to live at home as long as possible," she starts as she reeks of nervousness. Fumbles for the next sentence. The Puppy is about to take over, but the Bitch collects herself; I can hear her pulse steadily rising as she speaks:

"The problem is that 'as long as possible'"—she stops for a second to make stupid, catlike scratching motions in thin air—"might be here soon."

"Might actually have been here for a while," the Puppy mumbles, and it gets quiet again. Even quieter.

"So, you want to put me in a home?" Mrs. Thorkildsen says, calm and ice cold.

"We just want you settled in a place that's more suited to your needs," the Bitch says. "Jean spends quite a lot of time worrying about you, you know. *I* worry about you. I can understand that you don't want a cell phone even though it would be very practical for everyone. Dad is the same way—we bought him three different cell phones and he couldn't get the hang of any of them, but can we at least get you a safety alarm?"

"Suited," Mrs. Thorkildsen repeats as she slowly nods. As I've done many times before, I catch myself wasting time and attention on confusing stimuli, so I command myself to settle into a kind of calm under the coffee table. I'd prefer to lie low, and Mrs. Thorkildsen's puppy took the spot in the Major's old chair without asking anyway, as if it were the most natural thing in the world.

As soon as I've nestled my snout into the carpet, I can sense that sweet Mrs. Thorkildsen is now hiding a seething, white-hot rage under her calm exterior. Had she been a miniature schnauzer, I would have backed off at this point, tiptoed away slowly without taking my eyes off the dog. You can't tell just by looking at Mrs. Thorkildsen that she is furious. No, she's just sitting there in her chair with her glass and her frozen little smile as she teeters on the edge of murderous wrath, and not a single one of the other humans in the room has any idea of the danger they're in. As for me, I'm nauseated with excitement. What will Mrs. Thorkildsen do now? Well, what options does she have, really? The Major's old pump-action shotgun, the one he loved so much, is still lying under their bed. Clearly Mrs. Thorkildsen doesn't pose a physical threat to any of the three guests on her own, but give her a pump-action shotgun and things might look different. Still, Mrs. Thorkildsen remains seated:

"Well, I'm here," she says with astonishing clarity and poise, "and I'm going to stay here for the little time I have left. That's all there is to it."

The Bitch sighs. Then Mrs. Thorkildsen adds, bless her:

"And what about Tassen, anyway?"

I could shout a triumphant *Ha!* but I keep it to myself. End of discussion, thank you and good night. But no:

"We can't let the dog be the deciding factor here," the Puppy says.

I can hardly believe my ears. What kind of rule is that?

"And who's to say we can't find a place for you that will allow dogs? We're not talking about an *old folks' home*, Mom, we're talking about a fully equipped accessible residence. With no stairs. Practical and easy to take care of. Preferably here in the neighborhood."

"Yes, preferably," the Bitch echoes.

"I can handle stairs just fine, thank you," Mrs. Thorkildsen says, friendly words that don't sound the least bit friendly. The Puppy tries a new plan of attack:

"Not to be morbid here," he says, "but what will you do if something happens and you can't handle it for some reason? How will you go grocery shopping, for example?"

Grocery shopping? I think.

"Then I'll get my groceries delivered. No big deal. I do have a telephone. Had you forgotten that?" Mrs. Thorkildsen's tone has turned short.

"Okay," the Bitch says. "But, again, what about Tassen?"

I'm almost starting to wonder what about Tassen myself. I don't mind being an item of conversation—who doesn't like a little attention?—but this conversation, with its "What about Tassen?" mantra and a homicidal Mrs. Thorkildsen, is a bit unsettling. I'm seriously debating whether I should start whimpering. There's no dog noise like the whimper for making humans lower their shoulders. People who should know better say "Awwwwww" to even the ugliest pit bull's mug if only the dumb animal can muster up a whimper.

And I don't know anything about that biting stuff. Call it cowardly, but I kind of draw the line at biting. As I said, I would have done anything to defuse the nauseating tension roiling in Mrs. Thorkildsen's living room, but I would never resort to biting. Never. I might be mistaken, but I'll leave that up to others to judge.

"Now let's have a toast!" Mrs. Thorkildsen says, and there can be no doubt that's what's going to happen. This is another part of Mrs. Thorkildsen's magic—an almost frightening ability to predict the near future.

"Now Tassen's going to take a bath," she might say. "No, I don't think so," I might reply, but she always ends up being right. It can get a little creepy at times, and she seems totally unfazed, almost oblivious to this special talent.

"What are we toasting to?" the Bitch asks, holding her glass aloft.

Mrs. Thorkildsen thinks for a moment. She looks at the Bitch, then at the Puppy:

"To the one who makes it possible for me to live here, and to live a good life. To my rock. Cheers to Tassen!"

All three of them look at me, but I have a feeling only one of them likes what they see.

8

THE THEME OF THE DAY in Dr. Pill's office: *My racist father has to learn to accept the minorities in the family.* As usual, I can't understand a word being said, but Mrs. Thorkildsen sums it up for me with a heartfelt "Oh, dear!"

"It's a good thing I'm not long for this world," Mrs. Thorkildsen says.

Mostly just to start a conversation I ask, "How did it go? Did he learn to accept the minorities in the family?"

"I don't think so," Mrs. Thorkildsen says. "In fact, I think it's not easy for anyone to learn acceptance. I'm afraid he'll always be a racist, unfortunately."

"But is that so bad? I mean, I'm a racist, and that doesn't seem to be a problem for you, right?"

"Of course, that's bad! What do you mean, you're a racist?"

"Sure I am. You know I can't stand German shepherds, for instance."

"Oh, yes, I know that all too well. But does that mean you think a German shepherd is worth less than you are?"

"That's not a fair comparison. Remember that the Major got me at half price. Cash."

"What I mean is, do you think you're a better dog than a German shepherd?"

"Well, that depends what you want to use us for. For example, I'd like to see a German shepherd who's a better swimmer than me. On the other hand, if I were to bite the nearest bad guy in the shin, I doubt he'd even notice much of anything. So, yes, in some cases certain dogs are better than others. At least that's my opinion."

"But you all come from wolves. You're all brothers!"

"Wolves can be put to many uses. And what they can't do, they can slowly adapt to and learn. You see, flexibility is our trademark. A wolf for every need."

"So, I guess you're a cuddle-wolf, then," Mrs. Thorkildsen concludes.

To be honest, the conversation depresses me a bit, as existential questions often do. Afterward, I lie in the hall, mindlessly munching on a hiking boot before drifting off and dreaming a dream about being in the woods, unable to move while scary smells wafted in from every direction. Since I've woken up, I've been feeling a little weak and queasy. Mrs. Thorkildsen, on the other hand, has been in a great mood all afternoon, which is becoming clear in her light and springy step even after darkness has fallen. Now she's reading a book.

"What are you reading?" I want to know.

"*In Search of Lost Time* by Marcel Proust," Mrs. Thorkildsen replies. "I've read it before."

"What's it about?"

"Good question . . . I suppose the basic story line is that a man suddenly catches the scent of a cookie."

"Promising. Then what happens?"

"Well, *happens* is a bit of a stretch. The scent makes him remember everything that's happened since he was a child, which makes us think about the flow of time and how time changes—and *doesn't* change—people."

"Sounds deep. Any dogs in the story?"

"None in a leading role, I'm afraid."

"Well, do you know any stories where dogs play leading roles?"

"Hmmm. I have to think about that one. I can't come up with anything on the spot, except this one book we read in school: *Just a Dog* by Per Sivle."

"Sounds sad."

"I do recall it being pretty sad stuff. And then there's *The Hound of the Baskervilles* by Conan Doyle."

"Oh? What's that one about?"

"I don't think it's actually about dogs, really. But I can't think of any others, besides children's books."

"And you've read all the books there are?"

"Far from it."

"So there might be a story about dogs you haven't read?"

"*Lassie!*" says Mrs. Thorkildsen, sounding pleased with herself.

"Who's that?"

"Lassie is a Scottish sheepdog who . . ."

"Scottish sheepdogs *are* primitive and tiresome creatures. Lots of genetic challenges there."

"You really are a little racist, aren't you? But, anyway, Lassie was the world's most famous dog, and they made a bunch of movies about her. I thought Lassie was just a Hollywood invention, but one time the Major and I were driving around England and we came across a small town in the south of Cornwall, and it turned out to be the town where the original Lassie had lived. And I can assure you that she was no Scottish sheepdog—she was a mixed breed."

"Even better . . ."

"When a ship was torpedoed out in the channel during World War One—which is a different world war than the one the Major fought in—the bodies of the dead sailors were dumped in the cellar of the local pub. The pub proprietor was the one who owned Lassie. As the story goes, Lassie went over to one of the dead sailors and started licking his face. They tried pulling her off, but she wouldn't move away from the body. A few hours later he came back to life."

"And?"

"There's no 'and.'" Mrs. Thorkildsen takes a pause. "Other than the fact that the sailor came back to the pub later on to thank the dog who had saved his life."

"So the mutt became a star just because it could smell the difference between a dead and a living person?"

"I think so. At least that's the story we were told. I saw the Lassie movies when I was a young girl. They were usually all about Lassie finding missing kids, as far as I recall. But other than that . . ."

Mrs. Thorkildsen takes a trip to the kitchen. If I hadn't been stuffed I might have followed her, but I lie still in my spot, listening to Mrs. Thorkildsen as she opens the fridge, finds the bottle she opened earlier, pours a glass, returns the bottle to the fridge, grabs the glass, and plods back to the living room, where she delivers the following short and declarative message:

"Amundsen's polar expedition!"

She says it with a certain decisiveness, half an exclamation point, calm and confident. Then she falls silent, as if that small comment explained everything.

"What is Amundsen's polar expedition?" I ask.

"When I was growing up, everyone knew that story. About the Norwegians who made it first to the South Pole, because they used dogs, right under the noses of the British men who were sure *they* were going to be first—since they were a larger group, with tractors. It was a real underdog story. Ha!"

"Why was it so important to be first to the pool?"

"*Pole*, Tassen. Not *pool*. Roald Amundsen and his men drove sled dogs to the South Pole, which is . . . well, the South Pole. How can I explain that? The South Pole is the spot at the very bottom of the globe. It's on a giant continent covered by ice."

"Ice in the south?" Has Mrs. Thorkildsen gotten confused?

"When you get far enough south, you see, it starts getting colder again. On the other side of the world, it's just as cold as here."

"Whichever way you turn, your rear is always behind you."

"You might say that," Mrs. Thorkildsen says.

"What does it do?"

"The South Pole? Well, I suppose it doesn't do much of anything. It just sits there, I think. The Last Place on Earth, they called it. Once upon a time, it became important for people to get there. First. And that's what Roald Amundsen and his dogs managed to do. But I don't think the South Pole is actually much more than a white spot in the middle of a big white landscape."

"What kind of dogs?"

"I don't know. Sled dogs."

I patiently avoid telling Mrs. Thorkildsen I've assumed as much.

"Could they have been Greenland dogs?" I ask, and now I'm suddenly interested, in spite of myself and despite the lackluster premise of the story about Roald Amundsen and his dogs, who were first to get to nowhere. Greenland dogs, you see, are something else.

Calling a Greenland dog tough is like calling a cat dumb. A gross understatement. There isn't a dog on this double-ice-capped Earth who more closely resembles a good old-fashioned wolf, but I'm not even sure if a wolf can measure up to a Greenland dog on home turf. And on one hand, home turf can be anywhere, as long as it's covered in snow and ice. On the other hand, its home turf is strictly defined. A Greenland dog stops being a Greenland dog when it leaves Greenland. That's common knowledge, or it should be.

"They ate dogs," Mrs. Thorkildsen continues.

"Who ate dogs? And why in the world would they do that?" I try not to let any of my suddenly simmering feelings rub off on Mrs. Thorkildsen, staying calm although those two words, "ate dogs," run like an electric shock through my skull and all the way down to the tip of my tail.

"I seem to recall that they did," Mrs. Thorkildsen says. "I think there was talk of them slaughtering some dogs to get the vitamins they needed to survive. There's nothing to eat at the South Pole, you see, only ice and snow."

"How many?"

One of Mrs. Thorkildsen's best qualities is her ability to unabashedly admit the following: "I don't know." She has no qualms saying that, for the next thing out of her mouth is: "But I'm sure we can find out."

9

MOST DOGS AREN'T AS GOOD at feeling guilt or shame as people like to believe. That's what I would claim, but I'm not alone: in a scientific study, the human guinea pigs—I love that expression—were shown a picture of a dog and tricked into thinking it had done something wrong. No sheep massacre, more along the lines of knocked-over trash cans or doody on the living room rug.

Truth be told, the dog in the picture was most likely innocent. The picture had been snapped in a candid moment, and if the dog was thinking about anything at all as it faced the photographer, it most likely wasn't what it had done wrong in life. It was most likely thinking about whether there was food on the horizon. Still, people invariably read "guilt" or "shame" in the dog's eyes.

Sure, dogs lay themselves flat. Raise your paw, anyone who's never laid flat! But in most cases, this has very little to do with ethics or morals—it's usually a result of the dog being smarter than it looks. It recognizes that people are unhappy and dissatisfied. If it makes you feel better, you might call it empathy. And if Bonzo is really smart, he might even realize that it *could* have something to do with the couch cushion he emphatically murdered while his master was out.

To feel guilt, the dog would need a clear understanding of the difference between right and wrong. And it has no such thing, although it may be able to convince you otherwise. If you're lucky and the dog is really smart, it might be able to distinguish between "preferred" and "not preferred" behavior.

I'm not saying us dogs are psychopaths, by all means. We are sociopaths. Like every other amoeba on the planet, we're born with an ambition of lifting the "King of the World" trophy above our heads. No one can argue that humankind is the current owner of that perpetual trophy, but they seem to have forgotten that the title is up for grabs.

However adorable and harmless a tiny handbag-size puppy may seem, its natural instinct is to install itself as leader of the pack. The only reason it doesn't do so is the endless consideration of possible ways to take charge that's constantly playing out in the dog's head. Then there are those who are incapable of making these calculations: Chihuahuas and even smaller dogs, who bare their teeth and snarl aggressively at dogs who could swallow them in one bite. There's plenty of humor in that scenario, but switch out the tiny dog with a Doberman, and the road to eternal hunting grounds suddenly seems shorter. And this happens all the time. The dog who pushes the boundaries, who slowly but surely gets control of first the kids, then Mom, and if its balls are too big, makes a move for Dad. They can't help themselves. And one fine day when the family is gathered around the dinner table, Fido thinks the time is nigh. He leaps onto the table, lowers his head, looks Dad right in the eyes and snarls so Mom and the kids scurry off, and a chill spreads through the room. Fido doesn't want to fight, not really. A peaceful transition of power is the best option for all parties and, *hey*, haven't there been some great walks through the years? Surrender calmly and gracefully, walk away from the table now, and no one has to get hurt.

Dad pulls back. He knows he doesn't have a chance. Then again, he does have a shotgun.

Volka nogi kormyat, the old Russian proverb goes. *The wolf feeds off its legs.*

It's true of people, too. Humankind's ability to move in packs until they found themselves on the other side of the globe was what made it possible for these not particularly fast, naked apes to not only survive, but climb to the top of the food chain. Dogs and humans lived in perpetual motion, and together they could travel to places neither one would have reached alone.

I don't know which one of them first realized that the other one was useful. Whether it was the wolves who initially discovered that humans left a trail of food scraps in their wake, or whether it was the humans who understood that having wolves nearby meant never having to worry about other enemies in the wild.

So they lived in the shadows, man and wolf, in unspoken mutual respect. Roved the same terrain to hunt for prey without catching more than a rare glimpse of each other. If the two met in the woods, each raced off in the opposite direction. Perhaps they should have kept it that way.

Maybe it was a lone wolf who one day broke out of the pack, a wolf low in the ranks who thought that instead of putting up with harassment and humiliation, he might as well try his own luck. The infamous Lone Wolf™! Or was it a group of human puppies who found some wolf cubs and ran home to beg their parents to keep them? *Pleeease!*

All I know is how it definitely *didn't* happen: with a pack of wolves just running into a pack of humans one day.

Maybe that's precisely why we ended up together? In the recognition that each of us, one by one, is precious and helpless, but together we become a dangerous mob? The human being is beautiful, but humankind is hideous—is that what it's all about? I suspect that Mrs. Thorkildsen might see it that way. Hanging from the little corkboard in her kitchen is a joke she's read aloud to me many times:

I love human beings. It's people I can't stand.

At least it used to be a joke, once upon a time. These days it's more like a motto. And I'm no better than she is. We've grown pack-shy in our old age, Mrs. Thorkildsen and I.

Me.

Me and you.

Trouble.

10

THE DOORBELL RINGS. Mrs. Thorkildsen sets down her coffee cup and squints at the clock on the wall.

"Well, who in the world could that be?"

As for me, I bark my heart out without speculating very much over who it might be out there on our doorstep. Mrs. Thorkildsen reties the belt on her bathrobe and plods down the hall behind me to open the door. I stop the barking as soon as the door is opened, just in case a wolf is out there. But, luckily, there isn't. There is, however, a giant glow-in-the-dark man who is a scary sight, but still smells wonderful. I have the urge to drive my snout into his trouser leg and take a big belly breath, but Mrs. Thorkildsen cuts me off with her slipper.

The delicious-smelling man holds out a green bottle.

"You have to stop throwing bottles in the trash," he says. "This is the third time. If it happens again, we can refuse to collect the garbage."

Mrs. Thorkildsen looks at the bottle, back up at the man, then back to the bottle again:

"Is that for me?"

She takes the bottle from the hands of the giant man, who suddenly seems unsteady.

"Wow . . . is it my birthday today?" Mrs. Thorkildsen's amazement is clear. So is the Garbageman's. But the ball is in his court, and he has to come up with something, so he says:

"And you have to do a better job of tying up the dog's poop bags." He looks at me. "They stink!"

Rude bastard, I think. Ringing the doorbells of respectable old ladies early in the morning to harass them and talk bullshit. If the Major were alive, the guy would end up in the Dumpster himself. But the Major is no longer around. It's all me now. It's up to me to make the right calls.

"Get the shotgun," I tell Mrs. Thorkildsen.

"Can you wait one moment?" Mrs. Thorkildsen tells the glow-in-the-dark Garbageman, and without waiting for an answer, she moves purposefully through the entryway door and shuts it behind her, probably out of old habit. This causes a somewhat awkward situation. I am practically locked in a tiny cage with my nemesis. Thoughts race through my head. How long will it take Mrs. Thorkildsen to get the shotgun out from under the bed? Does she have the right ammo? What's for dinner? I give a half-hearted bark mostly to buy some time, but the Garbageman calmly sinks to his knees and begins saying sweet things to me.

"What a gooooood boy," he says, and before I have time to bark in response, my tail is in full swing, and then, there's that smell. Before I know it, his gloves are off and I get a few good scratches just above my hip bone. This is a man who has run his fingers through a dog's fur before. Right on par with the Major. I squirm under his hand and forget where I am for a second, before I hear the door click behind me.

"Don't shoot!" I'm about to shout, but Mrs. Thorkildsen is there armed not with a rifle but with a coffee cup and a cinnamon roll.

"Congratulations!" she says.

"Eh . . . it's not my birthday," the Garbageman replies as he unfortunately stops scratching.

Mrs. Thorkildsen laughs heartily:

"I know that, silly. It's our wedding anniversary."

Afterward, Mrs. Thorkildsen is so pleased she has to call a few cousins right in the middle of the morning to tell them about the showdown that ended with the Garbageman slowly pulling away with a cinnamon roll in one hand, safely convinced that Mrs. Thorkildsen had lost it.

"Wasn't that kind of wrong?" I ask when she's done with her victory lap on the phone. "I have heard you say that we should never lie about illness, because then you get sick."

"Lie? Who said anything about lying? All I did was deliver him safely into the hands of his own prejudices. If I'd been young and behaved that way, he would have assumed I was a drug addict. If I'd been African, he would have thought I was acting in a strange African way. Since I'm old, he jumped to the conclusion that I'm senile. And speaking of dementia: *Bring it on!*"

"I'll remind you of those words later."

"You'll have to, won't you? I'm going to tell you a secret." Mrs. Thorkildsen lowers her voice slightly. "Namely, there are many old folks who aren't as foggy as they pretend to be."

"Sure, but to be fair, you have to admit there are plenty of old folks who are considerably more confused than they look, too. Clean clothes and combed hair may hide spiritual ruin, but you can't fake the scent of a clear head."

"The point is that when it's used correctly, old age opens up surprising opportunities for mischief. No one expects an old rascal, and that can be used to advantage. Uncle Peder, for instance, lived to be almost a hundred and became a formidable tax evader in his golden years. One day the tax collector turned up on his doorstep, and Uncle Peder graciously invited him in. He asked the man to take a seat in the living room while he made coffee, and then Uncle Peder went to his bedroom and simply went to sleep. When he woke up, the tax man had left. The same thing happened again with another tax collector and the same result, and after that, Uncle Peder had no issues with the tax man."

11

MRS. THORKILDSEN HAS HAD A good day, and she claims it's thanks to me. It's been a pretty confusing day for me, and I would argue that Mrs. Thorkildsen is to blame. It's my word against hers, but this is what happened:

This morning, as far as I can recall, everything was within what we broadly speaking might call "normal." Eggs, milk, crispbread, and coffee. No surprise appearances in the obituaries. In hindsight, I guess I might say Mrs. Thorkildsen was being a tiny bit secretive.

"Today we're going to make packed lunches," she said. "It's going to be a long day."

"That sounds like a good idea," I said. Compromised as I am by my eating habits, it didn't occur to me to ask Mrs. Thorkildsen *why* we might be facing a long day. The knowledge that there was a treat awaiting me somewhere out there in the long day was enough of an answer to any questions I might have.

So I felt secure in my immediate future as we sat on board the tunnel train, Mrs. Thorkildsen and I. The tunnel train was delightfully free of little kids and dogs and feet, and I enjoyed the trip. At least until Mrs. Thorkildsen unexpectedly got up and pulled me behind her out of the train, which now seemed to have stopped inside a house, but I barely had time for a few whiffs of its complex and exciting mosaic of smells before Mrs. Thorkildsen, with exaggerated purpose, pulled me up a flight of stairs, and then we were out in a boiling chaos, at least seen from human knee height.

Mrs. Thorkildsen, who was naturally superior to any dog in a situation like this, teeming with people, noisy cars, suffocating gases, and an overall clattering cacophony, steered us calmly through the crowd until she reached her destination. A spot on the sidewalk, not unlike any other spot on the sidewalk. She stopped and stayed still.

I didn't know why we were paused in a place where it was so uncomfortable to stand around, and had a moment to worry whether Mrs. Thorkildsen really knew what she was doing, before she again blew me away with her paranormal ability to predict the future. Perhaps she sensed I was feeling a little insecure, because when I needed it the most, she bent down, gave me two pats on the head, and said:

"We're going to take a bus now."

No sooner had she uttered the words than an enormous red bus rolled up in front of us, and Mrs. Thorkildsen climbed aboard with the wheelie bag and me in tow, and found a spot in the back of the old clunker. I didn't even bother to try climbing onto the seat next to her, it was both too high up and probably forbidden.

The bus stopped, spat out some people, rolled on, stopped again, spat out more people, and rolled on again until Mrs. Thorkildsen and

I were the only passengers left on board. Finally, Mrs. Thorkildsen announced:

"This is our stop!"

"Our?" I asked.

"We're getting off here," Mrs. Thorkildsen replied.

We climbed off the bus. Mrs. Thorkildsen and the wheelie bag and I stepped out into the wind that came roaring in heaving bursts from the ocean, which seemed scarier than I had imagined. I remembered then and there something the Major had said on a few occasions, that I was built for duck hunting. Possibly, but not in this weather.

Still, our destination on this voyage wasn't the frothy, whitecapped sea in front of us, but an enormous building that didn't resemble a building at all. A steep, pointy roof stuck out of the earth and straight up into the gray sky above us. The building seemed oddly unsettling to me, although I'm not able to say exactly why now. Negative vibes, plain and simple.

"Are dogs allowed here?" I asked.

Mrs. Thorkildsen didn't answer my question, she just started making her way toward the front door with small, trudging steps. The wheelie bag squeaked, squeaked, squeaked until we were standing in front of the door and I could see that right in the middle of the glass, someone had taped up a sign:

"Let's not go in here," I said, a little anxious, to be honest.

"Now, what is this nonsense you're saying?" Maybe she hadn't registered the ominous sign. The Mrs. Thorkildsen I know would never have set foot in a house with that sign on the door, but since she had come all this way it seemed wrong for her to have to turn around because of me. I tried to weasel my way out of the situation.

"I'd rather stay out here and enjoy the weather," I lied, and added a quip: "Since it's raining cats and dogs, heh-heh. Tie me up to the fence over there, and I can stay there in peace and quiet while you're inside doing . . . come to think of it, what exactly are you doing here?"

Mrs. Thorkildsen still didn't listen. Kept pulling me onward, attached to the wheelie bag. I was mortified at the thought of entering a territory where I so obviously wasn't welcome, and if I could have turned myself invisible as easily as I could keep quiet, no one would have seen an inch of me.

We went straight over to a window where there was a relatively young man with no fur on his head, who smelled like lemon and hemp and the same stuff that killed the Major. Mrs. Thorkildsen smiled her friendliest smile, wished him good morning, and asked for a senior ticket.

"Dogs are unfortunately not allowed here, I'm sorry," the man said, in such a friendly tone that the contrast to his aggressive message was all the more striking.

"Did you hear that!" I said to Mrs. Thorkildsen, with more than a hint of reproach. "He even said 'unfortunately.' I think we should be content with that."

"It's a service dog," Mrs. Thorkildsen told the man in the window.

"Service dog?" he replied, before getting to his feet, leaning forward, and peering down at me; I could have sunk into the floor in shame. I had no idea what kind of pose or expression was expected of me. I took a chance and wagged a little, slowly and cautiously. But no sooner had I started getting my rear in gear than it occurred to me it might be a little unprofessional—perhaps service dogs don't wag, especially not at work?—so I cut it out at once, which just made me feel even dumber. The man stared at me for a while, then he looked back at Mrs. Thorkildsen.

"Do you have poor eyesight?" he asked.

Mrs. Thorkildsen chuckled:

"No, I don't. It's not a guide dog. I don't think Tassen would be much use as a guide dog, no, but it is still a service animal. It can sense when I'm unwell, so I don't feel safe without it," she said. As much as I resent being called "it," I was of course happy to hear what she had to say after the humiliation of being written off as a guide dog. Still, I was a little surprised to hear that I was a service dog. She could have told me that earlier.

It grew quiet behind the window.

"Well, well," the man said. "It's quiet here today, so . . . But you have to keep it leashed."

"Thank you very much," Mrs. Thorkildsen said. "How kind of you. Tassen has been looking forward to this."

Now Mrs. Thorkildsen was lying straight to the poor man's face. I wouldn't have thought her capable until the episode with the Garbage-man this morning. I mumbled a thank-you while I tried to keep moving in the style of a service dog, as best I could.

It wasn't easy, bound as I was to Mrs. Thorkildsen's wheelie bag.

Luckily, she parked the bag at the end of the counter. She didn't assume anything, but politely asked the man in the window whether she could leave it there.

"At your own risk," came the reply.

I'm still wondering what he meant by that.

Mrs. Thorkildsen grabbed the leash, and it immediately became easier to impersonate a service dog. I pulled with all my might and laboriously dragged Mrs. Thorkildsen farther into the strange premises, which had yet to make a definite impression on my nose. Newly washed floors with significant chemical traces don't give you much to work with. We might have been anywhere, but we were somewhere very specific.

I had expected the ceiling to be high, but it was red and sloped oppressively down toward the floor, and the floor in the middle of the room was dug out so the ceiling wouldn't crash into it. A strange design, and no place to hang around. I kept pulling to drag Mrs. Thorkildsen onward, expecting some resistance, but before she had time to pull the leash back, I stopped dead in my tracks. In front of us, raised on its hind legs, just a few feet away, was a polar bear. Yes, a stinking polar bear. A huge monster of a polar bear with claws and teeth and a dead stare.

I was terrified, of course, and instinctively wanted to flee this grotesque madhouse. I should never have set paw in here, but Mrs. Thorkildsen was ice cold. Her little heart kept beating at the same rate, and with a voice as calm and pleasant as if she were in her own cozy living room with a cozy blanket pulled around her shoulders and a cozy drink in her hand, she said:

"Well, isn't *that* a scary polar bear! Do you see that? I bet it would eat you for breakfast if it were alive!"

She kept walking toward the polar bear, and I had no choice but to follow. Not alive? What was it, then, if not alive? With no prior polar bear experience, I was no expert, of course, but it didn't exactly seem dead as it stood baring its teeth at us.

"What's wrong with it?" I asked.

"It's taxidermied," Mrs. Thorkildsen replied.

"What does that mean?"

"It means it's dead, and everything that was inside the bear—heart and lungs and intestines and muscles—that's all taken out and replaced with . . ."

Mrs. Thorkildsen took a pause so long that I had time to think, "There goes that thought," but then:

"I'm not sure, actually. Sawdust, maybe? Yes, I think sawdust is what they use."

"Let's keep going," I said.

So we kept going, but there was an endless parade of new signs for Mrs. Thorkildsen to read and objects for her to gawk at. Pretty boring, really. Go. Stop in front of next sign. Read. Boring. Go. Stop. Two taxidermied dogs. TWO TAXIDERMIED DOGS!! And not just any dogs. Greenland dogs.

"What the hell?" slipped out of me.

Mrs. Thorkildsen said nothing, and good thing she didn't, since in the blind rage that now washed over me, I might have torn anyone to shreds (not Mrs. Thorkildsen, of course, but I might well have accidentally nipped her in the calf in all the excitement) for the sole reason that they belonged to the same human race that stuffs dogs full of sawdust.

I should probably have more instinctive solidarity with the polar bear; I am more closely related to it than I am to Mrs. Thorkildsen, for instance. I should probably have taken it personally and sat down on my hind legs right away, but I admit that it wasn't until the sight of the taxidermied dogs that the gravity of the situation clearly appeared to me, like fresh piss on new snow.

They were two large, statuesque former Greenland dogs exuding raw power and grit, invincible, indomitable, proud, with dead eyes and, apparently, stuffed with sawdust. Saying it was a sad sight is a gross understatement. The dogs were as dead as can be and even deader than that; still, I didn't feel totally safe that they wouldn't at any moment leap over the rope separating the little tableau in the corner from the rest of the room.

How on earth does a scruffy old dog end up stuffed full of sawdust, on display for all the world to see? What could he have done wrong? Chewed up one slipper too many? Wiped his ass on the forbidden sofa?

Mrs. Thorkildsen wanted to keep going, up two flights of stairs that looked dauntingly long. We managed the first flight one way or another, but as we attempted the second, Mrs. Thorkildsen's steps grew slower and slower, and her little heart was working hard. But again, with her small, trudging steps, Mrs. Thorkildsen made it to the top. She stood still there for a while, waiting for her heart rate to settle down.

"You see?" she said. "That's the *Fram*."

"It's a boat."

"It's a ship," Mrs. Thorkildsen said. "A polar ship."

"What's a boat doing inside a house?"

Mrs. Thorkildsen had no answer to that. She shortened the leash. And then we climbed on board.

12

YOU CAN OVERHAUL A VESSEL from keel to mast, store it indoors, and let tourists step all over it for nearly a hundred years, but you'll never get rid of the smell. The polar ship *Fram* lay there resting in its giant house, warm and plump and dry, while she oozed fear and resentment.

I can sense the stench as we plod up the little footbridge. It doesn't smack me in the face exactly, but it's there. It doesn't take much. I'm reminded that my species can easily find any amount of drugs, no matter where on your polar ship you hide them.

Dust and dirt and old varnish, layer upon layer of faint odors and scents and aromas, and then, like a dull nail suddenly shoved up into my snout, an old but disturbingly sharp odor of sheer and simple terror. I don't know what kind of yardstick humans use to measure that, but we're most likely talking craploads (the Major's expression) of fear buried in the ship's hull. It's everywhere, and everywhere is a pretty big area—the deck of the polar ship is the size of a small park.

"I want to go home," I say.

Mrs. Thorkildsen is either enraged or surprised, I can't quite tell. She responds in a tone that would make you think I had just left a steaming doody right in the middle of the polar ship's deck.

"What nonsense! We've come all this way to the Fram Museum for your sake. And we've lied to the nice young man in the window for your sake."

For my sake. There's the cat out of the bag.

"I feel sick," I say. "And I never asked you to bring me to this terrible place. Had I known we were coming here, I definitely would have parked on my hind legs and refused, you can be sure of that. Maybe there's a reason they put that sign on the door downstairs. It never occurred to you that it might be out of consideration for dogs, not people?"

It takes a lot for me to call Mrs. Thorkildsen careless. But I can't find a better word for the way she chooses to ignore my objections. This whole damned boat makes me unsettled and afraid, but it seems to make Mrs. Thorkildsen thrive. Where is this sudden energy coming from? What does this energy want with this small, feeble human?

"Just think, this is the boat they used to sail from Norway to Antarctica a hundred years ago, with a whole pack of Greenland dogs, ready to conquer the South Pole. Just the sled ride to the South Pole and back was almost two thousand miles, can you imagine."

For some reason, Mrs. Thorkildsen wants to see the ship's interior. I do not. I don't have many remedies at my disposal, but as Mrs. Thorkildsen clambers her way over the highest doorstep I've seen in my whole life, I resign myself to passive resistance. I simply sit down, pulling a classic "sitting on my hind legs." Mrs. Thorkildsen doesn't register what's happening until she tries to move farther in and the leash grows taut.

"Come on," she says in her sweetest voice, but her tone changes as soon as I refuse to respond to her plea.

"Come on, now!"

More or less the same words, but her heart rate pushes the irritation level up.

"I can't get over that massive doorstep."

If Mrs. Thorkildsen can play senile, I can certainly play weak and cowardly.

"Nonsense. And guess what? I have a treat for you in my purse."

Mrs. Thorkildsen never bluffs. Not when treats are involved. The revolution can wait.

Second Bite

If the dog is happy, everything is fine.

ANTARCTIC PROVERB

13

MY TRUST IN HUMANKIND HAS been reduced just a fraction of a point. I try to tell Mrs. Thorkildsen she shouldn't take it personally, that it's just a natural result of our mutual striving, but Mrs. Thorkildsen has always taken life personally and has no intention of stopping now. After a relatively dry period, she has now upped the dragon water intake. Sure, a polar expedition now and then is fun, but I'm not so sure that dragon water is the solution for Mrs. Thorkildsen in the long run. Or in the short run, for that matter.

"It would probably be better for you if you were a stupid mutt who didn't know any better," she slurred before staggering off to bed last night. I don't know whether it was meant as nastiness or concern, but I'm afraid it's mostly an indication that Mrs. Thorkildsen thinks it would be better for *her* if I were a *Canis stupidus*. It would probably be easier for her to give me a smack with the newspaper if I were dumb as an ox or a goose. Really, if I were more of an *animal*.

The line between people and animals is the first tentative sketch of the food chain in which humans have climbed to the top. The whole hegemony is built on hunting and taming animals—how convenient, then, that all creatures on the planet except for them fall into the category "animal."

I must admit that people don't shy away from treating each other like animals, but that only strengthens my point. According to humans, all species can be divided into two categories. In one category you have one species; in the other you have all the other species.

If it really is true that humans eat animals on a large scale, while animals only rarely eat people, it would be more advantageous, according to our friend Charles Darwin (may he rest in peace), to be a human than to be an animal. So how does an animal become human? Or, more accurately, exactly where is this crucial line drawn? What is it in the eyes of humans that makes an animal an animal?

Take, for example, the co-worker of the human in space: the chimpanzee. Not so many years ago, after years of filming chimpanzees for entertainment, humans came up with the original idea to study how they behaved when they were allowed to let down their hair and just be themselves in their own homes. Perhaps humans shouldn't have done this, at least not if their goal was to preserve their own sovereign place atop the pyramid. With the very first report back from the kingdom of the chimpanzees in Africa's forests, one of the oldest and most common methods of distinguishing between humans and animals was shattered. They used to say that animals couldn't use tools! An easy and convenient dividing line that was quickly erased when the chimpanzees in Africa broke the rules of the game and used tools they had fashioned themselves.

After this, language became the humans' last resort. Animals don't understand human language and, even worse, it's impossible to understand a peep of what *they* say. That's the basis of the whole doctrine. In other words, it's all come down to the shape of the tongue.

And this is where the chimpanzee—with its opposable thumbs— starts showing it can talk with its hands. First it learns to point, which it doesn't do in nature, and in time it has learned to communicate pretty well with sign language. The question, dear people, is: How many words must the chimpanzee learn before it is taken seriously? What will people do when the chimpanzee eloquently stands up for its own rights in Hollywood and in the jungles of the Congo?

"Can you please stop cutting down our forests?" for example. Or: "We demand a union contract and benefits. And bananas."

What will people do then? Accord them full rights, shield the forests, and put an end to drugged chimpanzees in unflattering diapers?

Let's go with that.

"Who were those dogs?" I finally ask Mrs. Thorkildsen, who seems to have decided to stay home today. Or maybe she hasn't even decided, maybe it just turned out that way. It can be difficult to tell the difference.

She's sitting in the Major's old chair, cradling a big glass in her hands and doing nothing, which you rarely see Mrs. Thorkildsen doing, and it's rarely a good sign. She's not reading, sleeping, or watching TV—just sitting there like a golden retriever.

"What dogs?"

"The ones who were full of sawdust."

"Amundsen's dogs? What about them?"

"How did they end up there?"

"I have no clue."

"Is there a book about them?"

"Hmmm, I would think someone has written that story."

"Think? I thought you knew everything about books."

"Not those kinds of books."

"What kinds are those?"

"Polar literature. I don't know anything about that. Not sure whether it's even good literature. Whether it's literature at all."

"All literature is good literature in the sense that all literature is better than no literature."

"Says who?"

"Says you. When you're shit-faced."

"I'm never shit-faced!"

"Really? Drunk, then?"

"I don't get drunk! Have you ever heard such baloney!"

"Buzzed, then? Tipsy?"

"Tipsy is okay."

"So what is this polar literature about?"

Mrs. Thorkildsen drains her glass with warp speed:

"It's about Fridtjof Nansen and his descendants."

"Okay. Who's Fridtjof Nansen?"

"A groundbreaking scientist who saved millions of refugees' lives. And a Nobel Prize winner, to boot. But what is he remembered for?"

"I don't remember."

"A ski trip! He went straight across Greenland and became a national hero. Tried to go to the North Pole, too, but didn't make it—not that that put a damper on the hero worship. He didn't have to succeed, you see. Polar heroes don't have to succeed. Their fiascos, not to mention their downfalls, can be just as attractive as their victories when the thermostat reads forty below Celsius. If you have to cut off a toe or two when the cold sets in, you can use them as chips in the game of glory and honor. Forever. Amen. Who is the most famous polar explorer of all time?" Mrs. Thorkildsen continues.

"Are you asking me?"

"Robert F. Scott. And what did he do?"

"Well, what *did* he do?"

"He perished, that's what he did, in his attempt to reach the South Pole first. The Norwegian Amundsen came first, and the Englishman Scott came last and died on the way home along with the rest of his expedition. Total victory versus total fiasco. But still, Scott is the one who's remembered, and the base on the South Pole today bears his name alongside Amundsen's."

"The things you know!"

"I only know because there was some racket on TV because the Queen is going to the South Pole. I've never been particularly enthused about that woman, but I must say it's pretty impressive to make the trip to Antarctica when you're past seventy. That's worthy of respect."

"What in the world is the Queen going to do at the South Pole?"

"It's the anniversary. A hundred years since Roald Amundsen became the first man to reach the South Pole."

"And his dogs."

"And his dogs. But what's the Queen going to do? Well, she's going to mark our ownership down there, I'd imagine. Little Norway lays claim to a fifth of Antarctica, they said. That's an area much larger than

Norway itself. Pretty ridiculous, really. But I suppose that was part of the reason to be first, that you could lay claim to the land."

"So we're talking territorial pissings?"

"More or less."

"But in that case, the Englishman would be the winner! If he and his dogs came later and pissed out the markings left by the Norwegian and his dogs, his markings would reign supreme!"

Mrs. Thorkildsen thinks for a moment, and then delivers a triumphant point:

"Scott didn't have dogs."

Well, no wonder he perished, I almost say. But I don't. Instead I say:

"But men aren't the only ones who brag about all the terrible things they've been through. When you talk on the phone, the lines are full of sorrow and travesty."

Mrs. Thorkildsen gets a little defensive, which adds a tightness to her voice, though she probably doesn't notice it herself:

"Well, that's different. We don't brag about our struggles!"

"Weeeeell . . ." I say, unsure whether we should head down that path.

14

THOSE WHO ARE HUMAN MIGHT understand how words become actions, long after they're spoken, long after you thought they were forgotten. It was my words, you see, that had slowly but surely led us to the door of the Library, and I had to be reminded that I had uttered them.

"Who were those dogs?" I asked once in a distant past, and although "I have no clue" was an answer I very well could have lived with, the question obviously continues to burn in Mrs. Thorkildsen's mind, because she thinks I'm still going around asking myself the same thing. Kind of like two people chasing each other's tail.

Once again, my high expectations have betrayed me. The Library is nothing like what I imagined. I had pictured an older, monumental building based on Mrs. Thorkildsen's reverent description of this temple of knowledge. In the Library, she boasted, lay the answers to all questions, including potential questions about taxidermied dogs, and houses with boats inside them. And I let myself be carried away.

Instead, it turns out, the Library sits at the top of a worn gray flight of stairs inside a nondescript two-story house in close proximity to Mrs. Thorkildsen's usual hunting grounds at the Center. I've walked past it countless times without realizing it.

The next surprise is the scent that hits me right away when Mrs. Thorkildsen cracks open the front door on the ground floor. I must admit, I haven't spent much time pondering how a library might smell. A library, as far as I could tell, was a house full of books, so it shouldn't smell too different from home, I figured.

Instead, a rush of hearty laughter and bitter tears wafts out the door, strongly laced with the scent of plants swaying in the wind on the other side of the world, plus human sweat. And, like an invisible haze hanging above the floor: old, stale dragon water.

"I don't think I've been here in ten years," Mrs. Thorkildsen says. "And there's the Tavern!"

Mrs. Thorkildsen has made it halfway up the stairs, and she stops dead in her tracks. She stands still, gazing at the door at the top of the stairs, which may be closed but tells a story through the intense aroma that seeps through it.

"We used to go to the Tavern and drink beer on paydays," Mrs. Thorkildsen says.

"Those were the only days I went to the Tavern, you didn't want to spend a lot of time there. They had good patty melts, too. Overall, I got the sense it was a real quality kitchen. Simple, but quality. Better a simple patty melt than a fancy pâté with all the fuss."

"I'll take both, please," I say.

The door with the restless smells isn't the door to the Library, as it turns out. The Library has its own, more modest door right beside it, and as soon as Mrs. Thorkildsen opens it, the smell is more reminiscent of home. The sticky scent of dragon water is clear inside the Library, too. It mingles with the aroma of dusty books to create a pretty good satire of the smell in our home.

It's not hard to feel at home in the Library, though I'm still not entirely sure I'm welcome here. At least there was no sign on the door. There was one, I had noticed, on the door of the Tavern.

Mrs. Thorkildsen stays glued to one spot after the door swings shut behind us. The Library looks empty, but my nose tells a different story. I hear steps approaching from farther down the hall, and had I not been so anxious about being kicked out, I naturally would have given a warning bark or two. No howling, just a small, barely audible *woof!* to wake up the senses.

The Librarian! Young, barely full-grown, hasn't given birth, and isn't drinking milk. Ovulating. Safe, friendly, and welcoming. She's obviously a surprise to Mrs. Thorkildsen, and when she's surprised, Mrs. Thorkildsen loses her grip on reality a little. Both her body language and her speech grow jerky and stuttering. Mrs. Thorkildsen stays still a bit too long, gawking at the Librarian before uttering the timeless words:

"Are *you* the Librarian?"

"Yes," the Librarian says, smiling wide enough to reveal a shiny white set of teeth bordering on threatening. "How can I help you?"

I nearly pee a whole puddle in relief.

Finally!

Finally, someone's offering Mrs. Thorkildsen a little sorely needed *help.*

Where should we start? There are so many things Mrs. Thorkildsen could use help with. She could use help in hunting, for one. The size and quality of her bounty is markedly lower than before, or maybe it's just my aversion to the little oven on the shelf that says *Pling!* and kills almost all the scent in the food. Fortunately, my diet mostly consists of good old-fashioned dog food these days. And then there's the housework, the dragon water collecting, the phone chatting, and the diary writing. Truth be told, there are quite a few things she could use help with, now that I think about it, but instead of taking the Librarian up on her generous offer, Mrs. Thorkildsen begins telling an elaborate version of the story she told me on the stairs, about paydays and patty melts, and completely ignores the Librarian's generous offer of help before capping it all off with a question of her own.

"Aren't you a little . . . young to be a librarian?"

"I'm twenty-nine," the Librarian responds. Means nothing to me. "I finished my library science degree last spring. This is my first job."

"I'm six," I say.

"I was forty-four when I started working as a librarian," Mrs. Thorkildsen says. "I was a housewife for ten years before starting my library science degree. The sixties, you know. Do you like it out here?"

The Librarian hesitates, shuffles from one foot to another, and folds her arms across her chest.

"It's nice here, but the branch is being closed down in November, and that takes its toll on the job. There's a lot I would have liked to do, but it seems a bit . . . meaningless when we know we're closing soon."

Mrs. Thorkildsen, I can tell by the tone in her voice, is quite seriously perturbed to hear this. Before long I can smell it too. Her pulse is on the way up when she asks two questions:

One: "Closing down?"
Two: "Are they crazy?"

The Librarian giggles. More questions from Mrs. Thorkildsen:

Three: "Who made that decision?"
Four: "Was it the county?"

"Yes, apparently it's the county. They're shutting down a whole bunch of neighborhood libraries, and unfortunately we're one of them."

Eighty-eight: "But what will happen to you?"

"I'm not worried. It's easy for newly educated librarians to find work, with better pay than I make here. There have been so many jobs in the private sector lately that I can basically choose whatever I want, but I'd prefer to work in the public library system."

It's mainly Mrs. Thorkildsen who does the talking. And so much talking! I can't remember the last time I heard Mrs. Thorkildsen talk with such joy and force. The Librarian listens, asks questions when there's a rare opening, and tells little stories of her own, shorter and more to the point than Mrs. Thorkildsen's. Mrs. Thorkildsen asks nosy questions. When she likes another human, Mrs. Thorkildsen becomes a mental cannibal.

"We'd love to know more about Roald Amundsen's trip to the South Pole," Mrs. Thorkildsen finally says.

"About the dogs," I add.

"About the dogs," Mrs. Thorkildsen says.

"The South Pole?" the Librarian says. "Let's see."

Her fingers start tapping away. It's simply incredible what one can accomplish with the help of fingers, I'll admit. The Librarian's fingers are able to locate the book Mrs. Thorkildsen needs without her even knowing what she was looking for.

"I'm getting a lot of results for Roald Amundsen and the South Pole . . . tons, in fact," the Librarian says without taking her eyes off the screen. "But . . . I can't seem to find anything about dogs specifically . . . *The South Pole* by Roald Amundsen is the first result here. Two volumes. First published 1912. That might be a little old?"

"No, no," Mrs. Thorkildsen says. "It might not be a bad idea to hear from the boss himself, what do you say, Tassen?"

I don't respond. I see right through Mrs. Thorkildsen's empty social graces. She doesn't really care what I think, even when she asks my advice.

"Do you have a library card?" the Librarian asks.

And that sets Mrs. Thorkildsen off. To the untrained eye, it might appear that she's not well, but all we witness is her librarian's laugh, an almost inaudible laugh that manifests itself not as sound, but as a series of convulsions that seem to completely take control of her small body. She leans forward in her chair as she shakes, and might seem to be in great pain, but this is simply how Mrs. Thorkildsen expresses joy after her long and faithful service in the public libraries. An old work injury, you might say.

"I didn't even think about that!" she giggles at last. "No, I don't have a library card, so I do need one."

The Librarian laughs too, so all must be well.

After an interrogation so riddled with numbers that one has to wonder whether it was designed specifically to prevent dogs from signing up for library cards, our errand at the Library is done and it's time to make our way home.

Now we're halfway there, I think to myself. Good boy.

Mrs. Thorkildsen, however, has other plans. Or not really. For once, Mrs. Thorkildsen is following an impulse. I could see that it was an impulse, because she was already leaning her body weight into the first of many small steps down the stairs and home, when she caught herself, stopped abruptly, made a decision, and told me:

"You know, I think I'm going to have a patty melt and a beer at the Tavern."

"Are dogs allowed in the Tavern?" I ask, and I know the answer.

"I don't think they're allowed, no," Mrs. Thorkildsen says.

"So we'll drop it, then," I respond. "Let's go home and be cozy instead. Dr. Pill probably has something exciting on his show today. Maybe that pedophile grandfather you really liked will be on again today!"

"No!" Mrs. Thorkildsen says with a resolve that is surprising, beautiful, and frightening all at once. "I *am* going to have a patty melt and a beer. Waiting for half an hour won't hurt you, Tassen. And he wasn't a pedophile, by the way. His stepdaughter just wanted revenge on him because he had a new girlfriend."

I can hardly believe my ears. I patiently wait for her while she goes hunting; that's for the common good of our little fellowship. The struggle for survival. It's no small sacrifice, but it's necessary for our existence, it's part of the deal. What's *not* part of the deal is Mrs. Thorkildsen tying me up and slamming the door in my face, just so she can stuff her face with patty melts. I'm speechless. And I'm alone.

15

THERE WAS ONCE AN OLD ESKIMO, the oldest one in the tribe, who didn't want to live in the new way. He wanted to live the way he always had, the way his forefathers had, with dogs, hunting for food in the cold, snowy wilderness. His family, his pack, did what they could to convince the old man to move into a house, but it didn't help, for none of them could explain to him *why* he should stop living the way he always had.

They took his old tools and weapons. They took the knives, the ropes, the sled—so he had no choice. Without tools, even an Eskimo can't live in the cold.

The old man begrudgingly agreed to sleep in the house—on one condition. Like most old people and dogs, he considered it an abomination to do his business indoors. To shit in the house like any old cat! The old man still wanted to go out whenever he needed to pull down his sealskin trousers.

When night fell, he would stand on the stoop of the old house with a hot beverage in his hand and wait for the time to come, and when it did, he emptied the cup's remaining contents into the snow and went out into the dark to take care of business.

One winter night, when the cold was even more biting than usual, someone registered that the old man hadn't returned from the toilet, and they went out to look for him. They followed the old man's tracks to where he had relieved himself. But there was no trace of his activities there, and the tracks kept going to the dog yard, where they beheld a sight that told the oldest among them what had happened:

The old man had stood out on the stoop with his coffee, waiting for the right moment to go into the darkness. When he poured out the small splash of hot drink that was left, he could see it was cold enough. The warm drops froze into ice before they hit the ground. This was all the old man needed to know. He went to his usual spot, but instead of letting it fall to the ground, he took the warm mass into his hands. Just as he'd learned from his grandfather, who had learned it from his grandfather, he began to meticulously shape the dough. He kneaded and spat until his shit slowly began to take the shape of a knife.

When the knife was sharp and solid enough, he walked over to the dogs. He picked out two of them, and without it making a sound, he cut the throat of one of them and drank his fill of the blood that gushed forth. He butchered the dog and ate his fill of fresh meat before using the remnants of the dog's hide and bones to build a small sled. He made reins and a whip out of the intestines. The old man let the second dog eat his fill of dog meat before strapping it to the sled, cracking the whip, and disappearing out into the polar night.

That's the kind of man Roald Amundsen was. So Mrs. Thorkildsen says. The Chief, she calls him. At first I thought this was an expression of her somewhat unsophisticated ironic sense of humor, but she could parry the fact that Roald Amundsen's own men called him that—so why can't she?

Mrs. Thorkildsen shows me a picture of a man surrounded by white and wrapped in the fur of an animal I don't immediately recognize. This is the Chief. The Chief has skis strapped to his feet, and leans forward onto his poles as he gazes majestically out over the endless white.

"What in the world is he wearing?" I ask Mrs. Thorkildsen, who is friendly enough to hold the book open right in front of my snout.

"Wolf," Mrs. Thorkildsen says. Silence.

I feel a mix of revulsion and awe. What kind of man dresses himself in wolf hide, and what is a poor mutt supposed to do if he encounters such a man along the road?

Keep in mind that Mrs. Thorkildsen is not particularly enthusiastic about the Chief. Sure, the man might be a polar hero and a national icon—Mrs. Thorkildsen doesn't dispute that. But, as she determined early on in her studies of what she's taken to calling "The big trip to the middle of nowhere":

"The Chief is a liar!"

Well, who isn't? Mrs. Thorkildsen also resorts to lies on occasion, like when she says she's just ducking out for a little bit and is gone for years on end, or when she fools the nice Garbageman into thinking she's senile, but I know it would be futile to discuss. For some reason, Mrs. Thorkildsen seems personally offended by the Chief.

"His poor mother thought he was studying to be a doctor, and he let her believe that, even if he barely knew how to crack open a book. She was a widow, too. Roald Amundsen was sixteen when Nansen came home after traipsing across the Greenland ice, and the sight of the hero greeted by cheering crowds gave him his life's calling. Not to be a polar explorer, as he himself claims, but to be celebrated. He wanted to be a star. A polar star!"

"Well, okay, so what if he didn't want to be a doctor?" I object, but Mrs. Thorkildsen barely notices.

"Fortunately for him, his mother dies. And, sure enough, the Chief might be a little embarrassed but ultimately thanks his good fortune for clearing this obstacle out of the way. Since he had it in his head that he'd studied medicine, the Chief didn't think it necessary later on to bring a doctor on his expeditions. He managed to convince himself he was a good enough doctor."

"Well, okay," I say. "Most people seem to think they're born veterinarians, so why not?"

"The whole trip to the South Pole was a lie. He said he was going to the North Pole!"

"Well, okay, so maybe he didn't want to go to the North Pole after all. I can sympathize with that."

"But that's the point! He never had any intention of going there, it was all a bluff. The North Pole had once been this big trophy but, as it happened, two other men both laid claim to being the first one there, and it turned into a real dogfight. Pardon the expression."

"I beg of you."

"The Chief hustled up some money, borrowed a boat, hired a crew, bought a pack of dogs, and set sail letting everyone think he was headed north. Where else would he be going? The Chief wanted to go where there were no other people," Mrs. Thorkildsen explains. "Not to settle there. No, if the Chief went somewhere, it was with the intention of leaving it behind."

These are the kinds of places called "no-man's-land." You find them everywhere, but the Chief preferred a "no-man's-land" that was far, far away from anywhere else, so cold that no humans could live there.

"I still find it hard to understand, even when Amundsen himself explains it, what is so great about exhausting oneself and putting one's life in danger," Mrs. Thorkildsen says. "On the other hand, they only gambled with their own lives. That's how it was with the Major's fly-ing, too. I was anxious for him, but in the end he was only risking his own life. And he was a good pilot, anyway. Survived four or five plane crashes relatively unscathed."

"If a pilot crashes four or five times, how good can he really be?"

Mrs. Thorkildsen overhears me. She likes to talk about the Major:

"It was only after he stopped that I realized how much the flying had meant to him. I wouldn't say he became a different man. But it became possible to picture him helpless."

Mrs. Thorkildsen is a little emotional now. And a little thirsty. She plods out to the kitchen, and for a moment I consider following her (you never know when a little treat is in store), but I lie still. Don't want to get off track, and I know myself well enough to know the tiniest bit of sausage makes me forget everything else. In fact, just the thought of it makes my mouth water. Self-control. *Stay!*

Back in the living room, glass in hand, Mrs. Thorkildsen picks up the story as she's crossing the floor on the way back to her chair.

"That is to say, at first he compensated for the flying by buying a motorcycle. Not a big loud showy motorcycle, but a nice yellow one, just the right size for the two of us. A Honda. We used it intensely for a few weeks, took a few long rides and visited friends all the way out in Enebakk. And then it was left in the garage to get dusty, until he sold it to Neighbor Jack across the street. But I think the worst thing for him was giving up his driver's license."

"You make him sound like a control freak," I interject. "That's not how I remember him."

"He was just a man, like any other man. Just like the Chief, that's what I'm trying to say. And I don't think you could ever use the word 'freak' to describe the Major," Mrs. Thorkildsen continues. "He hated freaks and gave his own son a massacre of a haircut on several occasions. Plus, he thrived on chaos. Like most men, he sought control over life by collecting tools and equipment and technical gadgets. And weapons, of course."

"Of course."

"His weapons bothered me from the start. They jutted out of dressers and drawers and scared the living daylights out of me. But there was nothing to be done about it. He slept with a revolver under his pillow until we met. He didn't know I knew that. When he got old, it felt oddly comfortable to keep weapons in the house. Or at least less uncomfortable. I think he would have felt terribly vulnerable without them, and he had trouble enough sleeping as it was. But in the end there were no weapons or tools that could help him, and he became as helpless as I had feared he would become. It didn't bother me, actually. In fact, it was good for me. Our marriage was a sacred, ordinary, wretched marriage, but in many ways the last years were the best. In the last ten years, we probably spent more time together than we had in the first thirty. No one wants to wither and die, of course, but I know part of the Major enjoyed getting old. Not to have to worry about surviving at any cost."

"What happens if one of us gets old?" I ask, but Mrs. Thorkildsen is lost in thought. A while later, after I've stopped waiting for her to say more, she chimes in:

"What a drag it is getting old."

16

WOULD PROBABLY NOT HAVE SURVIVED the sail to Antarctica. That's what Mrs. Thorkildsen thinks. I would have kicked the bucket before even making it on board the good ship *Fram*, she says. If I'd survived the five-month boat ride against all odds, I would probably have met certain death in the three-month-long march to and from the South Pole. And even surviving that was no guarantee of making it farther. Did I still want to hear more?

"I want to hear about the dogs," I say.

"It does no good being impatient. The story of the dogs is part of a bigger story. A story within a story, so to speak. There are things you need to know."

"About what?"

"About ice, for example."

"What is ice, other than solid water?"

"Antarctica is mostly made up of water. So much water," Mrs. Thorkildsen says, "that nearly all the drinking water on Earth can be found there. Almost ninety percent."

"Is that a lot?" I ask.

"It's a lot," Mrs. Thorkildsen says.

"Compared to what?" I say, feeling smart.

"Compared to almost anything, I'd say," Mrs. Thorkildsen replies, and I no longer feel so smart. Mrs. Thorkildsen thinks for a moment. When she's done thinking, she gets up and goes into the kitchen. I follow—you *never* know when there might be a treat in store—but she's only going to pour herself a glass of water. Two glasses of water. Three glasses of water. Four glasses of water, and another and another and another and another and another and yet another.

Afterward Mrs. Thorkildsen goes out to the laundry room and gets her wonderful tea trolley, the one she normally uses only when she has company. She meticulously places the glasses she has poured on the trolley, then she wheels it slowly, slowly into the living room, for once without launching into the waiter's battle cry:

"All in one trip!"

This doesn't unnerve me; on the contrary, it seems like a sensible solution that will save her many risky trips to the kitchen when the dragon water makes her unsteady later on. But then something gives me pause. Instead of setting the glasses on the table, which I'd been led by all past experience to believe she would do, Mrs. Thorkildsen parks the wonderful wheelie cart in front of the fireplace, where she begins unloading the water glasses. One by one, she places them very gingerly on the floor.

Mrs. Thorkildsen places the glasses like this:

O O O O O O O O   O

Like a spirit passing over the waters, Mrs. Thorkildsen sweeps her arthritic hands over the glasses in large, circular motions as she guides me through mathematical mysteries to which I don't think many dogs have been exposed.

"All these glasses," she says as she waves her hands, "that's a hundred percent. A hundred percent is everything. Do you see?"

"One hundred percent is everything," I repeat like a brainwashed cult member, and that's all the encouragement she needs to continue.

"This," Mrs. Thorkildsen says, placing a finger on the glass standing apart from the others, "is all the drinking water on Earth that's not at the South Pole, while this," she points to the rest of the glasses, "is the drinking water on Earth that you find in Antarctica. Ninety percent. Nine out of ten."

"That's ninety percent?"

"That's ninety percent."

"And what's the one glass?"

"Ten percent," Mrs. Thorkildsen says. "Of all the water. Do you see?"

"I think I do," I respond, but I don't have a clue.

Imagine if I did!

Considering hers is a life where nothing happens, I'd say there's quite a lot of activity around Mrs. Thorkildsen these days. There may not be that many people showing up at the door since the Major vanished, but it's as if every one of them, other than the Puppy's puppy, causes significant change in our lives. And like most changes, there are pros and cons to each of them. Many pros and cons. There may be changes that are purely good or purely bad, but I haven't gotten the scent of them.

In Mrs. Thorkildsen's case, it can be hard to tell the difference between a "pro" and a "con." Both of them unfold mostly in silence, in the same surroundings. A good day is a day without rain, and on a bad day she's asleep. Personally I have nothing to complain about—even on rainy days, the food bowl is filled and Mrs. Thorkildsen opens the door so I can take a walk around the backyard on my own. Which is just fine, even though I don't like getting wet. Not in that way.

Although it knocks her out, it's also mostly the dragon water that gets Mrs. Thorkildsen out of the house at all. It's when the supplies of dragon water are dwindling that Mrs. Thorkildsen equips herself for an expedition. And if we're going to the dragon's cave, there might also be a trip to the Library in store. One accompanies the other, the only question is who came first: Hangovers or literature?

Every time the Librarian mentions that the Library will close in the new year, Mrs. Thorkildsen gets just as upset. It's as if her mind contains a drawer where she can stuff and forget undesirable thoughts like that. Like the thought of calling the bank, the thought of the Library closing, and many other thoughts she can have all to herself.

And so we go home with another book in the wheelie bag. That is, first Mrs. Thorkildsen goes to the Tavern to eat a patty melt and drink a beer. These Tavern visits are a mixed experience as far as I'm concerned.

At least I'm no longer tied up on the street, brutally exposed, I'm shielded from the worst of my fears of suddenly being assaulted by grabby human kid hands or loudmouth mutts. But that doesn't mean I can let my guard down. You never know what might come out of the Tavern doors, or what mood it might be in.

There's a friendly bowl of water placed in the corner for me, but I never quite manage to settle down and be calm in front of the Tavern's gates. And I'm not the first poor dog to be left out here in limbo. Through the chemicals smeared all over the stone floor, I can pick up on the distinct scent of lonely dog.

Sometimes it feels comforting that other dogs get left out here, sometimes not. As with so many other things in life, it depends on the dog. There's something about the whole situation that brings out the most pathetic part of us. A little dutiful sniffing around, followed by every dog for himself, in awkward silence and endless strain that mostly consists of avoiding one another's stares. In a revolving-door pack like that, when anyone could come and go at any moment, staring is just an invitation to trouble, but you can imagine how hopeless it would be to avert your gaze once you've locked eyes with someone. Awkward and drawn out, except one time, which actually made all the other times worth it. One time, which arrived in the form of a greyhound-family mongrel bitch with black and white hair. Her name was Janis. I'll never forget her.

Janis was unhappy. It wasn't her own fault, of course. Janis's happiness was like that of most dogs—entirely in the hands of the creature at the other end of the leash. At the other end of Janis's leash was a troll.

The first time I met Janis, I honestly didn't really notice her. It was the Troll I noticed, with her fluorescent hair and giant stomping feet. And then I noticed that the Troll hadn't tied up her dog before she went into the Tavern, she'd just left her loose outside with a few calming words of warning before she disappeared.

"There we go. Good girl, Janis. Janis, Janis, Janis. Wait here, Janis. Mom will be back soon."

"That's what they all say," I chimed in after the Troll had slipped into the Tavern, but Janis wasn't interested in striking up a conversation, not just then. She lay down on the floor with her snout on her front paw and her eyes relentlessly glued to the door. She got up each time someone came out through the door, even when Mrs. Thorkildsen showed up, full and content.

After that, I don't think about Janis any more than I think about other dogs who come my way, but that changes the next time we are at the Library, where Mrs. Thorkildsen wants to discuss food and place an order for a book before ducking into the Tavern for her patty melt and her pint.

"You don't need to tie me up," I say when Mrs. Thorkildsen goes to strap the leash to the banister by the stairs. "I won't run away, if that's what you're afraid of."

"I thought you preferred to be tied up," Mrs. Thorkildsen says.

"That depends on the situation," I reply. "Sometimes it feels good to be tied up, sometimes it doesn't."

"All right, it's up to you," Mrs. Thorkildsen says.

So I sit there, untied but bound by invisible chains, and think about the Fenris-Wolf. Keep thinking about the Fenris-Wolf until the front door opens down there and I am given something else to think about. Suddenly, beyond the usual soundscape of cars and screaming kids, the most wonderful scent you can imagine streams in from the street. It is as if life itself had come through the door to say:

"Wake up! It's time to live."

I immediately recognize the Troll's stomping steps. They sound like an avalanche in reverse coming up the stairs, and for an instant I think the heavenly aroma is coming from her. But of course it is Janis, who slowly and elegantly tiptoes up and lies herself down right after the Troll disappears into the Tavern. It is just the two of us now, us and that chaotic, overwhelming smell of hers.

Don't ask me what happened, but it happened, oh yes, it happened! Janis's scent completely overpowers my nervous system and I turn into an old dog and a little puppy all at once. I can't think straight while the scent is brutally instructing me to take up a position behind Janis, who does absolutely nothing to hide the source of the smell. On the contrary. I simply have to get a taste, and the taste that unfolds across my tongue removes any doubt about what I have to do. And so I did. And then I did it again. No harm done, and it feels profoundly meaningful even though I'm not quite sure what it is all supposed to be good for. But most of all, it is delightful. And just when I think I am really getting the hang of it, Mrs. Thorkildsen comes out of the Tavern early for once in her damn life, and before I know it I am tied to the wheelie bag and strolling streetside, and the whole mysterious miracle is behind me.

Like clockwork, visitors have again arrived while we were at the Center. As we step through the gate at home, two women, one fully grown and the other young, come walking down the driveway toward us. I do my job right away when I spot them, letting out a few appropriately scary barks that make them freeze on the spot. Before I have time to check with Mrs. Thorkildsen whether she also wants me to tear them to pieces, the older woman says hello, and Mrs. Thorkildsen barely has time to say hello back before the woman asks:

"Do you know the Lord Jesus Christ?"

I have no immediate associations with that name, but it seems to ring a bell for Mrs. Thorkildsen.

"I do," she says. I can see that this delights the older woman, who is about to speak up again, but Mrs. Thorkildsen cuts her off:

"And I can't stand the guy."

What are the odds? Complete strangers approaching a complete stranger, and it doesn't take more than a moment to establish that they have a mutual acquaintance. These are the kinds of things that remind a dog what extraordinary powers human beings have, after all.

Naturally, I am very curious about what this Jesus might have done, given that women of all ages are now going door to door looking for him, but the fact that Mrs. Thorkildsen doesn't like him is obviously a blow to both of these women's happiness, since, after offering Mrs. Thorkildsen some reading material in vain—and she loves to read!— they plod out the gate and across the street looking dejected on their way to the neighbor's house across from us.

17

THE ATTACK OF THE HOME HELPER. It's raining tonight, and Mrs. Thorkildsen isn't feeling well. Not in the least. Mrs. Thorkildsen is lying on the bathroom floor again, and I can't get through to her. She talks to me on and off, but she won't look at me, and all I can hear, the only word I can make out from what she's trying to say, is my name.

"Tassen," Mrs. Thorkildsen says.

"Chavanaguhrrr chatzz buzz Tassen!"

After giving it some thought, she adds: "Hoo-wah!"

She flails her arms and legs around a little, but her body, so flimsy and so heavy, mostly stays put where it is.

It's the Home Helper who is responsible for this disaster but, if I know myself, I'm sure it's my fault as well. I should have insisted that Mrs. Thorkildsen take me out for a walk even when it rains, and I should have done so long ago. But she doesn't do that anymore—she hasn't for a long time. If it rains, which it naturally does from time to time, she just opens the door so I can go into the backyard and do my business. But had I forced Mrs. Thorkildsen to put on her coat, shoes, scarf, and hat, and do her duty as a dog owner, maybe things would have looked different tonight. Yes, I should have taken her out for some air, then this never would have happened. But, as I said, I maintain that most of the blame lies with the human who bears the extremely misleading title of Home Helper.

The Home Helper was the Puppy's idea. He was as proud as a bird dog with feathers hanging out of his mouth when he stopped by to proclaim that Mrs. Thorkildsen now, thanks to his persistent efforts with the municipality (I have no idea), was entitled to a home helper. Naturally, Mrs. Thorkildsen first tried to give him the impression that she had no desire whatsoever for a home helper, just like she didn't want a cable guy, but perhaps it was the positive experience with the cable guy that eventually made her put her indignation and stubbornness aside and decide to welcome the Home Helper into our lives. I thought it sounded like a brilliant idea. I could use a little home help myself, come to think of it. My hair is long overdue for a good brushing, and I can't remember the last time my nails were clipped. I promise not to bite again.

This morning we awoke to the rare sound of the alarm clock.

"The Home Helper is coming today" was the first thing Mrs. Thorkildsen said.

She'd laid out the clothes she was going to wear, but didn't get dressed before going through a solid morning ritual with her newspaper and coffee and toast. She'd retrieved a bag of cinnamon rolls from the winter cabinet and laid them out to defrost. I offered to check whether they were done defrosting.

"I'm sure they'll be just fine. We're going to have some when the Home Helper gets here."

"Don't you think I should check one, just to make sure?"

Mrs. Thorkildsen laughed, and that meant it was settled. I got my cinnamon roll. She watched me with a clever smile as I gobbled up the treat.

"Well, was it edible?"

"Hard to say when you've only had one."

"I think we'll just have to take that chance," Mrs. Thorkildsen said.

As the magical hour of the Home Helper's arrival drew nearer, Mrs. Thorkildsen got more and more restless. It was contagious. She couldn't focus on Dr. Pill, could only sit through the first five minutes of *My ex-wife claims I assaulted our daughter who ran off with her boyfriend* before she was back on her feet to check that everything was in its proper place. Everything was in its proper place, and it was still a long time until the Home Helper was due to arrive.

The strange thing is, the more you anticipate something, the more you've pictured in your mind how it's all going to turn out, the more surprised you are when it finally shows up. When the doorbell finally, finally rang, we both jumped out of our seats, but I was the only one who barked. Mrs. Thorkildsen didn't like that. Worst of all, the Home Helper didn't like it either. To put it mildly.

How is it possible to have a job with so much responsibility when one is so massively prejudiced against dogs? I only got a momentary glimpse of the Home Helper between Mrs. Thorkildsen's calves, a tiny woman with dark skin and dark hair and instinctive anxiety shining in her eyes. Before Mrs. Thorkildsen had time to open the door, the

Home Helper had already run down the stairs and partway down the driveway, where she unabashedly stood and shouted for the whole neighborhood to hear:

"Afraid of dog! I'm afraid of dogs!"

"Oh, I'm sorry!" Mrs. Thorkildsen said, as if she had anything to apologize for. "Wait a second!"

She pulled the door shut and asked me to sit. No problem. I'm glued to the spot.

"You'll have to stay in the bedroom, I think. The Home Helper is afraid of dogs."

"It's a trap!" I say. "The Home Helper only wants me out of the way so she can rob you in peace and quiet. I've heard about all that."

"I think we're going to have to take that chance. You should go take a rest, it wouldn't hurt you."

"Well," I said, "don't complain to me when she molests you."

And molest she did. The Mrs. Thorkildsen who, after an eternity, came to let me out of the bedroom was a completely different person than the Mrs. Thorkildsen who had shut me in. She seemed deflated, plain and simple. She was no longer restless and wired, but slow and lethargic in her movements. She said nothing.

"How did it go?" I asked, although I could see it hadn't gone well. Mrs. Thorkildsen didn't respond. She plodded into the kitchen, where the wheelie cart was positioned precisely as it had been before the Home Helper arrived, and I followed. Mrs. Thorkildsen found a mug and poured herself coffee from the pot.

"Can you believe it? She didn't want a cinnamon roll," Mrs. Thorkildsen said.

Didn't want a cinnamon roll? Were there people who didn't want Mrs. Thorkildsen's cinnamon rolls?

"She didn't have time," Mrs. Thorkildsen said. "And it was almost impossible to understand what she said. But she did a fine job with the laundry, I'll give her that."

Mrs. Thorkildsen had been promised help, and she thought she would get help she *needed*, but no. She'd get help doing the laundry, though she could very well have done that herself, and had the house not been vacuumed already, she could have gotten help with that as well. But what she really needed help with, being the best version of herself, she couldn't get help with.

Mrs. Thorkildsen was feeling blue. I know her so well that she didn't need to tell me that. And depression plus TV plus dragon water minus an evening walk equals Mrs. Thorkildsen on the bathroom floor. That much math I know.

It stinks. Mrs. Thorkildsen stinks, and it stinks in the hallway. That last part is technically my fault. Mine, plus a tray of cinnamon rolls. What was I supposed to do? Mrs. Thorkildsen was in the living room drinking away unsettling memories and stressful home helpers and the wheelie cart was just sitting there full of cinnamon rolls. There was, I thought, no point in that.

Mrs. Thorkildsen didn't see me help myself, and when the cinnamon rolls began to make their presence known in my stomach it was too late—she had already gone horizontal in the bathroom. I tried to let her know, I nudged her with an insistent snout and gave a little woof, but none of this brought me any closer to the door. In the end there was nothing I could do. What happened happened.

The house stinks of dog shit and forlorn drunkenness. *This* is when we could use the Home Helper.

I'd like to say something clarifying and enlightening about the sense of smell. Something that could reveal a tiny corner of the mystery, the way Mrs. Thorkildsen did with her water glasses, but I don't know where to begin. I might as well begin with the eyes, which are about as underdeveloped in dogs as they are in humans. How would you explain not only *what* you see, but the fact *that* you see, to a person who can't see? The answer is most likely that you're well-mannered enough not to do that. I can't imagine what the world would be like without the information that smell carries. How would you know anything at all?

"The smell was indescribable" is something you often hear, and truer words were never spoken, but let me try anyway. It's an enormous challenge to convey anything at all to a creature who doesn't have a sense of smell, but thinks it does anyway.

Three things you should know about smell when you don't have a sense of smell:

One: Smell is three-dimensional.
Two: Smell never disappears, it only takes new forms.
Three: Smell never sleeps.

You didn't hear this from me.

18

GREENLAND IS THE THEME OF the day for Mrs. Thorkildsen. The second-largest block of ice on Earth, just a bus stop away from the North Pole. The world's largest island and a tough place to live. The humans who settled there might be the hardiest on the planet, but they couldn't have done it without their dogs. Or the other way around, for that matter. The Chief ordered no fewer than one hundred such dogs from the west coast of Greenland—promptly delivered to a small island in the south of Norway, Mrs. Thorkildsen explains. And I have to ask:

"One hundred?"

"Yes, one hundred."

"Is that a lot?"

"I didn't think you cared about things like that."

"Okay, well, maybe I do."

Mrs. Thorkildsen doesn't respond, but she makes it impossible for me to doubt that my words are at work in there, my thoughts are making her thoughts move, divide, and merge again into new constellations, which turn into words and actions. The action at the end of Mrs. Thorkildsen's line of thought is for her to get up from her comfy chair and go into the room behind the bathroom, the one we never use anymore. In there, she rummages around in the drawers before returning to the living room with quick, almost eager steps and settling down at the dining table.

Mrs. Thorkildsen sits at the dining table and writes. Is that what she's doing? Instead of the staccato sound of her words, when she scratches them into the pages of her diary there is the sound of a pen trying to complete a continuous, controlled arc over a sheet of paper. And another sheet. The same arc again and again, and it's almost soothing—I've assumed a relatively flat position at Mrs. Thorkildsen's feet. My rest is promptly cut short when I hear one of the scariest noises I know in the universe:

The scissors.

"Snip, snip," the scissors and the paper sing in unison. "Clippy clippy clip!"

Mrs. Thorkildsen cuts, and the longer she cuts, the more delicate the sound of the scissors through the paper grows. It slices more and more slowly, until finally it's not slicing at all. It grows quiet. Mrs. Thorkildsen lets out a short, wordless noise that tells me she's satisfied. She gets up from the table, and I get up from my place at her feet.

"Do you see that?" Mrs. Thorkildsen asks and reaches out her wrinkly hand, holding a piece of paper that smells like nothing but paper. "Do you see what it is?"

Despite my best efforts, I can't see what it is—but that doesn't seem to worry Mrs. Thorkildsen. She moves over to the low table by the couch, the one she strangely claims to be afraid of and thus keeps covered by a floor-length red tablecloth. She places the piece of paper on the red tablecloth so it stands upright, and asks again: "Now do you see what it is?" When viewed head-on, the piece of paper looks a little like the pointy shape of the house with the ship *Fram* in it, but when I circle the table and see it from the side, it looks a bit like this:

I stay still and gaze at the little paper shape on the table, still not quite comprehending what it's supposed to look like, but then I hear myself say, without having thought it over:

"It's a wolf. A paper wolf."

"Well, it's supposed to be a Greenland dog," Mrs. Thorkildsen says.

"That's what I said."

19

THE PUPPY MADE A SURPRISE visit today. With the Bitch. They presented it as a practical little detour since they were in the neighborhood, but the whole operation seemed more like an ambush to me. I have no idea what time it was, morning is morning, and Mrs. Thorkildsen was still sleeping her sorely needed beauty sleep. I lay in the hallway snoozing among the Major's shoes, dozing and dreaming and meditating over the mantra of "breakfast." My bladder was at ease and I was still looking forward to a solid nap when the alarm clock rang so earsplittingly loud I impulsively barked with gusto and stumbled to my feet before I was completely awake. To be fair, I bark with gusto whenever the doorbell rings, but this was something else. This was Code Red, and the captain was still passed out on the deck after yesterday's rough seas.

The sound of the key in the lock made me stop my barking. Before the door had time to open, I sprinted into Mrs. Thorkildsen's bedroom and resumed barking, although she was obviously awake. At least she was out of bed. That wasn't necessarily good news.

Mrs. Thorkildsen stared at me with bulging eyes and an open mouth. Her spindly, bright white legs protruded from her nightgown, her hair stood on end, and between those two points was mostly chaos. A skinny old workhorse on its way to the glue factory. For free.

I heard someone cry hello from the hallway.

"It's the Puppy and the Bitch," I whispered. The whispering that was meant to calm the whole situation only made it feel more urgent. Mrs. Thorkildsen's panic had already transferred itself to me. Just then I recalled something the Major used to say:

"Panic and paralysis are two sides of the same coin. It's better to make a wrong decision than to make no decision at all."

And just as the Major had promised, the panic disappeared the moment my decision was made. From fear to action in two heartbeats.

"Go back to bed," I sneered. "I've got this."

I chose to go out offensively, to harness the element of surprise, the trump card in every battle.

The swine in the hallway stood waiting for sweet little Tassen with the wagging tail, eager as ever to see a familiar face, but that's just how they know me. Makes you realize what's in a name. A name can hide a lot of things, no matter what they say.

My name isn't really Tassen, "the small one." Tassen is my slave name, given to me by the master who bought me. Actually, when I first came to this house, covered in my own puke, the Major said my name was Helmer. But Mrs. Thorkildsen called me Tassen from day two, and no one has called me otherwise since. Tassen Thorkildsen. Doesn't matter, really, because underneath it all I'm Satan Snarl of the Hounds of Hell.

It was Satan Snarl whose hair stood on end as he flashed his teeth this morning. He growled softly and bared his gums as he planted his feet deep into the carpet. Where that sound came from, I have no idea. I was almost a little frightened by it myself.

After a moment when it seemed like the Puppy simply didn't believe his own eyes, I could smell him getting anxious. Really anxious. Not "Ohhhh, look how fierce you are, Tassen!" in a silly voice. He went silent and his heart rate skyrocketed. Pulled his hands back, the coward. Seems the Puppy was a little afraid of dogs, too. Instead of continuing his path into the house, he pulled his leg back. Good boy. Take your bitch and make a quiet exit, and no one gets hurt. Slowly and quietly, I said.

The Bitch got the point right away, and turned her entrance into an exit without saying a word. The Puppy stood there alone, paralyzed by fear now, so afraid he cried out for his mother.

"Moooom!" he cried.

Mrs. Thorkildsen did not respond.

"Moooo-ooom!" the Puppy cried again then. I turned my head toward the bedroom and he immediately smacked me with the newspaper, rolled up and fresh from the mailbox. It sounds so innocent, giving the dog a smack with the paper, but it's more than enough to conjure up stars and moons and planets if the combination of accuracy and power is just right. The Puppy has that combination down, which I've known for a while, so I was finished on the spot. No more growling from me—but in its place, I absurdly enough felt shame.

Whining, I darted into Mrs. Thorkildsen's room with my tail between my legs, and the Puppy followed. Mrs. Thorkildsen struggled to put on her blue bathrobe and seemed even more confused at the sight of the Puppy:

"What in the *world* is happening?" she asked, and the Puppy chimed in:

"Tassen attacked us."

"What nonsense," Mrs. Thorkildsen snorted as she tied the belt around her bathrobe. "Tassen doesn't attack anyone."

"Oh, no? He was baring his teeth at us when we came in."

"Hear that?" I said. "That wasn't an attack, it was a warning."

"That wasn't an attack, it was a warning," Mrs. Thorkildsen said. "Tassen looks out for me. If you'd warned me you were coming, he wouldn't have reacted that way. But what do you expect when you come trampling in here like the Gestapo?"

Mrs. Thorkildsen had been completely blindsided, but she knew the tactics of war as well as him. And now the Puppy was the one put on the defensive.

"Put the kettle on and let me get ready!" she said. Emphatically. The Puppy backed out of the bedroom before Mrs. Thorkildsen had reached the word "kettle." I followed to make sure he obeyed her orders.

While Mrs. Thorkildsen took her time getting dressed, the Puppy and the Bitch rummaged through all the drawers and cabinets they could as they exchanged short messages through clenched teeth.

"She must have them somewhere," the Puppy said. "I just don't know where. She used to hide them in the linen closet, but now I have no idea. Have you looked in the laundry?"

"There's not a single empty bottle there."

"God knows where she gets rid of them."

God knows. Mrs. Thorkildsen knows. I know. The nice-smelling man in the fluorescent uniform knows. Why the Puppy and the Bitch needed to know, I'm honestly not sure, especially since they once again were here to talk about houses.

• • •

"I understand them all too well," Mrs. Thorkildsen says, finally secured in her chair with a glass in the pitch dark after a long day.

"Her, that is. As for Junior, I don't think he cares that much about living here. Why else would he spend most of his adult life overseas? But *she* has obviously decided this is where she wants to live, and like I said, I understand her all too well—this is still a nice place to live. A fantastic place to grow up, but can't they just be patient, the little bit of time I have left? I'm going to stay here until they carry me out cold, and I've never given them a reason to think otherwise. But what happens when I do my part to keep up the rate of decay? Then it's suddenly a problem that I'm not taking care of myself or something!"

The last words are spoken in a voice I think is meant to imitate the Bitch. She utters the words with a grimace. Stays quiet long enough to make me think we're done with the subject, but then comes:

"Take care of myself! That's what I'm doing. Taking care of my life. I'm living the way I want to live. I'm no child who doesn't understand the consequences. I understand. It's the ones who for the life of them can't understand that I don't necessarily just want to live as long as possible. Why should I? Live a gray boring life in hope of an even grayer and more boring life at the old folks' home? Why in the world should I take care of myself?"

"Well, for one thing, you've got a dog," I weigh in. "And that's a big responsibility."

Mrs. Thorkildsen smiles. "You're my constant comfort, Tassen. You know that? And I hope you know I'll always make sure you're happy."

"Always?"

"Always!"

"With cinnamon rolls?"

"With cinnamon rolls."

20

MRS. THORKILDSEN'S CUTTING AGAIN. I'm glad to see her on her feet and active, but to tell you the truth, she seems a little feeble. She should eat more and maybe drink less dragon water. And she knows it. I've even heard her say it. But she has no appetite and barely any food. We should have gone hunting today, although we have plenty of dragon water in stock, but it's getting dark now, and Mrs. Thorkildsen never goes hunting at night.

She cuts in silence and a hush spreads through the house, other than the sound of paper being folded and scissors slicing through it. Then the phone rings, and Mrs. Thorkildsen jumps, quietly gets to her feet, and staggers out to the hallway to answer it.

"Twenty-eight oh-six oh-seven?" she says, and I bet it's one of her friends calling, maybe a cousin. I can hear it in the way Mrs. Thorkildsen is talking. Not relaxed, exactly, but as relaxed as she ever gets with the phone pressed to her ear.

"Well, I'm just sitting here," Mrs. Thorkildsen says, and gives yet another brief summary of how her life looks since her husband went away. She describes a life with many empty hours, with no appetite and terrible prices and useless shit on TV that she never watches anyway. Overall, she paints a pretty tragic picture, but she never fails to deliver the final point:

"I don't know how I would manage without Tassen," she tells whoever is on the other end of the line, and I think to myself that I don't know either. Or how I would manage without her. We need each other. I'd starve without Mrs. Thorkildsen, and she'd drink herself to death without me.

She doesn't mention the Puppy or the Bitch at all. Nor does she mention the fact that we were at the Library and the Tavern today (Janis was there as well, but today she was suddenly both uninteresting and uninterested; she was pregnant, too), or the fact that she's sitting at the dining table cutting. Instead, she repeats:

"Nothing ever happens."

A strange thing to say. Here we are caught in the middle of an ice-cold drama between life and death, honor and humiliation, dogs and men, and she says nothing is happening? The Puppy and the Bitch barging in with fistfuls of papers that make Mrs. Thorkildsen overwhelmed and scared, isn't that something happening? Isn't the Home Helper happening? The patty melts at the Tavern?

I know what Mrs. Thorkildsen is doing. Mrs. Thorkildsen is not complaining. This, you see, is how Mrs. Thorkildsen complains. For Mrs. Thorkildsen, complaining isn't just a skill, it's an art form at the highest level.

"The best place to hide a tree is in the forest," the Major told me once, and since most of what he told me were things he'd already said to Mrs. Thorkildsen, I think she must have heard it, too. She's living by his advice, anyway. She disguises her lack of complaining with complaining. On the phone, she doesn't complain about missing other people, other times. Instead, she talks up a painful foot I've never heard a peep about. And then there's all that talk about those who have it worse than her, all the time. And the Home Helper. And all the useless shit on TV.

Afterward she goes over to the dining table, but she doesn't cut anymore. Just sits there quietly, staring through her glasses, not responding when I talk to her. Even her smell is barely there. Then Mrs. Thorkildsen goes to bed without so much as saying good night.

21

IT TAKES THREE NIGHTS. On the third night Mrs. Thorkildsen gets up from the dining table, cleans up the paper scraps, puts the scissors back in the kitchen drawer, goes out into the hallway, and calls my name. Always happy to go for a walk, I am ready at the front door before Mrs. Thorkildsen can grab her coat—but then the old hag tricks me. I hear the door to the living room shut behind me, and Mrs. Thorkildsen is already on the other side. It takes me so completely by surprise that I don't really have a reaction. I choose to believe it is a misunderstanding, which will soon be cleared up.

I wait for so long, taking into consideration both Mrs. Thorkildsen's flighty spirit and her rickety physique, but there are limits. I bark. Nothing happens. I bark again. And again. Mrs. Thorkildsen doesn't answer. It's not in my nature to bark for my own sake; I've been programmed— by *people*!—to warn them about threats that lie in wait. And, naturally, I am concerned about what Mrs. Thorkildsen might do when left unsupervised. Older people do, as the Bitch has pointed out, have an unfortunate tendency to burn down the houses they live in. Or break their hips. What if Mrs. Thorkildsen goes senile in there behind the closed door, I think, or forgets that I'm standing here in the hallway? Alone. I'll starve to death. Or more likely, die of thirst. There are enough shoes here to sustain me for a while, but there's no drinking water. The drinking water is at the South Pole.

Then, in the middle of my stream of thoughts, the living room door slides open. I have such a good start with the barking, it is becoming nearly as autonomous as a Chihuahua's, so a few barks slip out even after Mrs. Thorkildsen opens the door. There is a brief and slightly dumb pause. I fear the worst, but Mrs. Thorkildsen isn't mad at my barking.

"There, there, Tassen," she says. "It wasn't *that* bad, was it?"

I am about to respond that, yes, it was *that* bad, but Mrs. Thorkildsen has already proceeded to her "Come on, now," and I come. You never know when there might be a treat in store.

On the floor by the fireplace, the results of three nights' hard work with scissors and paper stand on display. The lone paper wolf has become a giant pack.

"A hundred dogs," Mrs. Thorkildsen says. "That's how many there were."

A hundred dogs is far more dogs than I ever could have imagined, it turns out. It's more dogs than I've ever seen at one time in my whole life. I didn't know there were that many dogs in the world. It is a sight that explodes all boundaries in a simple dog's brain. The floor is filled with small paper wolves in neat rows, all of them different, all of them alike but, most of all, they are *many*.

"That's how many dogs the Chief bought in Greenland," Mrs. Thorkildsen says, gazing down at her creation.

"And that's how many"—she snatches one paper wolf up from its place on the floor—"died on the voyage from Greenland to Norway. A single one."

She stands frozen with the paper wolf in her hand, thoughtful rather than confused. I've learned to smell the difference by now. Mrs. Thorkildsen, who otherwise is a true master at predicting the future, is constantly wandering into little pockets of time where she simply can't make head or tail of what's just happened, or what's about to happen. Sometimes Mrs. Thorkildsen doesn't have a clue what Mrs. Thorkildsen has done or is about to do.

A decision is taking shape in her head, and she walks over to the fireplace and sets the paper wolf she is holding in her hand upon the mantel. White paper against white plaster, the only proof it is there is its shadow. A dead wolf on the mantel. The army of dogs stretches almost the whole way from the fireplace to the coffee table. The pack fills the whole space between the basket of firewood and the Major's chair, which is now my chair. We both end up with our gaze fixed on the lone wolf on the mantel.

"Where is it?" I ask.

Mrs. Thorkildsen thinks for a while before responding:

"Well, who knows? It's certainly not at the South Pole. But if it was a good dog, and I have every reason to think it was, I'm sure it went to a good place."

"Good dogs don't make it to the South Pole?"

"Unlikely."

Of course I am pining for Mrs. Thorkildsen to call me a good dog, but you don't ask for these things. That's like *asking* for respect. The moment you ask for respect, you've lost all respect. If Mrs. Thorkildsen, based on our joint daily life, concludes that I'm a good dog, it'll have to be up to her to tell me so on her own terms. So I ask:

"How did it die?"

"Hmmm, not sure," Mrs. Thorkildsen says. "It's strange, actually, that there weren't more of them who perished on the journey. The Chief had hired two Eskimos to watch the pack, but it was easier for a dog than for a native person to leave Greenland. The dogs' fates were left up to chance, crammed together in a dark cargo hold with no supervision."

"That whole giant pack was crammed together in a ship's cargo hold?"

I was speechless.

"None of the crew knew anything about dogs. Men at sea typically don't have to. They stayed away from the cargo hold. They threw food down the loading chute, and it was up to the dogs to share it among themselves."

"Uh-oh," I say.

The survival of the fittest is brutal enough in the wild, but if you're fast enough, you might be able to escape any immediate threat. To hide. How the survival of the fittest might play out among Greenland dogs scared shitless in the crowded cargo hold of an old hulk wobbling its way through the North Atlantic is unimaginable. To put it mildly, it's a miracle that only one of them perished on the journey. On the other hand, it may have been the luckiest dog in this whole tragic story.

22

THE SICKNESS HAS A NAME. Mrs. Thorkildsen suffers from loneliness. It's a chronic ailment that Mrs. Thorkildsen bears silently and bravely, but sometimes, once in a rare while, usually when the day has been a long one, she confides in me:

"I'm so lonely, Tassen," she says. It makes me feel terrible, because *I* don't feel lonely. I have Mrs. Thorkildsen, and that's more than enough for me. Mrs. Thorkildsen, on the other hand, only has me, and that's obviously not enough for her.

Mrs. Thorkildsen would have been happier as a dog, I think. (I think most humans would, for that matter.) As a dog, she'd be able to thoroughly greet everyone who crossed her path, whether she knew them or not. Every chance encounter on the street would smell like zesty information and tasty stories. Not to mention how much more exciting it is to sniff each other's groin than it is to vaguely nod as you pass each other, as people usually do—that is, if they greet each other at all.

Yesterday, Dr. Pill ran a show called: *My mother-in-law is sabotaging our marriage with false accusations.* For once, Mrs. Thorkildsen couldn't bear to finish the program. Mid-sentence, mid-scream, she grabbed the magic wand and cut both the mother-in-law and Dr. Pill off with her mighty thumb. I lifted my head from my lying position, awoken from my daily dose of Dr. Pill by the massive silence that followed the human cackling. Mrs. Thorkildsen sat still, glaring at the dead TV screen. She stared into the darkness and listened to the silence too long. Far too long, I thought, so I asked:

"Do you want to talk about it?"

"No," Mrs. Thorkildsen said. "There's nothing to talk about."

"It feels better if you talk about what's bothering you. You've said that yourself."

"Who says I want to feel better?"

Mrs. Thorkildsen sucks nutrients out of the letters on books' pages like my intestine sucks nutrients out of pork fat, but the reading causes problems, too. What goes in—whether in brain or intestine—must come out. Mrs. Thorkildsen gets constipated in the head if she doesn't also have an outlet for whatever it is books are putting in her head. The words from books flow through Mrs. Thorkildsen like a river that turns the country it runs through fertile and fruitful, but what happens if the water can't find an outlet?

Floods. Ruined crops. Desert. Sometimes I'm afraid Mrs. Thorkildsen will turn into a desert.

Mrs. Thorkildsen, I'm afraid, is smitten by the Chief's insanity. She thinks she's going to the South Pole. Step by step, word by word. With a single dog pulling the sled.

The Chief is a liar. That was and is the premise and conclusion of

Mrs. Thorkildsen's tale "The Antarctic Odyssey," and now, full of schadenfreude and a quick glug of dragon water, she's gotten to the moment when he reveals his lying nature to the world. This is Mrs. Thorkildsen's exhibit B in her case against the Chief. (Exhibit A, that he demonstrably lied to his mother, will always be Mrs. Thorkildsen's most damning argument.)

· · ·

The Chief stands before the *Fram*'s aft mast with his hands behind his back. It's early in the morning in the harbor of a small island in the Atlantic. The *Fram* is farther from the North Pole than she has ever been. From the mast hangs a quadratic map unlike all other maps. The map shows an island. The coast is outlined in detail. Inland, the occasional mountain range, but toward the center of the map, not a single topographical feature is filled in. Most of the map is a blank space where all the lines run together to the exact same point, like on a dartboard. Another way to read the map, which might be what the Chief does, is to see a blistering light radiating from a point in the center.

The Chief speaks. About the South Pole. The place where the lines run together, or radiate from. A shining star, or a black hole. All or nothing. The Chief doesn't even need to say it: first or last. There's no room for the in-between. Nor does he need to say anything about what awaited those who didn't come *first*. Someone was already on the way to be first. Firster than first, that was the Chief's goal. Any questions?

No questions.

"He lied to everyone he ever asked for money, he lied to the man he borrowed the boat from, he lied to his king, and he lied to his first mate. Told him he was going to the North Pole. He could even explain *why* he wanted to go to the North Pole. Explain with so much clarity and force that men were willing to suffer the loss of seven summers' leaves on the trees in order to run with the ice across the polar seas."

"Is seven summers a long time?"

"Half a dog's life."

"So if you left a young dog at the height of his powers, it might die of old age before you made it home?"

"That's how it was," Mrs. Thorkildsen says. "My father set sail for three years at a time. I first saw him when I was three years old, the next time when I was six, and then I had him at home for a whole year when I was nine. Then he left again. Went back toward China, but disappeared on the way. No one ever found out what happened. Mother thought it was the crew that had done him in. 'He was too tough,' she said."

I'd like to know what Mrs. Thorkildsen's mother meant by "tough." The Chief, for instance, must have been a tough man, but obviously not *too* tough. Tough enough to turn the world upside down, to break his promises and sail a ship on which he'd conned his way right into the history books. Tough enough to commandeer a pack of Eskimo dogs out into the great beyond, but obviously not so tough that he got beaten to death by his own crew and chucked overboard. It's a fine balance.

The Eskimos taught the Chief to drive sled dogs. Eventually he learned to chastise every mutt who wouldn't submit to him, and he learned how quickly you can nurse a tired, famished sled dog back to one with its tail in the air, longing to pull on the harness with all its might. He learned what happens if you drive the dogs too hard, and after he'd shot and slaughtered a dog who didn't want to pull one day, he learned that Greenland dogs are cannibals, taste good, and ward off disease. A dead Greenland dog, the Chief thought, might very well be a good Greenland dog.

23

NORMALLY, I WOULDN'T BE ABLE to quote any of the poetry Mrs. Thorkildsen reads aloud to me from time to time, with the best of intentions. There are many reasons for that. The first is that the poetry reading usually takes place late at night, after a certain amount of dragon water consumption. The diction, in other words, isn't always the clearest.

The other reason is that the poems she reads are mostly totally incomprehensible. I'm not saying they're bad, it's just that they don't speak to *me*. And when it comes to poetry, I think it's best to trust your gut. It might just be that dogs don't understand poetry, but I do wag enthusiastically when a poem first gets me excited. This, for example:

A rose is a rose is a rose.

That's what I call poetry. Cards on the table, no bullshit, cut to the bone. (It's been a while since there's been meat served on the bone in this house, by the way.)

Mrs. Thorkildsen has been kind enough to show me how poetry is made, though I haven't asked. The secret of poetry, Mrs. Thorkildsen explains, is simply to make the words a little obscure. She uses a tailor-made metaphor to spark my interest: it's like choosing to take the most exciting route through the park instead of the most direct one, she says.

For example:

> *Your bum's*
> *behind you whichever way*
> *you aim.*

That's all there is to it, according to Mrs. Thorkildsen. Good luck!

Sometimes I have to remind myself that Mrs. Thorkildsen isn't a dog but a human, with all the flaws and weaknesses that come with the species. I've often had to remind her that this is a story about dogs, first and foremost, but now it's finally gotten through to her. And why has it? Because Mrs. Thorkildsen has discovered—apparently to her own surprise—that the South Pole dogs had *names.* I'm sure they had names long before they were crammed into the cargo hold in Greenland, too, but those names were left behind when the ship glided out from the dock in the bright summer evening.

It's the crew members who give "their" dogs names, and Mrs. Thorkildsen is very concerned about these names. Each time she discovers a new dog name, she gets happy and excited. Then she takes the time to stand and plod across the floor over to the pack of paper wolves by the fireplace, and pick out an individual whom she then places on the table. Then she stops by the fridge, since she's already on her feet.

With her glasses perched on her nose and a ballpoint pen in hand,

she writes names on the paper wolves one by one as she discovers
them.

That one is Siggen, that one is the Corpse, that one is Maxim Gorky,
which makes Mrs. Thorkildsen laugh, and then there's Fridtjof, Teddy,
and the Colonel. The Major makes us both laugh.

Bella, Bolla, Lasse, Eskimo, Balder, Fix, Lussi, the Angel of Death,
Gray, Brum, Lucy, Jacob, Jack of Clubs, Tiger, Rat, Mischief, Emil,
Baldy, Hellik, Adam, Rascal, Slap, Grim, Suggen, and Mrs. Snapsen.

Tiny, Kaisa, Kaisa-Boy, Uranus, Neptune, Esther, Sarah, Eva, Olava,
the Clock Maker, Lola, Elsie, Siv, Maren, Cook, Bone, Fancy-Pants,
Helga, and Peter. Madeiro. Thor.

Those are the names I remember. Probably less than half of them.
I don't have the memory of an elephant. I've never pretended I do. To
make up for it, I produce small, presentable droppings that a reason-
ably fit retiree can harvest with a plastic bag without difficulty. It all
works out.

"Can you imagine," Mrs. Thorkildsen asks, "what chaos it must
have been on board the *Fram* with all those dogs, in the middle of the
Atlantic?"

Yes, I can. Better than she can, I think. I can imagine how the moist
deck of a ship, wobbling across the blue marshes, would be hell for a
Greenland dog—well, for any dog, I'd think. I've visited that deck. And
I've smelled it.

The men who were unfamiliar with Greenland dogs—that is, most
of the men on board—found them scary and primitive, simply repulsive
as they stood there, with dirt in their mustaches and hunger in their
eyes. If the dogs were angry, they bit. If they were hungry, they bit. If

they were scared, they bit. And it wasn't possible to teach a single one of the dogs anything at all on board the ship. The *Fram* was a floating zoo filled with more or less wild animals. And, like the animals in a zoo, none of them were supposed to be there.

"This is animal abuse," I point out. "To strap polar dogs to the deck and then sail the ship through the tropics, that's a bit much!"

"Just wait," Mrs. Thorkildsen says with a smirk, "it gets better."

"I'm guessing they start dropping like flies."

"The Chief had counted on losing half the dogs over the course of the voyage from Greenland to Antarctica."

"Cynical bastard."

"You might say that. But guess how many dogs there were when they arrived after five months at sea?"

"Fourteen hundred and ten thousand? What do you expect me to say? But let's say the Chief was right. I'm under the impression that he was the kind of man who's usually right. Let's say half."

"Fifty percent?"

"Percents are good. We like percents. Let's say that."

"Just wait!" Mrs. Thorkildsen says, suspiciously cheerful and secretive, and wouldn't you believe that she has a little surprise in store.

"Sit!" she says. I sit. Easy peasy. I sit like a speeding bullet.

"Stay!" she says. I stay, of course, but I'm starting to wonder just a little. Might there be a little treat in store? I'm sorely in need of a treat right now. I feel a little empty and my stomach feels restless. Mrs. Thorkildsen walks into the kitchen, and my tail starts to move, all on its own. It's very impractical to wag while you're sitting.

She's back, but unfortunately not carrying a treat, unless it's extremely well wrapped up.

"Now you'll see," Mrs. Thorkildsen says, and of course she's right again.

She walks over to the pack of paper wolves by the fireplace, and now I see what she has in her hand. More paper wolves!

Mrs. Thorkildsen places them in the pack one by one. Human babies come from the stork, paper wolves come from Mrs. Thorkildsen. There are many of them. Every time I think she's placed the last one, there's another. And another. I lose count after four. When she's finished, Mrs. Thorkildsen stays still with her hands on her hips—the preferred pose of humans when they feel they've accomplished something. Which I would say Mrs. Thorkildsen has. She's earned those hands on her hips now.

"One hundred and sixteen dogs," Mrs. Thorkildsen says. "That's nineteen more than there were when they left Norway."

All I can do is trust that she's right.

"There were puppies born on board constantly, you see. All the male dogs that were born while the ship was at sea joined the trip to Antarctica. But can you guess what happened to all the bitches who were born on board?"

I can feel myself getting a little nauseated before she's even finished asking the question. I can almost smell the scent of roasted Greenland bitch with rosemary, gravy, boiled vegetables and potatoes.

"Eaten . . ." I venture, and what I feel isn't even rage, just emptiness. Mrs. Thorkildsen, on the other hand, laughs!

"What's so funny about eating little puppies?" I ask, hoping my irritation is obvious enough.

"You'll have to excuse me, Tassen," Mrs. Thorkildsen says, and in the middle of all the wretchedness it's good to hear what the laughter does to her voice. "No, they didn't eat the puppy bitches. But I really shouldn't laugh—what they actually did to them wasn't much better. When a bitch was born, they took swift action. She was thrown overboard before she had time to open her eyes."

"They drowned?"

"I should think so."

"Just like that, plop, plop, they were gone?"

"The crew cried 'Fish food!' when a newborn was thrown overboard."

"Scoundrels."

"Not necessarily. I think you should keep in mind, Tassen, that these men weren't dog haters. You might think a man capable of grabbing a newborn Greenland dog by the scruff and throwing it over the railing while its mother watches must have a heart of stone, if he isn't pure evil. But that's not necessarily the case. It's enough for him to have a goal. And if the goal requires bitches to be sacrificed, then they're sacrificed. According to the Chief, who had learned from the Eskimos, too many bitches in the pack would only mean trouble. The Norwegian South Pole expedition was, overall, not a great place for women."

She can say what she wants. Newborn puppies being drowned isn't much better than newborn puppies being served for dinner, if you ask me.

"Just listen to what the Chief writes about those who called this animal abuse," Mrs. Thorkildsen insists, her glasses perched at the tip of her nose. She reads in a deep voice, as deep as her vocal range will allow her, but I still don't think she sounds like a hardy polar hero. She still sounds like a hardy librarian:

"*If only I had these gentle people under my care. Hypocrites, all of them. Goddamn it! I can safely say the animals love us.* Do you hear that, Tassen, the Chief thinks you're a hypocrite! What do you say to that?"

The animals love us. Yes, they do, but not because you're kind and gentle, Captain Amundsen. They love you because that's what dogs do. That's our job. We love humans, even when they give us no reason to do so. We love you, with all the worries and calamities it brings. And every time we think we've had enough, we come back for more. You'd actually have to torment a poor mutt quite thoroughly and quite early on to break them of that instinct. The dog won't turn from friendly to hostile, but from friendly to scared, and good luck coaxing them out of that corner once you've forced them into it. What does he imagine the dogs would have done if they hadn't been happy—other than die, that is?

24

THE DAMNED PAST BITES ME in the tail once again. It does so because I don't understand the damned future.

One day long, long ago, Mrs. Thorkildsen said something completely out of the blue as she did the dishes after her modest breakfast:

"You're going to have to manage without me a few days next week."

"You know I can't stand being alone," I replied. "And why on earth should I be alone?"

"I'm going on a trip," Mrs. Thorkildsen said. "With a few of the old library patrons in the association. We're going on the boat to Denmark."

"On a boat? In the ocean?"

"Yes, of course. We're going to Copenhagen."

"What in the world will you do there?"

"Well, not so much 'do,'" Mrs. Thorkildsen said, and she laughed in the slightly teasing way I can't quite stand. "It's mostly just for the trip's sake. We'll only be in Copenhagen for a few hours before we set sail back to Norway."

"What's the point of *that*?"

"Well, there isn't so much a 'point,'" Mrs. Thorkildsen said. "I'm going to relax with good food and drinks, in the company of old friends."

"Well, that sounds right up my alley!"

"Unfortunately dogs aren't allowed in Copenhagen," Mrs. Thorkildsen said, trying to sound like she was sorry about this.

"Well, can't you do it here instead?" I insisted. "It's far too long since you threw a real party. You have plenty of food in the fridge and dragon water in the linen closet."

I'd almost said *hah!*, but let it be. Mrs. Thorkildsen didn't answer that one. Of course she didn't—the discussion had ended and I had won. So I thought the case was closed, until yesterday, when she started rummaging around in drawers and cabinets. I asked her what was happening, but Mrs. Thorkildsen was too single-mindedly focused on her own endeavors to respond. She was nervous and cheerful all at once, and that's not like her, at least not when she's home alone.

Today, she declared at last, she is finally going across the sea to Copenhagen, only to come right back home again. Wise, sensible Mrs. Thorkildsen—what kind of a ludicrous idea is this? For the first time I find myself sharing the Puppy and the Bitch's concern for her mental health. I haven't seen any signs of decline otherwise, but it's now becoming clear that something is seriously wrong. You don't just leave your dog like that, at least not if you're Mrs. Thorkildsen! I'm not thinking of myself, of course, far from it, I'm not that kind of dog. I am only concerned for Mrs. Thorkildsen's safety.

"Take me with you," I say. "I can stay on the boat while you make a quick trip inland. It'll be fine. Don't worry about me. Think about yourself."

Not that I want to leave home—the thought of a boat on the high seas makes me slightly sickened, and I have no idea how I would survive the lonely hours in Copenhagen while the librarians do their thing—but I am willing to stick it out for Mrs. Thorkildsen's sake. But she ignores me. Keeps on packing her suitcase, even more excited now.

"You'll be just fine," Mrs. Thorkildsen says. "Someone will come and let you out twice a day, and make sure you have food and water."

"Who?" I ask, sharply suspicious.

"Neighbor Jack."

"Neighbor Jack!" I say. Or perhaps shout. "What does that hillbilly know about taking care of dogs? Have you lost your mind, woman?"

If you met Neighbor Jack, you'd share my consternation. The man lives most of the year in a suit he claims is made of beaver nylon, but after smelling the thing, I can promise you there's not a thread of beaver in that suit, no way. Neighbor Jack smells of oil, gasoline, diesel, and liquor—all kinds of liquids that can make things move. He's always in motion. Draw your own conclusions.

While the Major was still active, Neighbor Jack would help him with things that needed moving, preferably with the help of machinery. He'd plow the snow in the driveway (with a tractor, of course), take the wheels off our car and put them on again, every spring and every fall. He helped with both procuring and consuming dragon water, and no matter where he was and what he was doing, he was always smoking the same eternal cigarette. Neighbor Jack is the only man I've ever heard yell at the Major. The fact that the Major didn't tear him to shreds is all thanks to Neighbor Jack's handyman skills. Neighbor Jack is the best of what humanity has to offer, at least in the Major's opinion—Neighbor Jack is a *jack-of-all-trades*. He hammers and drills and lays bricks. He knows how to *make* things. According to Mrs. Thorkildsen, he also takes care of his old mother, who lives one floor below him, but is that supposed to make me feel better? Taking care of a mother is one thing, but a dog involves another level of responsibility.

"Has he ever looked after a dog in his life?"

"I have no idea," Mrs. Thorkildsen says, "but I should think so."

"*Think so?*" I ask, but that was all she had to say on the subject.

So here I am, alone and abandoned on a bed of dead man's boots and shoes. Of course I feel sorry for myself, would you expect otherwise? I mean, who else is going to feel sorry for me when I'm all by myself? I miss Mrs. Thorkildsen and I wonder if she'll ever come back, but I don't miss her worries. Thankfully, she's taken those with her on board.

25

HATE TO ADMIT IT, but Neighbor Jack turned out to be a perfectly adequate dog sitter. More than that. I'd claim that the man has potential—undeveloped, but still—to be a first-rate dog owner. He didn't quite stick to Mrs. Thorkildsen's planned regime of regular feeding and walking, but I'm not complaining.

After a long morning with icy tension between us, Mrs. Thorkildsen disappeared, headed for Copenhagen in a taxi with all her odds and ends, fueled by three glasses of dragon water. She tried until the last minute to make me accept the injustice I was about to face, flattered me and filled my bowl until it ran over. It took all my self-control not to dive headfirst into the meal until she was out the door, dragging her suitcase behind her.

"I'll be back before you even notice I'm gone" was the last thing she said before leaving. What a strange thing to say. And it turned out to be false. I took her at her word, and earnestly sniffed through the house with a degree of optimism as soon as she left, but she wasn't there. Either the claim had been a lie, or something had occurred to

Mrs. Thorkildsen along the way. Both devilish alternatives. The thought of Mrs. Thorkildsen being able to lie was always the worst.

In short, I was in a gloomy mood as I lay on the shoe pile in the hallway. It's embarrassing to admit, and I tried with all my might not to explode, but then I gave in and found a moccasin to console myself with. This was not meant as revenge against Mrs. Thorkildsen. If I'd wanted to take revenge on her, I would have chewed her favorite slippers to pieces. I know it's wrong to nibble on shoes; it's almost embedded in my instinct after a few unlucky episodes early in my career that aren't worth revisiting here.

Shamefully, I must admit that chewing on shoes brings its own special kind of peace. It works about the same way dragon water does for Mrs. Thorkildsen, I think, just without the wobbling and slurring of words. If Neighbor Jack had stuck to the plan, I could easily have made my way through a whole pair while Mrs. Thorkildsen was out sailing. But instead of coming by to refill my food while I did my business in the yard, he took me by surprise.

The key in the front door told me it wasn't Mrs. Thorkildsen outside. She always fiddles with the key before she slots it into place and twists it around gently when she arrives, but the person now arriving attacked the lock quickly, decisively, and powerfully. In that moment I forgot all the instructions about walking and feeding. Time to panic!

Still, I couldn't get a bark out. The job description is clear on this point: when strangers break into the house, you're supposed to bark at full volume. But now that this nightmare scenario is actually happening, I'm paralyzed. Is there any point? Barking to scare off intruders and simultaneously warn everyone in the house—of course I see the point in that. But barking to defend an empty house—is there really a point in that? I'm *man's* best friend, not the house's.

The door swung open and the smell of Neighbor Jack reached me before he had time to open his mouth, although he was not dressed in fake beaver.

"Come on now, boy. We got a party to git to," he said.

Party. Turns out I'd never been to a party before. This is how a party works: you gather four grown men plus another guy around a salon table in a house where a cat used to live. You can never get rid of that stench. Of the cat, that is. You put out dragon water, nuts, and potato chips (heavenly!) on the table. The salon table. And at this salon table, you eat hot food. If only Mrs. Thorkildsen knew!

There are voices and laughter and smoke and music in the air, and I feel so heavy and light all at once that I don't know whether I'm sinking into the ground or flying up to the heavens. I'm hungry as a dog, too, no matter how many sausage bites the gentlemen sneak me. I don't know why, but the word "fat" keeps churning around in my dog's brain like a mantra, and I'm a wolf, the last in a long line that can be traced back to the very first wolf. I'm awake, but dreaming the dream of life. I wish Mrs. Thorkildsen were here. For her own sake. So she could drink and smoke and laugh and yell, too. She could have sung along with the choruses. A guitar and another guitar and suddenly the whole congregation is singing, singing with rusty voices, and drinking even more dragon water and smoking more spices, while they misunderstand and love one another at a furious pace.

A lot of it is hazy in retrospect, but I remember that at one point one of the humans thought I'd turned into a statue.

"Tassen's stoned!" the hairless one said, and as if that statement wasn't absurd enough, he added for good measure: "Stoned as a monkey!"

Humans speak in strange ways when it comes to animals. "Pearls before swine." "Quiet as a mouse." "The elephant in the room." "Free as a bird." "Happy as a clam." "Loan shark." "Slippery as an eel." The whole damn language is a menagerie. (By far the dumbest use of animal as metaphor? Not surprisingly, it involves the infamous cat: "Kitty cat." *Kitty cat?* What the hell is a kitty if not a cat, and vice versa? I mean, you don't exactly go around saying "Doggy dog," do you? Stupid felines.

As I lay there in a haze on the floor, rolling around in a cow's hide jacket someone had been kind enough to leave right there, I thought of all the animals, one by one. Of the blue whales in the ocean and the fleas in my fur, and all the creatures in between. Of how we're all connected, and connected to all those who came before. The whale is the flea and the flea is the whale and I am Mrs. Thorkildsen. Mrs. Thorkildsen wouldn't have been lonely here. Maybe she's not lonely where she is, either. Right now there may be no place that's lonely.

That would be sweet.

I woke up and didn't know where I was at first. The important thing is that you wake up at all, no matter how strange you might feel. Perhaps especially if you feel strange. Take a moment to appreciate that.

The hairless one was asleep on the couch, and I could hear snoring sounds from a room farther into the house. A soft calming hum emanated from the loudspeakers, a distant electronic echo of the ventilation system in the home, back in the day. Maybe I should have worried, but I was just thirsty. Incredibly thirsty. I thought I remembered a water bowl in the kitchen, and got to my feet. Stretched my legs, back, tail, and tongue, plodded calmly into the kitchen—and who did I meet there, if it wasn't Neighbor Jack. He'd changed his hair, looked more like a poorly groomed schnauzer waiting for a new home.

"So, the gentleman is out walking?"

"I could say the same to you," I said, and located the water bowl.

After lighting his good old cigarette, which had been resting on top of the overflowing ashtray, Neighbor Jack said:

"Let's go for a walk, Tassen."

I thought he'd never ask.

Go for a walk we did, and the walk was long. Longer than any walk I've ever taken with Mrs. Thorkildsen, or the Major for that matter. Through morning-dazed villa roads, across frozen grass lawns, and through forests, we walked as dog and master. God bless Mrs. Thorkildsen, but she can't tire me out walking, I see that now. I need to move more, and she needs to get out more. Two conclusions upon which we can keep building. This brief separation, which I resisted so fiercely, may have done us both good. We've had a few new impulses, a fresh breath of air in a life together that, let's be honest, is often stuck in a rut. "Well, here we are," as Mrs. Thorkildsen says, and we have to rely on other people's stories to feed our conversation. I mean, what the hell do Mrs. Thorkildsen and I have to do with Antarctica? I can only hope her expedition has been as fruitful as mine. And I'll know soon, now that the boat to Denmark has docked, and Neighbor Jack has gone to help Mrs. Thorkildsen with her bags while I protect the car from strange humans. It's a never-ending hell.

There's Neighbor Jack. And Mrs. Thorkildsen. Not walking, but sitting in a chair with wheels that Neighbor Jack pushes with one hand while he rolls Mrs. Thorkildsen's plaid suitcase behind him with the other. Mrs. Thorkildsen, poor thing, is completely exhausted and more or less lying flat in the wheelchair. It must have been a rough journey. A hurricane, I think to myself. At least.

"Mom is shit-faced," Neighbor Jack says as he opens the door. He says it in a half-irritated, half-exasperated way, and maybe it's this lack of engagement that provokes me.

"No, she's not. She's seasick," I say. Neighbor Jack doesn't respond. With one yanking motion he lifts Mrs. Thorkildsen out of her chair and plops her into the front seat of the car. It doesn't look like a heavy lift. I whine and moan, trying to get close so I can give her a little lick on the cheek, but Mrs. Thorkildsen doesn't respond. Neighbor Jack gets behind the wheel and straps Mrs. Thorkildsen in, and now she finally speaks up.

"Guuuehhhhhh," says Mrs. Thorkildsen, and vomits all over her pretty green coat.

Definitely seasick.

26

PENGUINS ARE NOT THE NICE animals they've made the world believe they are. There's a reason they live on their own somewhere no one else wants to live. They live there because no other continent will have them. Penguins, it turns out, are dubious creatures with a far better reputation than they deserve. Humans think the penguin is among the animal kingdom's most charming beasts, a sweet little thing in a tuxedo that's literally neither fish nor fowl.

The penguin has accomplished the impressive feat of becoming one of the world's most famous and revered animals, despite the fact that the truth about its nature would disgust most decent people who have ceramic penguins sitting in their windowsills. If you have such a penguin, it might be best to put it in the trash before we go on. Or if the stupid penguin is that important to you, you can skip the next page. But in that case you're living a lie, just so you know.

It is Mrs. Thorkildsen who breaks the ice. It happens with the help of her preferred tool: a book. The books are back, and that means Mrs. Thorkildsen is back, but I couldn't tell you which came first.

She tells me about George Murray Levick, a poor guy whom Captain Scott ordered to spend a season among the penguins in the middle of the Antarctic winter. The stay was itself an inhuman hell of frost and bad weather, with lard as the only firewood and food. Black with soot, with runny eyes and lungs seared after breathing in lard fumes for months, Levick scratched out his observations about *la vie pingouin*.

Homosexuality. Pedophilia. Necrophilia. Rape. Murder and assault. Levick was deeply disturbed by what he called "depraved" conditions in the penguin colony. Horny young male penguins mated with whomever—and whatever!—it might be. When they couldn't find a female penguin to rape, after the corpse of the last gang rape had started to freeze so it was no longer possible to fuck it, well, then they sodomized one another. They sodomized chickens. They did it all with a bestiality that would make Genghis Khan's most bloodthirsty generals turn away in shame.

The frightful conditions in the colony were of a sort that later, to prevent the contents of the report leaking out to the public, the material was translated into Greek and the English version destroyed. And so the penguin was allowed to roam freely on the world stage. It's one of the greatest deceptions in world history, and like all the most successful acts of deceit, it took place through silencing. It wasn't until a hundred years later that Levick's notes were found and translated back into English. The truth will come out one day.

My point is that nothing has changed. Penguins are still the same perverse creatures, susceptible to all the vile behavior listed above and more, but they face no consequences! When they finally published Levick's report, you might have expected it to cause a paradigm shift in humans' relationship to the bird-fish/fish-bird, that the ceramic pen-

guin in the windowsill would be silently removed, like a swastika on
the lapel the day before the war ended, but that's not what happened.
The penguin is so cute and charming in the eyes of man that all sorts
of explanations and excuses for the penguin's horrorocracy suddenly
popped up. But as for Mrs. Thorkildsen, the cup runneth over. She
hates penguins now, at least to the degree that Mrs. Thorkildsen is capable of hating anything. But Mrs. Thorkildsen's found a new hero now, a
dark-haired feisty little guy with a funny mustache. His name is Adolf.

Mrs. Thorkildsen's had many and often strange heroes throughout
her life. It might have something to do with her father leaving but, as
I mentioned earlier, I'm no expert in those kinds of things. I'm under
the impression that most of Mrs. Thorkildsen's heroes are somewhat
sad, small gentlemen who are most comfortable behind rolled-down
curtains in small, sad rooms where they scratch out thick, sad books.
In that sense, the Major was on the opposite end of the spectrum. He
was never timid, not even with bullet holes in his body, and although he
loved to read, he loved not writing books even more.

In Mrs. Thorkildsen's eyes, the Major was first and foremost a master
in the art of survival. The bullets and the airplane crashes might have
been good motivation to believe that. And he knew what hunger was.
That was the most important thing. The Major had lived like a dog: in
a cage, at the mercy of strangers and unable to hunt for his own food.
That left its mark.

"I fell for him the first time I went home with him and discovered he
had a whole cured and salted leg of lamb hanging in a kitchen cabinet
in his apartment," Mrs. Thorkildsen says. She tells me this so I'll be
able to better understand her fascination with her new idol.

Adolf Henrik Lindstrøm is the full and complete name of Mrs.

Thorkildsen's new hero, but she just calls him Lindstrøm. Tenderly. According to Mrs. Thorkildsen, he's the biggest hero in this whole story. Perhaps the only one. That's how it often is with Mrs. Thorkildsen's heroes. They're the biggest of all, and unlike anyone else. Her villains, too.

Naturally, my curiosity is piqued when I hear Lindstrøm's job description during the South Pole expedition: *jack-of-all-trades*. But I suspect that Mrs. Thorkildsen's enthusiasm about Mr. Lindstrøm is indelibly linked to the fact that he was also the South Pole expedition's chef.

Lindstrøm was the kind of man who got pleasure from seeing others enjoy things, especially when the outlook for enjoyment looked poor. With modest means and lots of energy, Lindstrøm managed to create small pockets of pleasure wherever he went. The worse it got, the better he did. Not unlike Mrs. Thorkildsen at her best.

Whether Lindstrøm understood other people I'm not so certain— raise your paw if you understand people!—but he did have the rare ability to get along with everyone. Because he understood what they needed.

With his stout, round body, he was the only one in the party who went ashore in Antarctica with no ambition of setting foot on the South Pole. He stood apart from the hierarchy and observed it with deep solemnity and a lopsided grin. People like that become a natural rallying point. In extreme circumstances, such as in a small, snowed-in cabin a little north of the South Pole, they're the key to surviving with dignity.

One time, a young guy who smelled like tobacco, sperm, and bacon came to ask the Major a bunch of questions about the war, the kind of questions Mrs. Thorkildsen never asked him.

"What would you say is the main reason you survived?" he asked.

The Major responded so quickly you'd think he'd been sitting there waiting for the question since peace broke loose:

"I kept my ass clean."

The bacon man laughed, but stopped laughing when he realized he was the only one. The Major continued:

"If I had water, the first thing I did was to wash my private parts. If there was any left over, I drank it. Many of those who ran aground did so in their own shit. Once you start slacking on your hygiene, it all goes to hell. You get sick, and that makes you even more apathetic. That's what captivity is all about, to turn you into an animal. The guards would pass pornographic pictures around to the prisoners as part of their psychological methods. When you're in that situation, the thought of sex can only bring you sorrow. The guys who rubbed one out after the porno pictures slowly lost all their willpower and resistance. Self-respect. Plus, you can't afford to lose the protein in your semen."

• • •

When it rains, as the common old saying goes, it tends to pour. Books are that way, too. One leads to another; the last one leads to the next one. Apparently there's no such thing as a book that just tells it all like it is, once and for all, period, full stop. There's a book about everything and everyone. About Lindstrøm, too, and it surprises me a little how deep an impression he's left on Mrs. Thorkildsen through that book. But, like I said, it's a book about a chef, possibly the only book about a chef from northern Norway that Mrs. Thorkildsen has ever read, so I give her a bit of a long leash.

"Lindstrøm's recipes were refined and thorough," Mrs. Thorkildsen muses, "but his recipe for keeping a calm disposition was simple: always be observant, ready to serve, and patient, with a sense of humor . . . he may have been a bit . . . *simple*."

"Simple?" I ask. "Is there really such a thing as a 'simple' man?"

"Most men are simple," Mrs. Thorkildsen replies, "but many of them make even *that* complicated. Lindstrøm, on the other hand, simplified what was complicated. And do you know why he did that, Tassen?"

No, I suppose I don't.

"Let me try to explain. When men work together in a pack, they have to establish a ranking order so that the pack will function properly. That order doesn't need to be explicit, but it has to be established and respected so that the pack will work from day to day. Just like a pack of dogs."

"When the farmer, back in the day, as part of his business strategy, started to demonize the wolf to legitimize its massacre, it became imperative to depict the wolf pack as one big snarling hierarchy of power and discipline. A society, no less. The rule of the mighty built into a system, with the alpha male as supreme leader based on his ferocity. But it's not like that. Should you encounter a wolf pack—and what are the chances of that, Mrs. Thorkildsen?—what you'd really be meeting is a family out for a walk in the park. Family values. That's what it's all about."

"I'm sure you know this better than I do."

"Right? A wolf pack is rarely more than a dozen individuals, and they're connected by family bonds. And you must know that under such circumstances, it's not the father, but the *mother* who's boss. She's neither the largest nor the strongest, but in a well-organized wolf pack,

Mom is the leader, and she assumes that position without having to constantly slit the throat of anyone who challenges her."

"Hmmm . . ." Mrs. Thorkildsen says.

"Gave you something to think about there," I say.

"You did," Mrs. Thorkildsen says, "and I think what you're saying might be the explanation for the Chief's success. And for the demise of the British men."

"And there you've lost me."

"I can see that, Tassen. The point is that Lindstrøm, in the pack of men who sailed south together, represented the mother figure in a way. Not least for the Chief himself, you see. Lindstrøm wanted to keep things clean and tidy, he kept everyone's spirits up, he was endlessly patient, he nursed the sick, and, not least, he served up the most delicious meals."

"Not least!"

I can feel all this talk of food starting to affect me.

"Lindstrøm decorated for Christmas nicer than Mom did. Every year, he built a new Christmas tree with his own two hands, since there weren't any trees where they were. On Christmas Eve, they sat there in the frozen tundra, around a table that was more plentiful than they would have at home. And just like Mom, it was Lindstrøm who woke first in the morning in the little cabin on the coast of the South Pole that lay buried in snow. Only the chimney stuck up over the snow. Lindstrøm was the first to rise in the pitch-black polar morning. He lit the stove with the help of a generous squirt of gasoline, put the coffee on, and then the Chief could wake up, and they would drink their morning coffee together.

Lindstrøm was the only one who *almost* knew the Chief, the only one in whom the Chief dared confide his doubts and his fears over a coffee cup in the kitchen. Lindstrøm listened, said only those few encouraging words that were needed, and if there was scolding to be done, he was the only one who could give it to the Chief. Or at least the only one the Chief could take it from. And you should know this—Lindstrøm was the dogs' favorite."

"Well, that makes sense," I say. "He smelled like food. When you smell like food, you're well on your way to making friends with any mutt you meet."

"Yes, but I think it was more than that. He'd learned from the Eskimos how to use dogs. Lindstrøm and the Chief lived among them in the Canadian wilderness for two years. They both learned how to discipline Greenland dogs, but Lindstrøm understood the dogs on another level, too. He was good at driving the sled, better than the Chief."

"I'm amazed the big Chief let him drive."

"In order to become as famous as the Chief did, I'm afraid you have to spend a lot of time thinking about yourself. That is, you can't afford to spend too much time reflecting on others and what they want. That's why people like that become so dependent on others. The Chief was dependent on people who took care of all the finances and correspondence and all the other drivel that came with life in civilization. Truth be told, the Chief didn't care much for civilization, but where else can you hear ovations?"

The Chief had seen it with his own eyes—how robust men, chosen as the best of the best, could degenerate into filthy, feeble weaklings passively slipping further into a misery of their own making. Men who stop washing their asses. That didn't scare him. He couldn't imagine himself in such a condition, but he learned to watch out for the danger signs out there in the cold. The most obvious one had to do with hygiene. A man who doesn't take care of himself can't take care of others.

"Lindstrøm was an artist!" Mrs. Thorkildsen says it emphatically, and it's not just the dragon water talking, but I can hear the echoes underneath.

"Survival . . ." Mrs. Thorkildsen takes a dramatic pause. "Survival demands that human beings draw on some of their most civilized qualities and, at the same time, that they're able to throw off some of their civilization. You have to be able to live as the animal you truly are, when required. To handle your own smell. Your stench."

"What would you know about stench?" I'm tempted to ask, but now is not the time for sarcastic quips. Mrs. Thorkildsen is excited, and it suits her.

"On the other hand, you can never let go of your decency and culture," she continues unabated. "You're there because you're human, you're there to be human. Otherwise there'd be no point. So you need something to remind you of who you are when you're not an animal. Such as a mille-feuille. Or a seal steak cooked to perfection. Profiteroles? Fresh-baked bread and rolls. Pancakes. Coffee. Canned pears with whipped cream. A tiny nip of schnapps to top it off, perhaps? Cheese and port wine. It takes so little, and Lindstrøm had plenty of it."

I took note of one of Lindstrøm's sayings, since it was also one of Mrs. Thorkildsen's. It goes like this:

Always have at least one extra bottle hidden away.

I've waited long enough now. I've listened patiently to Mrs. Thorkildsen's uncritical praise of Lindstrøm, who obviously was a man after her own heart and who surely had plenty of great qualities, but still must be judged for the actions he took:

"So how could such a fine man put dogs on the menu?" I ask, with a slight sneer.

Mrs. Thorkildsen laughs her librarian laugh, even though we're all alone and there's not a soul to disturb.

"Poor Tassen. Did you think they were sitting there eating dogs for dinner constantly? Dog steak à la Lindstrøm? No, no, Lindstrøm neither served nor ate a single dog. It was only the ones who traveled to the South Pole who did that. Lindstrøm stayed behind in the cabin for the months the journey took, together with the dogs who weren't going to the Pole, and they all had plenty of food to eat. But he wasn't completely innocent. Do you remember the stuffed dogs at the Fram Museum?"

"As much as I'd like to forget them," I say, feeling the discomfort that still lingered.

"Lindstrøm was the one who put those to sleep and prepared them while the others were at the Pole. He was an expert at it, too. There are lots of stuffed animals that Lindstrøm left behind in the university's collections."

"But he's in the clear as far as being a dog eater?"

"Absolutely. Lindstrøm is innocent on that score."

"So let's find the guilty parties."

"Just one more thing about Lindstrøm?"

"We have a South Pole to get to."

"I think you'll like this one. Listen: Lindstrøm, you see, is the one person on the crew who comes nearest to dying on the South Pole expedition. And he has himself to thank, I'd say. For what does Lindstrøm do when the Chief and his chosen men finally take off, and he's alone at last? What does a good Norwegian do when the sun is shining on the sparkling, snow-covered fields? Sure enough, he straps on his cross-country skis and goes for a run—and that's what Lindstrøm does, so far and for so long that he goes snow-blind, far away from the snowed-in cabin."

"What do you mean, snow-blind?"

"If people go out for a long time in the snow under the sun without protecting their eyes, they lose their eyesight. It returns after a while, but it's quite painful. Like sandpaper under your eyelids, or so I've read."

"Perhaps an indication that they—unlike Greenland dogs, for instance—are in the wrong place?"

"Perhaps. Without being able to see, Lindstrøm—who's terrified now, you have to understand—roams around the frozen landscape aimlessly. He listens for the howling of the Framheim dogs, but it's too far away and the sound carries poorly across the snow. He has to find his way home without anything to guide him. Every route except for the most direct path from here to the cabin will lead to certain death out in the cold. Lindstrøm is history, for all intents and purposes; it's just a matter of time. But then he hears a dog bark."

"Ha!"

"And not just any dog, either. Lindstrøm can tell among all his dogs based on their bark. It's one of his favorites, who loves her freedom to run around during the day, always with a tail of suitors right behind her."

"A real bitch!"

"Calm down, Tassen. The point is that Lindstrøm manages to call the dog to him, and she leads him back to camp so he survives and dies an old man in Oslo a whole lifetime later. Isn't that a beautiful story?"

"Yes, really beautiful. Until they get back to the cabin and Lindstrøm strangles the poor beast and prepares it for taxidermy."

27

THE RETURN OF THE HOME HELPER. I may have accidentally underestimated the Home Helper. In more ways than one. The Home Helper, it turns out, has the power to completely change its appearance. Today the Home Helper isn't a hysterical dog-hating woman, but instead a perfectly cheerful man with absolutely no fear of "dog," who even knows how to *scratch*. Mrs. Thorkildsen may not understand much of what the Home Helper says today either, but he has a fierce appetite for cinnamon rolls, and he has time to listen to Mrs. Thorkildsen and give me scratches, as I mentioned—and that takes care of a lot. Most things, actually. The three of us have had a lovely morning, and the Puppy has just arrived, too. The Puppy doesn't say no to a cinnamon roll. This is starting to look like a party—if only Mrs. Thorkildsen could get out her dragon water and some of that spicy tobacco.

"I thought I could drive you to the store," the Puppy says, and for once Mrs. Thorkildsen seems to think he's had a good idea. At least, she doesn't start discussing it with him. She goes off to get ready, and the Puppy moves closer to the Home Helper.

"How do you think it's going?" he asks in a low, concerned voice. The Home Helper seems a bit surprised by the question, and his scent seems to indicate he's a little uncomfortable.

"Okay, I think?" he says, and that should answer his question, but the Puppy isn't satisfied.

"I'm worried about how she's getting on. It's a big house. And the store is far away . . ."

"She seems to be doing fine," the Home Helper says. "She keeps a neat, clean house, and the fridge is stocked with food. The dog seems to be doing well. At least, he's not too skinny. You know what they say—if the dog's happy, everything is fine." The Home Helper laughs.

I can't be bothered to speculate about what in the world the Home Helper might mean by "not too skinny." He's rather robust himself, so he might have meant it as a compliment. As if he can read my thoughts, the Home Helper says:

"Good boy."

How could I help but love a human with such good instincts?

"But what about all these paper dolls she has?" the Puppy asks the Home Helper. "Is it . . . healthy?"

"It must have been a ton of work."

"Sure. But do you know *why* she does it?"

"No . . ." the Home Helper says.

"For the dog!" the Puppy says, waiting for a reaction that doesn't come.

"Okay. What do you mean?" the Home Helper asks.

"Tassen is the best thing in her life, but sometimes I think she takes it a bit too far, that she treats him almost like a person. She reads aloud to him, for instance. She talks to him and he talks to her. She says Tassen thinks this and Tassen says that. That's why she's cut out all these paper dogs, to show Tassen how many dogs Roald Amundsen took with him to the South Pole. You see? Dogs can't count, she says, that's why she's teaching him this way!"

"They're Greenland dogs," the Home Helper says.

"Oh?" the Puppy says, his foothold slightly slipping.

"I worked in Greenland once, on the west coast among the Inuit. You can probably hear that I'm part Danish, so I seized the opportunity to earn some good money in my student days—and since then I've spent half the year up there. They still talk about Roald Amundsen's dogs there."

"I see. But you think it's okay that she cuts out these paper animals and talks to the dog?"

"I don't know your mother well enough to evaluate her. Nor is it my job to do that. As far as I can tell, she's a lady with her wits about her, who maybe isn't eating quite enough. She's not the only person who talks to her dog. I think most old ladies do that."

Then the Home Helper does something that makes the Puppy's scent change and his heart rate spike. He lays his hand on the Puppy's shoulder without saying a word. Just sits there for a long while with his paw outstretched, as if he's asking to be scratched or fed, then says:

"It's not easy. I know. Your mother isn't getting any better; there's no miracle diet or wonder cure that can bring her back to where she was yesterday or the day before. Nothing you can do, nothing we can do, except make her journey as pleasant as possible. I can see this is a house full of books, so do you know your Hamsun, by any chance?"

The Puppy nods his head, and his smell is difficult to interpret now. "The Nobel laureate," he says.

"Knut Hamsun," the Home Helper goes on, "described life by painting a picture of a man sitting on the back of a wagon, on his way to the gallows to be executed. The wagon is built in the simplest way, and there's a nail sticking out and gnawing at his ass cheek. So he moves over a bit, and it stops gnawing at him."

The Puppy gets quiet. The Home Helper keeps scratching my neck with calm, even movements. After a long while the Puppy says:

"My grandmother once told me she had made love to Hamsun."

"What?" the Home Helper says. "That's incredible."

The Home Helper is enthusiastic, and clearly wants to know more, but the Puppy places an index finger over his lips as Mrs. Thorkildsen returns from the bathroom wearing her outside smell and her outside face. She seems to be in a sparkling good mood.

"Well, gentlemen," Mrs. Thorkildsen says, "shall we?"

28

HOW TO BEAT A GREENLAND DOG. A short introduction by Captain Roald Amundsen:

> A confirmation often happens when one particular sinner has decided to be difficult and will not listen. It consists of, at the first available moment when the sled is stopped, going up to the dogs, removing the disobedient one, and smacking it with the handle of the whip. These "confirmations" can, when they become frequent, require many whip handles.

It's bizarre hearing these words come out of Mrs. Thorkildsen's friendly little mouth. The thought of Mrs. Thorkildsen smacking Greenland dogs so whip handles snap in half is beyond my wildest imagination. But of course they're not her words, but the Chief's. And he's got more:

> The whip had stopped frightening them long ago; when I tried to keep beating them, they'd huddle together, trying to protect their

heads as best they could, they didn't worry so much about their bodies. Yes, many times it proved almost impossible to get them going, so I had to get help for this work. Two of them pushed the sled forward and the third continued to whip.

Mrs. Thorkildsen falls silent. It's a trick. I've noticed that—as the atrocities detailed in the story of the journey to the middle of nowhere get worse—she increasingly prefers to let the books speak for themselves.

In the Chief's dispassionate tone, I soon get the story of one dog, then another lost to the great beyond before the journey from the winter quarters to the South Pole has even begun. It takes so little, since if there's one thing the expedition has plenty of, it's dog power. Dogs are killed for any reason you could possibly imagine—because they're too fat, or too horny, or too stubborn—but, most of all, because they are too many.

On the November day the Chief and his four chosen men finally swing their whips around and set out in a straight path toward the South Pole, Mrs. Thorkildsen and I have long since lost track of exactly how many dogs are alive and how many have fallen before the great march. It's becoming a large pack up there on the mantel, while the pack on the floor is larger than ever. Meanwhile, Mrs. Thorkildsen has taken the step of splitting it up. That is, it was really the Chief's idea.

She picks up about half of her paper dogs on the floor one by one, with slow, systematic movements. She freezes, her arms full of dogs.

"I can't say exactly what these ones died of, or when, but none of them survive in the long run. Some of them die of natural causes, I'd guess."

I'm about to ask what "natural causes" means for a Greenland dog in Antarctica, but then I hear Mrs. Thorkildsen say:

"Some of them run away."

Run away. These are the happiest words in this whole story so far. I want to hear more about the dogs who ran away, but Mrs. Thorkildsen doesn't dwell on them.

"Now it's all about these dogs," she says, pointing to the pack that's left on the rug. "Fifty-two dogs, Tassen. That's two more than the Chief thought they'd have left when they arrived in Antarctica. And those fifty-two are split into four groups . . . like this."

Mrs. Thorkildsen never ceases to amaze. After sorting the dogs into four equal groups, standing in rows two by two, you see, she goes to fetch the sleds. They're made of paper, too, constructed on the same principle as the dogs. They look like small ships, and I suppose that's what they are, after all. Ships to cross frozen seas.

"And they're ready to march," Mrs. Thorkildsen says. "It's summer, but it's still colder than the middle of winter here. Minus twenty-five degrees Celsius. Perfect conditions for the dogs. And the dogs are happy—at least, the Chief claims they are."

"He might be right about that. Unfortunately."

"The dogs enjoy pulling?"

"Enjoy? Greenland dogs live for it. It's the only thing they know how to do in this world. They long with all their hearts to pull and pull until there's blood in their mouths—and even beyond that. That's what's so practical about us dogs, you see. If you have a plan and the patience to keep going for a few generations, you can breed an animal specially designed for the most evil or stupid purposes. Just think of all the absurd varieties the Germans and hillbillies have come up with throughout history. You have to be pretty sick in the head, and have a pretty malicious spirit, to come up with the Doberman pinscher, or the pit bull, or an alligator, don't you think?"

I'm telling the truth. Sled dogs enjoy pulling, as long as they get to pull at their own pace. Go too fast, and they get exhausted and sit down in the track. If you're very unlucky, you never get that pack to pull again. Go too slow, and you'll end up with yapping and confusion. But when the dogs get into a good galloping tempo, a human has to be a good skier to keep pace.

"So you're not upset about the dogs pulling the sled?" Mrs. Thorkildsen is relieved.

"Nah," I say, mulling it over. "Greenland dogs are simple souls, and when they're enjoying themselves while pulling the sled, one might as well take advantage of it, right?"

But if they're enjoying themselves, why would the Chief need to beat them?

If it's not clear already, let me assure you that Mrs. Thorkildsen is a relatively thorough woman. You may also have realized that she's a woman with a flair for the dramatic, and it's these two qualities that converge, for better or for worse, when she tells the story about the Chief's dogs. She tells me far more than I need or wish to know. For instance, Mrs. Thorkildsen knows the exact number of biscuits packed onto the sleds and into the depots that were sent southward before the winter set in. So then I have to ask:

"Depots?"

"Well, how do I explain it?" Mrs. Thorkildsen says. "It's probably similar to when a dog buries a meat bone to eat later on. Do you remember how unhappy you were when we gave you the giant lamb's knuckle? You circled the house restlessly for days, while whining and holding that giant bone in your mouth, endlessly searching for a hiding spot. I don't know how many times we found that lamb bone behind the couch cushions. What happened to it in the end, do you remember?"

"I buried it, but I don't remember where."

"So that's what they were doing down there at the South Pole, or something similar. The summer before they set out on the sled trip, they'd laid out depots along the route to the south so they had food and fuel waiting for them. It's almost inconceivable that they managed to find them again. White pyramids of snow out there in a landscape that was entirely white. There was no terrain they could use to draw a map. Flat, white, and that was it. To find the depots, they marked them with black flags."

"I wouldn't say it's a miracle, exactly, that they found their treats again. I mean, if the dogs went the same way they'd gone the year before, all they had to do was follow the scent."

"In that cold? After a winter? I don't think so, Tassen," Mrs. Thorkildsen lectures me.

"What do you know about it? Stupid old lady."

"Useless mutt."

From Mrs. Thorkildsen's point of view, the purely nutritional is the most fascinating side of the Chief's whole South Pole project. That's not so strange, perhaps. Once a chef, et cetera.

"It's all an equation, you see," Mrs. Thorkildsen explains.

"No, I most certainly don't," I say, which is the truth.

"All these dogs have to eat," she says, turning to the four packs on the floor. "And they have to eat every day. The longer the journey lasts, the more food they have to bring. And since there's no food to be found along the way, they have to carry all their provisions with them. If they bring too much, their sleds grow unnecessarily heavy, and the dogs get hungrier. If they don't bring enough, some of them will starve."

I have a suspicion about who will inevitably be the last to starve, but I keep it to myself.

"And that's why they counted the biscuits, tens of thousands of them, several times. They weighed out the precise daily rations for themselves and the dogs, and by adding up what they had on the sleds and what they had in the depots, they could know how many days' worth of supplies they had. And then there was another factor . . ."

It gets eerily quiet. Then, at last, it comes out:

". . . and that factor was the dogs."

"So dog meat was part of this 'equation,' too?"

"Yes."

"Fucking fuckers."

"If it wasn't initially, dog meat became part of their calculations after a while. But before I say more about what came next, there's a few things I have to remind you of."

"Do you *have* to?" I object. "Your reminders are always so boring. Can't we just go straight to the part where they eat the dogs?"

"You have to remember that it wasn't just the men eating the dogs, Tassen."

Okay, but something smells here. Didn't Mrs. Thorkildsen say that there were no other life forms of any kind on the inner Antarctic ice fields?

"The British men?" I suggest, for lack of a better idea. "Maybe their ponies ate dogs? I've never quite trusted ponies; I think it's likely they suffer from many of the same breeding issues that affect smaller dogs."

Mrs. Thorkildsen slowly shakes her snow-white head.

"The dogs that weren't being eaten, well . . . *they* were eating dogs."

I permit myself a moment's disappointed silence. "*This* is what you needed to 'remind' me of? That 'eat or be eaten' is the law of nature? Of course the dogs ate one another. Dogs—like humans—eat anything once they're hungry enough. And dogs are almost always hungry enough."

Mrs. Thorkildsen continues down her track without further comment. "The yardstick for the dogs' level of hunger was when they started to eat each other's shit. Human shit had been on the menu ever since the *Fram* was on the open seas. The toilets in the winter quarters were a giant snow grotto that was kept squeaky clean by the dogs who fought over this privilege. But as I said, when the dogs start to eat their own or each other's shit, that's a warning sign."

Perhaps, like me, you think it's a bit conspicuous that Mrs. Thorkildsen doesn't comment on the organization of the pack dogs. I mean, Greenland dogs are driven in fan formation in Greenland. Perfect for an island like Greenland, where no vegetation grows beyond mid-calf height. In forest terrain the so-called Nome style is better, with the dogs paired up in two long rows. There's not much forest in Antarctica, yet the Chief still went for the Nome style. Since he rarely left anything to circumstances, I have to believe he had a reason for departing from the fan formation he'd learned firsthand from the Eskimos. With the dogs assembled in Nome style, lead dogs at the front, the Chief had instituted an artificial, human hierarchy in the open, frozen landscape.

I see a clear technique of domination here, but Mrs. Thorkildsen sees nothing.

What Mrs. Thorkildsen tells me, she gets from books. And the books come from her hands. Her hands are blue and white and wrinkly and gnarled and painful. They've been worse, and they'll get worse again, Mrs. Thorkildsen says. Before she quit being a librarian, she had such bad pain in her hands that she'd sometimes go to the restroom to cry a tear or two. Yes, she almost cries just talking about it. But those spindly fingers still have the power to navigate the books' pages and to find the puzzle pieces she marks with tiny yellow flags.

"Look what I found!" says the flag.

That's how they do it, humans. Plant flags by depots of wisdom and stories that await them when the right moment finds them and they're put to the test. Without these flags, I honestly don't know how they'd get along, even with opposable thumbs.

Every single book in this world has a different smell, as far as I can tell. It may be no surprise that an old, leather-bound edition smells different from a cheap paperback, but there's more to it than that. Every book takes on its smell based on who reads it, of course, and how it's read. And it pulls into it the smell of time passing. That was the smell I recognized over at the Library, the first time we were there.

What's odd, you might say, is that a good book smells no different than a bad book. The same is true of the contents. War and young love, philosophy and tall tales, it all pretty much smells alike. Cookbooks, and of course I mean *used* cookbooks, are an obvious exception. A good cookbook smells like food. If it doesn't, it's probably not a good cookbook. But no matter what book you choose, page 14 smells exactly like page 1003.

If it actually were possible to smell the contents of a book, I think the age of human hegemony over the library profession would be over. At best, librarians would be replaced by dogs. The customer walks in, doesn't know which book she's searching for, but Fido needs only a few quick sniffs of the hem of her coat, then he's on the scent whether the library patron needs comfort, excitement, fantasy, or a recipe for Dover sole. Fido drags the dog handler over to the right shelf and indicates a book like a drug-sniffing dog on a Colombian suitcase. The customer gets the right book. The dog gets a treat. The dog is happy. Everyone's happy.

29

SHIT!" MRS. THORKILDSEN CRIES. Both content and expression show me that this is serious, and I jump to my feet before I have time to consider what dangers may lurk in the kitchen, where the cry originated. When I get there, all I find is Mrs. Thorkildsen with a book in one hand and a giraffe glass of red dragon water in the other. Business as usual, I'd say. No bogeymen, no garbagemen to see or smell.

I have to ask what's going on, but Mrs. Thorkildsen has no time to respond—she's consumed by the book she's holding, the one that's made her exclaim, "Shit!"

"What book is that?"

"*A Life in the Ice*. The one about Chef Lindstrøm."

Of course it's the one about him.

"I've never seen you read a book that made you curse."

"Look at this!" Mrs. Thorkildsen says, holding the book open to a certain page, and I again feel the quick jolt of fear that Mrs. Thorkildsen sooner or later will lose track of daily existence, when I once again have to remind her:

"Dogs can't read."

Although no one knows better than Mrs. Thorkildsen that I can't read, it sounds a little embarrassing to hear myself say it. This reminds me that no matter how satisfied Mrs. Thorkildsen may be with me, she'd probably be even happier if I could read. Each of us sitting in our own chair, each with our own book in silence, only breaking it to quote a good phrase or refill a drink. A snack from time to time. On the other hand, she'd probably get sick of having to turn the pages for me. It all evens out in the end.

"It's red wine!" Mrs. Thorkildsen says, and I finally understand what she means. In the middle of the page is a circle whose colors blend together the colors of the flag. Red and blue, mixed up with a little white. I'm not sure what to call this color. Dragon water purple, maybe.

"Okay, so you spilled a little red wine in a book. It's hardly the end of the world, Mrs. Thorkildsen," I say as cheerfully as the occasion allows.

"In a *library book*!" Mrs. Thorkildsen says, and it's Code Red.

When it comes to your own books, you can wipe your behind with them if you so desire, but books borrowed from the Library are another category altogether. Those can't be damaged with a single stain or crease during their stay in your home. They must be returned safely to the Library with no more wear and tear than your eyes give the print on the page.

And Mrs. Thorkildsen, of all people! She's the one who has imprinted on me this reverence for library books. Well, well, it goes to show you that it can happen to the best of us. The question is: What do we do now?

So I ask Mrs. Thorkildsen: "What do we do now?"

"Yes, what do we do now?" she asks in return.

"Buy a new book?" I suggest. Constructive thinking.

"In the old days, I could have done that. I think I still have some of the old pocket cards lying in a drawer. All I'd have to do is glue one of those pockets onto the inside of the back jacket. Laminating the cover is a piece of cake to a librarian. I think I have an old stamp around here somewhere, too, so yes, we'd probably be able to turn a bookstore book into a library book. But these days . . ."

Mrs. Thorkildsen pauses, examining the book from all sides.

". . . now there are all these stripe things. Look."

Now she wants me to examine the book.

"What is it?"

"These stripes tell the computer everything it needs to know about the book. You just take some kind of electric pistol, point it at these lines, and then *ping!* But I have no idea how it works."

"Smell," I say. "Sounds like smell is the key to this."

"Smell?" Mrs. Thorkildsen says. "I can't imagine that. In that case you'd smell it"—Mrs. Thorkildsen sniffs the book—"and I don't smell anything here. Just the book."

"I don't think we should use your sense of smell as proof of anything at all," I point out. "You can't even smell it when you've stepped in a cow patty."

Had Mrs. Thorkildsen been more open-minded, I might have been able to teach her a little something about how smell works. It's not so different from the stripes on the book she has vandalized with dragon water. But instead of a quick *ping!* that probably can tell you the basic facts, you inhale deeply through the nose and experience the third dimension of smell: time. The past. The present. The future. Not necessarily in that order. That's why, you see, it can take some time to fully absorb a smell. It's not always enough to take a quick sniff—sometimes you need an intensive, sustained sniffing to get the whole picture. Try to remember that the next time you pull the leash impatiently.

30

THE ANSWER TO THE QUESTION "What do we do with the library book?" turns out to be "Nothing at all." It sits on the dresser, just like it did yesterday, and I won't be surprised if it's there tomorrow as well. For my part, I never mention that book again. The last time I did, Mrs. Thorkildsen turned gruff and somber and "forgot" to feed me before she went to bed. The book about Adolf Henrik Lindstrøm has become a *non-book* in my life, but that doesn't erase the question hanging over us, gnawing at Mrs. Thorkildsen: What do we do now? And a thousand more questions. What kinds of repercussions can we expect from the Library if we simply ignore our duty to return the damaged book? What kind of power do they hold over us? Will the Puppy and the Bitch find a way to exploit this? Can the Home Helper help us?

I calm myself down with the thought that we still have weapons in the house. But I'm sure that were Mrs. Thorkildsen to open fire on fellow librarians, it would be with a heavy heart, so I'm still hoping for a peaceful solution. I'd rather bite someone who truly deserves it.

"In Greenland, they drive the sled dogs in a fan formation," Mrs. Thorkildsen says. "I'll show you how it looks."

"Of course I know what sled dogs in a fan formation look like," I say, and hear the gruffness in my own voice. "What do you take me for? A Tibetan spaniel? You don't need to show me that. You don't need to show me the Nome style, either. Or the Nordic. I know all about that."

"My goodness," Mrs. Thorkildsen says. "How do you know that?"

"I don't know."

"You said you knew all about the various sled-pulling techniques?"

"I mean I don't know how I know it."

"Well, well, Tassen. What I was going to say is that the Chief didn't use the fan formation at the South Pole."

"I know."

"So that means you also know *why*?"

That word again.

"Because the Chief was a controlling bastard who forced his dogs into an unnatural hierarchical system to dominate them," I'm about to reply, and forcefully, but Mrs. Thorkildsen, on her first glass of dragon water, beats me to the punch:

"The ice they drove across may have looked like the flattest of dance floors, but the terrain on the way to the South Pole is dangerous, with deep crevices under the snow that could swallow a pack of dogs whole. So to reduce the chances of stepping into cracks in the ice, the Chief decided it would be best to move in a narrow formation, even though he didn't have to worry about vegetation. And this ended up saving the day more than once."

Well, damn him.

They called it the "Devil's Dance Floor." The cracks in the ice summon the only hint of pathos in the Chief's tale so far. He turns poetic, too:

These cracks are impressive when you lie on the edge and stare down into them, he writes. *A bottomless abyss that turns from light blue to the deepest black . . .*

There's a poet in the Chief too.

> *A*
> *bottomless*
> *abyss*
> *from light blue to*
> *the deepest*
> *black.*

"The Chief has a lot to say about these crevices," Mrs. Thorkildsen reflects. She's on the scent of something. Mrs. Thorkildsen smells blood.

"I interpret it as an expression of his own position as leader of a giant all-or-nothing project. The fear of falling, plain and simple. A typical man's fear. With every step he takes, the Chief is contemplating what awaits him if he doesn't become the first one to the South Pole and the first one back. Thinking of it that way, death by crack-in-the-ice might seem preferable."

"It might just be a cover-up for the fact that the South Pole expedition was actually pretty boring," I say.

Mrs. Thorkildsen does not disagree:

"Day after day, hanging on while a pack of dogs charges across the ice. Just as white and flat in every direction, the sun never goes down. The weather gets better and worse, but the cold is constant. The same routines every day. Down with the tent, the same distance to travel as the day before. Tent up. Eat. Sleep. Follow the plan. The dogs deliver their predicted amount of miles day after day, the food rations are adequate, and the depots appear where they're supposed to be. Had he not been living in a nightmare in which Captain Scott was already standing at the South Pole with his motorized sleds, the Chief might have enjoyed the expedition, as if it were a pleasant Easter ski trip."

"Well, isn't that what it is, after all? A ski trip. If a slightly more momentous one. All they're really doing is taking their dogs for a spin."

"Until they hit the wall."

"And when does that happen?"

"Now. The wall is ten thousand feet high. That's high," says Mrs. Thorkildsen, as high as the planes way up there in the sky, the ones I can never quite spot. The wall is built from ice over thousands of years, layer after layer of snow polished by the coldest winds that blow on Earth, and it's full of murderous crevices. Here, at the foot of the climb, was the final depot, this was where the map ended. The rest of the way to the South Pole was all that remained of "the unknown" in this world.

It was a game of chance. They could count every biscuit four times to make sure the margins were on their side, but the next step might lead them to death anyway.

Beyond being dead tired, the dogs grew terrified as one sled, then another, then another nearly disappeared into the cracks on their way up the glacier. After the restless, sick, or horny dogs are dispatched as the march across the oceanic ice continues, the pack on the mantel has now become the largest.

31

THE CURSE OF THE HOME HELPER. I'm really starting to like the Home Helper. In the beginning I found the constant transformations frustrating, but that was before I realized that mutability is precisely the true form of the Home Helper. And why should a noble soul like the Home Helper be tied up in a single persona?

Today the Home Helper is—as far as Home Helpers go—a relatively young man. He has a little daughter, a girlfriend who can't quite decide what she wants from him, and he has dreams of becoming an ambulance driver. I can smell all of this. Just kidding! But this much he's told Mrs. Thorkildsen, who listens in rapt excitement and goes to fetch more cinnamon rolls. The house is the way it always is when the Home Helper arrives, spotless. There's plenty of time for the only task she needs help with: bringing in the lawn furniture.

The Home Helper goes out to retrieve garden furniture, and I plod along after him, pleased something is happening. Anything.

Three chairs and a small table. It's not much of a job, but the Home

Helper still lets himself take a break in the shed afterward. Takes out a cigarette and lights up.

"You won't tell, will you?" he says, grinning. I don't respond. Better that than to admit I have no clue in hell what he's talking about. I wag my tail as calmly as I can, but it never seems calm enough. My goal is the swaying elegance of a large bird of prey, but the result comes out more like a windshield wiper at top speed.

Then the Home Helper exhales through his nose and something falls into place. He's sitting there in the white plastic chair smoking herbs!

"Of course I won't tell," I say.

The Home Helper coughs. I let him finish coughing. The Home Helper's heart rate skyrockets for some reason, and he stares at me with wide eyes as if I were the first dog on Earth.

"Just between you and me," I continue as he stares, "I was actually going to ask if you have any extra . . . whatever it is you have. I think it would be good for Mrs. Thorkildsen, you see. She drinks, as I'm sure you've gathered, far too much dragon water for her little body."

"You can talk . . ." says the Home Helper, getting to his feet.

"I will pay you for it," I say. "I know exactly which books Mrs. Thorkildsen hides her money in: *The Future in America* by H. G. Wells and *The Complete Works of Robert Burns*. Both of them are just to the right of the fireplace. She'll never notice. I actually think she's forgotten the money is there."

"You can talk!" the Home Helper repeats.

"I'd do it myself, of course, but as you can see I lack thumbs, and simply getting a book off the shelf is a losing battle in and of itself."

"You can talk!" says the Home Helper. Then he has to go, and does so at an incredible speed.

Mrs. Thorkildsen becomes the Angel of Death again once the Home Helper has left. With calm, measured movements, she picks paper dogs off the floor. One. Two. Three. She picks up four. Another one. Another one. And another one. And another. Another. Another. Another. Another. Another. Another. Another. Another. Another. Another. Another. Another. Another. Another. Another almost at the end and one at the very end, and now they're all gathered up in Mrs. Thorkildsen's wiry fist, the whole bunch of them.

"Twenty-four," Mrs. Thorkildsen says. "These were slaughtered at the top of the climb by the same men who were assigned to take care of them."

"A good old-fashioned bloodbath," I say, and I can hear myself sounding trite. But what am I supposed to say? That I'm shocked? I could say that, but the truth is I'm not. Mrs. Thorkildsen tells the story of the great massacre that took place when men and dogs finally stood atop the plateau, after an outstanding team effort, after days of exhaustion, and I'm not the least bit surprised. If I had Mrs. Thorkildsen's grasp on numbers, I could have just counted biscuits and rations to see that the math wasn't working out, that the Chief's strategy once again turned out to be based on having more dogs than he needed.

There will be a time for feelings, but that comes later. Facts are what matter now and, anyway, I've never been one to let my feelings run away with my manners unless I'm extra hungry, which I'm not right now. On the contrary, I'm nice and full. I'm warm. The likelihood of Mrs. Thorkildsen giving me a shot through the skull without warning feels lower and lower. I'm safe, and that's really all a dog like me ever wants to be.

"If they didn't realize it right away, the dogs must have eventually known what was going on when they were served their dead friends for dinner," Mrs. Thorkildsen says, flipping her way to one of the yellow flags in one of the books. What a strange experience it must be for a library book to accompany Mrs. Thorkildsen home, I think.

32

T ODAY ON THE DR. PILL SHOW:

They're closing down my local library, but at least I'm going to die soon!

Dr. Pill's show about Mrs. Thorkildsen would be called something like that, I guess. At least if she got to decide. If the Puppy got to decide, on the other hand, I'm afraid the show about Mrs. Thorkildsen would be named something like:

My lonely old mother is drinking herself to death, and I'm not sure how to feel about it!

The Bitch:

My mother-in-law is a feisty old witch who doesn't want us to have a good home, and she never looks me in the eye either!

The Boy Puppy:

Beep! . . . Beeeep! . . . Beeeeeep! Kabooom!

But what about my Dr. Pill show, what exciting title would we give it to entice the viewing masses? I must say the answer to that question will entirely depend on what day you ask it. Here are a few ~~fresh~~ suggestions:

> *I think I've had sex, and I'd really like to be sure of it, but the bitch wants nothing to do with me now!*
>
> *My owner sometimes forgets to feed me, and then has the nerve to complain when I fart!*
>
> *I'm too fat because I love people too much!*
>
> *The Rottweiler down on the corner is getting on my nerves and I wish he were dead!*
>
> *I'm afraid I'm going to starve to death! Now!*
>
> *The Librarian is in love with me and I'm afraid Mrs. Thorkildsen will die if she finds out!*

I added that last point to the list today. I'll return to this shortly, but first I must point out how my list of show title suggestions reveals my problem:

I lack clearly defined enemies in my life. Antagonists, as nonviolent people call them. I'm obviously pro Mrs. Thorkildsen, no question about that, but that tells me nothing about who or what I should be against in the world, other than her daughter-in-law and Our Lord and Savior Jesus Christ, God's only son. And truth be told, Jesus hasn't really bothered Mrs. Thorkildsen or me lately. That leaves the Bitch, who is and will remain Mrs. Thorkildsen's problem, and hers alone. I don't want to get involved in all that. Okay, I do hate the aforementioned Rottweiler down on the corner, but only for the short while I have to listen to his barking every time I walk past his house. I don't hate him otherwise, unless I waste my time mulling over the curses of the past or the curses of the future. He's just a stupid dog, anyway. The world is full of stupid dogs.

Could it be the Puppy who's my enemy, my antagonist?

I certainly hope not. I only have good things to say about the guy, except for how he makes his mother nervous with all his papers and his talk about the future. I certainly hope he didn't take the whole Satan Snarl episode personally.

The Bitch is no big fan of mine, but I don't take that to heart. Had I only experienced the opportunity to properly sniff her up and down, to smell what lies beneath all the antiseptic and camouflage stench, we might even have become good friends.

Like I said: "The Librarian is in love with me and I'm afraid Mrs. Thorkildsen will die if she finds out!"

This is the natural conclusion I've drawn after today's events. We've come home, which means we've been out. The Library/Tavern was the only destination for our walk today. The Puppy and Mrs. Thorkildsen left me alone forever while they went hunting this morning, and they came home with more dragon water than we've had in the house for a long time. The Puppy held the key this time, so he was the one to whom Mrs. Thorkildsen had to explain herself.

"I'm having the old girls over for dinner," she said, and put on her wistful voice for the occasion: "It'll probably be the last time."

"Don't talk like that!" the Puppy snapped, with an emphasis I've rarely heard come out of him. "You've got many good years left, Mom. But, damn it, you've got to pull yourself together a little more. How old was Grandma when she died? Ninety-four? Ninety-five? There's no reason you won't live just as long. Longer! People get older these days. You can't just sit here feeling sorry for yourself while you slowly fade away. Can't you just go to the Canary Islands? Have a little fun in the sun. Enjoy it. We'll take care of Tassen, you know that."

"I don't feel sorry for myself," Mrs. Thorkildsen said, and the room grew ice cold.

"You know we do everything we can so you can live life on your own terms," the Puppy said. Mrs. Thorkildsen said nothing. "But if we're going to do that, you have to hold up your end of the bargain. Be active. Think positive. Why have you fired the Home Helper, by the way?" the Puppy asked.

This was news to me. I peered up at Mrs. Thorkildsen inquisitively, but Mrs. Thorkildsen said nothing.

"Mom?" the Puppy said.

"He's the one who quit," Mrs. Thorkildsen finally answered. "They had finally sent me someone who both spoke my language and had time for a cup of coffee. Finally, I thought. So I sent him out to clean up the lawn furniture, and it's like something snapped for the guy. He came back totally disturbed. Couldn't get out of here fast enough, barely said goodbye, and you know what? I thought, enough is enough. If even the best Home Helper is raving mad, what's the point of waiting for the second-best one? I called the municipality and told them I won't be needing another Home Helper."

The Puppy sighed, but said nothing. Mrs. Thorkildsen kept going:

"I don't feel sorry for myself," she repeated. "If I did, I might need a Home Helper, but as a matter of fact I don't. Plus, you never know what kind of people they're going to send, they come from all over the world, after all. No, let those who really need a Home Helper get one. I'll be just fine."

The Puppy gave an even deeper sigh. Then he said:

"And what if we need it? Part of the point of the Home Helper, Mom, is that it actually makes me—us!—feel safer. Knowing that there's someone coming to check on you every other day might make a bigger difference to me than it does to you, so I wish you'd talked to me about this."

"I can't stand new strangers in my house two days a week, but thank you anyway," Mrs. Thorkildsen said. "And you never know what to feed them! Either they're allergic, or they have some kind of religion that forbids them from having a cup of coffee and a pastry while they're on the clock. I might reach the point where I need a Home Helper eventually, but I'm not there yet. And that's enough of that!"

Later, when Mrs. Thorkildsen, the wheelie bag, and I were strolling through suburbia toward the Center, I had to ask Mrs. Thorkildsen a question that had been weighing on my mind for a while:

"Are you lying to your Puppy?"

"Most certainly not," Mrs. Thorkildsen said. Indignant, I could tell.

"So it's true, you are having the old girls over for dinner?"

"Sure it is," Mrs. Thorkildsen said, and there was something about the way she said it that made me not want to let go, so I hung on like a German shepherd biting into the arm of a peace activist:

"When?"

"I haven't quite decided that yet."

"Ha!" I said.

"Ha yourself," Mrs. Thorkildsen said. "As long as I'm alive, I can say I'm having the girls over for dinner, and no one can prove that is not my intention."

"Well, then I don't understand why you're so furious with the Chief.

He could have said the exact same thing as you. I'm going to the North Pole, he would have said, just not today. Another day."

"I'm not furious with the Chief because he's lying! Imagine that. Every man I've ever met is a liar. Men lie about big things and they lie about little things, not all the time and not about everything, but they all do it. I'm not mad at the Chief, I just think he's a real dolt from time to time."

It's almost strange that we've never thought of it before. After Mrs. Thorkildsen has gotten her books and is having a quick chat with the Librarian, it's time for Mrs. Thorkildsen's regular visit to the Tavern, and a nervous wait in the hallway for me. But then the Librarian, bless her, says:

"Feel free to leave him here while you go get a sandwich."

I didn't realize she was referring to me until Mrs. Thorkildsen addressed me in the voice she uses only when she's talking to me out in public among people, the kind of voice I imagine she would have used if I were her slightly challenged human puppy:

"What do you say, Tassen? Do you want to stay here while Mom goes to get a sandwich and a beer? Does that sound good? Doesn't that sound gooood!"

"Yes, please," I said. "That sounds like a great idea, if you're sure it's not too much trouble."

That's a strange thing about people, how much they change when you get them one-on-one. Mrs. Thorkildsen is obviously the prime example in my life, but I think most people are like this. On their own, they're either better or worse.

The Librarian, who was already quite wonderful, became even better, and that's what bothers me a little as I lie here in the Major's leather chair watching Mrs. Thorkildsen obliviously read her book and drink her dragon water. Should I tell her about all the Librarian's cuddles and sweet talk? How she got me to roll over—I couldn't help it, it happened all on its own—and burrowed her snout into the fur on my neck as she made all kinds of sweet grunting noises. The Librarian thinks I'm a good boy, and she's not afraid to let me know it, and it strikes me that I'm not entirely sure whether Mrs. Thorkildsen feels the same way. That is, I think she does, but I've never heard her say it. That's what happens when a stupid mutt starts to rely on words.

Am I lying if I don't tell Mrs. Thorkildsen what happened and how wonderful I thought it was? Or, the other way around: What good could come from me telling her? If I know Mrs. Thorkildsen, she probably wishes she were young and limber so she could get down on her knees, the best position from which to enjoy a dog, but Mrs. Thorkildsen is old and she thinks getting old is a drag, so I think it would be best to leave it alone. To talk about something else.

"So what happened to the other dogs, who weren't butchered to make an example out of them?" I ask.

Mrs. Thorkildsen looks up from her book.

"Well, they made it to the South Pole. The dogs got to eat their fill and rest for a few days, and the rest of the dog meat was left at the 'Butcher's Shop' as provisions for the way back. Then they continued on with that gang"—she pointed to the paper dogs on the floor—"eighteen of them."

"What about this Scott? Did he make it to the South Pole?"

"The British men made it to the South Pole over a month after the Norwegians had been there, but where the Chief had fulfilled his dreams, Scott found his life's nightmare. 'God, this is a horrible place,' he writes. The Chief had registered no such thing. Do you know what really sank their spirits?" Mrs. Thorkildsen asks, and answers before I have a chance to say no. "All the dog tracks in the snow. There were so many of them. An advantage, in every sense."

"But the South Pole itself, it's actually . . . nothing?"

"Oh, there's nothing there at all. An X in the snow, framed by black flags that the Norwegians planted in every direction so no one who came to that place would doubt that someone had been there before them."

"Black flags. That's really it?"

"Yes, really."

This is how the Chief's map of the South Pole looked:

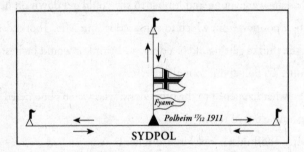

And this is how the map looks when all human installations are removed:

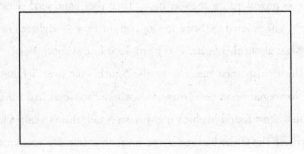

The topography of emptiness. In the middle of the map they plant another flag, too, in red, white, and blue. All the participants in the expedition lucky enough to have opposable thumbs grab the flagpole and drive it into the snow with all their might. Mark it with a flag. That's how humans are. Everyone's happy for a while.

The dogs, on the other hand, are indifferent. To them, the South Pole is just another stop. For some of them, the last stop. The flag has been planted, and the Chief explains:

> Helge had been an exceptionally skilled dog. Without any
> fuss, it had pulled our sled from morning to night and been
> a shining example in the pack, but over the last week it had
> simply collapsed and, by the time we arrived at the Pole, it had
> become a shadow of its former self. It simply rambled along in
> its harness, not pulling any of its weight. One whack on the
> head, and Helge was no more. Helge was dismembered on the
> spot, and within a few hours, only the tip of his tail and his
> teeth remained.

The Major had left the pack a few days earlier. He simply left and never returned.

I suppose it wandered away to die, the Chief writes in his diary. I'm not so sure.

Four days later, the Chief's favorite dog, Lasse, had to pay the price. *It had exhausted itself and no longer had any value.*

Lasse was cut into fifteen parts and fed to his friends. The next day, Per collapsed and received his blow from the hatchet. The Chief briefly dwelled on the death of this slightly "strange" dog who had no interest in fighting or playing with the other dogs, a "misfit" before he was put into the reins.

As a sled dog, it was priceless, the Chief writes, *but like most of the dogs with similar qualities, it couldn't keep going for long. It collapsed, and was beaten to death and eaten.*

As for Blackie, nobody seemed to miss him. The Chief writes in his diary a few days later, the night that dog was consumed:

A lousy specimen. Had it been human, would have ended up in juvenile detention and eventually in jail. It was relatively fat and was eaten with visible relish.

What is the Chief trying to do here, if not reveal what a moral vacuum the South Pole expedition is in his own mind? If he wants to bring us along on "Project Wandering Meal," he should at least rise above the act of commenting on the food's track record. As the Chief portrays it, the world has one less criminal once Blackie has left this world.

Had it been human . . .

33

IT SMELLS GOOD. A powerful aroma is slowly spreading through the house, growing in reach and strength as the time approaches. Time for what? Only the birds know.

I might get dangerous soon if I don't get a treat, but Mrs. Thorkildsen is blind and deaf to my humble demands, and we all know she has no sense of smell. The unknown dinner guest is in charge of everything now. A person who remains a mystery to me, whom I may never have met, has taken charge of my life remotely, and I think it's bullshit.

I have a full bowl of food, so there's no immediate threat of starvation. But food in your bowl is one thing, that's food you already have and thus can save for later. I'm more interested in the food up there on the counter.

"What is that I sense?" I ask.

"Venison steak," Mrs. Thorkildsen says.

"My goodness," I say.

"It should really be bear steak, preferably polar bear, but it's so hard to find."

"I'm sure that's fine," I say coyly. "Might it be possible to taste an ever so tiny piece? Just to check that the meat hasn't rotted? Apply my expertise?"

My salivary glands have already started the party. I'm on the verge of drooling. Mrs. Thorkildsen places her hands squarely on her hips, a sure sign of her confidence in both me and the steak. She tilts her head and smiles; I think the expression *roguish* might be appropriate here. Yes, Mrs. Thorkildsen smiles *roguishly*, and she says:

"As if you wouldn't have wolfed down any piece of rotted meat and then begged for more? You dogs really will eat anything. Even dogs!"

The Mrs. is being sarcastic. Well, two can play at that game:

"Well, who doesn't?" I ask, with the final touché: "I suppose I should be grateful you didn't put *me* on the menu tonight."

"Hmmm, maybe that would have been an idea? Marinated you in dark beer for a few hours before frying you up and serving you with onions and potatoes on the side? Tassen à la Thorkildsen."

Then she catches herself:

"I'm sorry, Tassen. But, you see, I intend to serve the famous 'beef à la Lindstrøm' tonight, and that's no joke."

"Who's laughing?"

"A hundred years ago this dish was served in some of the finest restaurants in Europe and America. The elite wanted to taste the polar chef's specialty. I found the recipe in a book."

Really? First he wins over Mrs. Thorkildsen's heart, and before you know it, Lindstrøm is running loose in the kitchen. A perfect example of one of the dangers of reading books. It may change you. Forever.

"Beef à la Lindstrøm must not be confused with beef Lindstrøm," Mrs. Thorkildsen warns me.

"Of course not," I say. I play along. I'm shameless when such a delicacy is at stake.

"The Swedish dish beef Lindstrøm is, by comparison, a rather pathetic affair," Mrs. Thorkildsen says. "A simple beef chuck camouflaged under beets and a fried egg. Swedish cuisine at its second worst. Doesn't begin to compare to a real beef à la Lindstrøm."

"Right?" I say, and start to get a little dizzy from all the B-words floating endlessly around the room.

"Beef! Beef! Beef!" it echoes. "Beef! Beef!"

"Real beef à la Lindstrøm, you see, must be made with game meat, and ideally with polar bear. But venison will have to do. The meat has to rest for a couple of days, marinate in dark beer after that, and then lots and lots of butter and heat takes care of the rest. Fry up some onion, pour it over the steak, and *voila!* Beef à la Lindstrøm. But we'll do that at the very end. You serve it with fries, and I don't mean frozen, mass-produced fries, Tassen, but handmade . . ."

The doorbell rings, and I start up. The old ritual. I bark, if not energetically, at least evenly and steadily until Mrs. Thorkildsen opens the door. The routine stops right there. I'm surprised, no, I think in this case one might even use the word "shocked." The shock makes my heart dance and my tail lose all control, unfortunately. I wish I could be ice cold now, when who walks in but the Librarian!

This raises the stakes.

So she's desperate enough to come knocking on my door late at night. I'm hugely flattered, of course, and completely unable to hide it, but what will Mrs. Thorkildsen say, and tonight of all nights, when we're expecting company?

"How nice, come on in!" Mrs. Thorkildsen says. "Tassen has been dying for you to come, haven't you, Tassen. Is Tassen happy now?"

Actually, Tassen is a little confused. It dawns on me. So it's the Librarian! She is this unknown, mysterious person who has ruled my life lately. Our lives. The last few months, come to think of it. The Librarian is our dinner guest, and that makes her a guest of honor when the host's name is Mrs. Thorkildsen, no less.

The two women hug, and it doesn't seem like Mrs. Thorkildsen smells anything fishy. To tell you the truth, I'm unclear on what exactly is so suspicious about the smell of fish, but I'm glad this won't present an obstacle tonight.

And then it's my turn. Not a moment too soon.

"Hiiiii, Tassen!" says the Librarian, squatting down in one quick, slinky motion, the kind Mrs. Thorkildsen crossed off her repertoire long ago. Before I was born. You almost have to wonder whether the Librarian does this right under Mrs. Thorkildsen's nose just to mess with her. But enough about that, it's not up to me to make her feel welcome. Snout to snout.

Had I known we were getting such a fancy visitor, I would have at least quickly rolled around in the compost heap before she came, but the Librarian will have to take me as I am. Mrs. Thorkildsen, on the other hand, has doused herself in perfume and put on her nicest dress tonight. She's gone all out with real earrings and a heavy string of pearls, and of course I should have seen it before, she's been to the good but cheap hairdresser who says she's allergic to dogs. The rest is color and paint, and the end result is that Mrs. Thorkildsen is no longer pale and blue, but warm and red.

The Librarian, on the other hand, is dressed like a librarian, in practical trousers and a high-necked sweater. She smells almost the same as she smelled the last time we were together. But not quite. One single small but giant difference. A new smell. On the contrary. An old smell. The oldest. The Librarian is in heat!

And theeeeere she's found the magical spot to scratch—the one that's just a little south of the back or north of the tail, depending on how you see it, and it doesn't really matter, because it's simply impossible to reach just that spot yourself. Without that magical spot, I think the relationship between humans and dogs would look very different. That was likely how the whole thing started in earnest—with that magical spot to scratch.

You can imagine how the wolf must have reacted. Not to mention how the news was received when he came home to the pack bragging about what he'd experienced. And what do you think he does the next day? After dreaming all night about five fingers on his back?

He's hooked now, he *has* to have it. He starts sneaking away from the pack to see if there might be any humans out wandering in the woods, people who might consider giving him a scratch, with no strings attached, of course. Family and friends can see that something has happened to the wolf. They see that he's happy, that getting his butt scratched simply makes him a better wolf, and so the other wolves probably think, if *he* has a magic scratching spot like that, well, isn't it possible that *I* might have a magic scratching spot like that, too? So the evolution has begun, and in the hands of a human, a wolf can be turned into a Chihuahua with astonishing speed. On the other hand, fortunately, it takes a long time to turn a Chihuahua into a wolf. More time than this planet has left, I hope.

I'm about to roll over onto my back, but catch myself as soon as I hear Mrs. Thorkildsen say:

"Well, haven't you two become good friends!"

Did I hear a hint of a sardonic tone? A suspicious tone? Did I hear any tone at all? What is tone, after all? My nose is of no help here. Mrs. Thorkildsen's odors are locked up inside a vault of perfume, but at least her heartbeat is regular and strong, and that's good to hear.

"Tassen and I are best friends now," the Librarian smiles.

I'm glad she chooses to be honest. Cards on the table. No more lies.

"Tassen's actually the first dog I've really made friends with since my own dog died," the Librarian says.

"His name was Robin. A golden retriever. Blond. A pretty stupid dog. He was hit by a train. And survived."

This last piece of information, about how stupid the golden retriever was, is of course superfluous—but the rest of it is interesting enough. So the Librarian has suffered a loss. Her dog died. And she's choosing to dwell on this loss. If she had a new dog, she wouldn't miss the dog that died. Old Robin would be a soft and tender memory. I'm sure he already is, but until the Librarian gets a new dog, the memory will be a sad and painful one. The foremost and often the only function of house dogs like me is to help their humans pass the time through all the sad, painful stuff that piles up over the course of their existence. I don't know if it's right to say that dogs take your mind off everything that's sad and painful, but I'm saying it anyway.

The dog is your comfort and your scapegoat.

• • •

The table is set, the aroma of food fills every nook and cranny with hallucinations, the fireplace has been lit and is now a sparking inferno underneath the paper wolves up on the mantel, and there's just the kind of piano music Mrs. Thorkildsen knows I enjoy. Like most dogs, I enjoy classical music, but I'm especially sensitive to string instruments. The sound of a Hardanger fiddle makes me howl. I can't help it, I don't know where it comes from, really, the drawn-out, bottomless wail that pours out of me, but I know it's ancient and I know that someday I'll die. Piano music, on the other hand . . .

When I eventually pull myself together, after Mrs. Thorkildsen has served sherry to the Librarian and the two are chatting louder than you would imagine possible for two small librarians, I can't help but be impressed by Mrs. Thorkildsen, who has managed to throw a surprise party right under my nose. When did they make this arrangement? It's a sheer joy, but a surprise, and I think that were I human, I might have seen this night coming. It's unbelievably lame for a dog who excuses his weakened instincts with his increased human wisdom. But enough about that—Mrs. Thorkildsen is in rare form tonight. That's the most important thing. She smiles and asks questions and laughs. Accepts the Librarian's compliments on the house in general, and especially the view. Since one wall of the living room is filled with books from floor to ceiling, interrupted only by the fireplace in the middle, I don't think the two of them will ever run out of conversation tonight. Maybe they're planning to read books after dinner? That would be nice. They speak, as they always do when they meet, about the Library at the Center, which will soon meet its demise, and Mrs. Thorkildsen gets a little touchy, but then she thankfully must excuse herself to go check on the food.

We're alone, the Librarian and I. For one charged moment.

The Librarian looks at me and I look at the Librarian and my tail wags, you can bet my tail wags.

"Yes, come on, Tassen," she says, but she can't possibly mean that. Mrs. Thorkildsen might come back from the kitchen at any moment but, on the other hand, we can probably sneak in a little petting and scratching if I just stand here at her feet. And she smells so good it's almost hard to believe, and there, it's happening again, and suddenly there are no thoughts, it just happens on its own, and it's hard to know how to respond. I see no better opportunity than to start with that leg there, to take it from there wherever it might lead us, and the whole thing would be a lot simpler if the Librarian would only stop laughing and instead help out a little.

"Tassen! GET DOWN!"

Mrs. Thorkildsen is back and she is mad as hell. I should have known this would end in shouting and drama. It always does. Love is an over-rated mess.

"No, no, it's fine," the Librarian laughs, which should have put the whole thing to rest, but the old biddy has climbed on her moral high horse now, a shabby, spotted old nag who should have been sent to the farm long ago.

"What in the world has gotten into you?" Mrs. Thorkildsen says to me sternly, and to the Librarian she says softly: "He never does that, really, I can't apologize enough. *Bad* boy!"

The Librarian laughs again, but she doesn't come to my rescue. Doesn't tell Mrs. Thorkildsen that she was the seductress and I the seduced, no, she lets me live with the shame alone. Traitorous woman.

• • •

"First, a little piece of gravlax. I cured it myself. And I hope you appreciate the mustard sauce. It's one of my secret specialties."

I don't know how the poor Librarian could be expected to give her honest opinion, the way Mrs. Thorkildsen raises expectations around her own culinary skills. It's in rather poor taste, to tell you the truth, and not at all like the Mrs. Thorkildsen I know. But she knows what she's doing. The Librarian chews until it crunches, and there it is. The little sound that says it all.

"Mnyeh . . . !"

That's about how the tiny gasp sounds, the one that reveals the Librarian, too, has now sold her soul to Mrs. Thorkildsen's kitchen. Well, at least she sold herself at a high price. Some people surrender over a simple cinnamon roll. The Librarian is at least getting three full courses. Perhaps she's thinking about how lucky she is, though she can't possibly know she is privy to an encore performance in a once-legendary theater that closed its doors long ago. She chews slowly and deliberately, and asks:

"What's the secret behind the sauce?"

"The secret," Mrs. Thorkildsen whispers secretively, "is that the sauce isn't a sauce at all, but a cream! Mustard and whipping cream, whisked together. The easiest trick in the book, but you can't beat it! You don't even need a recipe. But don't tell a soul!"

It's fascinating to watch what happens to people when they're fed. I don't mean the daily mouthfuls of sustenance, filled with whatever they may be, sealed in plastic and joylessly prepared in ovens that say *ping!*

No, I mean what's playing out right here and now, when two people sit down with time on their hands and eat as slowly as they possibly can. The Librarian's beautiful little grunt was just the audible part of the metamorphosis. The heart beats slower, the blood smells sweeter, and we're still only on the appetizer.

Mrs. Thorkildsen asks and asks and sips dragon water. Small and big questions that have accumulated in her over a long time. The Librarian answers and answers and sips dragon water.

"My parents were born in Vietnam," she responds to a question I didn't hear. "They were adopted separately as children, and met at a summer camp for adopted kids up north. Then they ran off to Oslo and started a family before anyone could stop them."

Mrs. Thorkildsen listens, rapt with attention.

"Then they got divorced. Dad went to visit his family in Vietnam and never came back. Now he's a businessman there. Apparently he's earning a lot of money. The strange thing is that between the two of them, Mom was the one who grew up in a home that emphasized her homeland's culture. Dad could barely point to Vietnam on a map, I think. But he could capture reindeer with a lasso. Not many Vietnamese people can do that."

"Not nearly enough," Mrs. Thorkildsen says.

The Librarian takes a fresh swig. I may have overestimated Mrs. Thorkildsen's special talent for drinking; new evidence would suggest that this is a more widespread skill. It would seem that librarians, in the course of their everyday work, are exposed to environmental hazards that predispose them to liberal engagement with intoxicating beverages. Once a librarian, always a drunkard. It's just a theory.

"Where does your mother live?" Mrs. Thorkildsen asks.

"Mom died two years ago. One day she didn't answer the phone when I called, so I went to her house and let myself in. She was lying on the kitchen floor, and I didn't need to look closer to realize she was dead."

"What on earth happened?"

"She lost her balance and fell while she was cleaning the top of the fridge. Her head hit the kitchen counter, and that was that. Broke her neck. Apparently no more than one second passed from when she lost her balance until she was dead."

"That is just the most horrible thing I've ever heard!" Mrs. Thorkildsen says, and she sounds like she means it.

"And here's the best part," the Librarian continues. "The autopsy revealed that Mom had been dying of cancer. She hadn't noticed a single symptom, at least as far as I know, but according to the hospital, she would most likely have died a slow, painful death over the next eighteen months."

"Well, that's just the most horrible thing I've ever heard," Mrs. Thorkildsen says, and it sounds like she means it again. A new personal record.

"It's not so bad," the Librarian responds. "I honestly think she might have taken her own life otherwise. Mom told me about an uncle she lived with in Vietnam after her parents died, before she came to Norway. Her uncle had six cartridges lined up on the mantel. His wife and the four kids in the house knew who they were intended for if the situation became . . . intolerable. Mom used to stare at the ammunition neatly lined up in a row on the shelf, and wonder which bullet was meant for her."

"Oh, dear!" Mrs. Thorkildsen says, clasping her hands together. "Well, it's time for the main course. Perhaps you wouldn't mind helping me in the kitchen for a minute?"

Life doesn't get much better than this. In the kitchen. Mrs. Thorkildsen, the Librarian, a couple of giant, juicy steaks of polar bear, and little old me.

"Oh my God!" the Librarian says when she spots Mrs. Thorkildsen's steaks. "And I'm a vegetarian!"

"Nonsense, you're no such thing!" Mrs. Thorkildsen nearly wheezes. "You're descended from a Neanderthal who chowed down on meat whenever he had the chance."

"Yes, but that was only because he was too dumb to fish," the Librarian replies, and they laugh again. I can't get Mrs. Thorkildsen to laugh as often as she should, and when it happens, it's usually by accident, and afterward I don't always understand what she was laughing at.

I love hearing her laugh. There's a whole human life echoing in that laugh, it's like the song of the whales in the ocean, shaped and reshaped year after year, slowly, so slowly that neither Mrs. Thorkildsen nor anyone around her realizes it happened, and is still happening.

Of course, I can make Mrs. Thorkildsen laugh. Every sofa cushion with self-respect and liver paste on the menu should be able to do that, but if I'm being honest, it comes down to cheap tricks more than subtle humor. A little nudging with my snout here and there, chasing my own tail a little, it doesn't take much. But the repertoire is limited, and some of the tricks are getting old. If I'm being completely honest, some of her reactions might be wearing off a bit, too. The laughter I can summon is a different laughter than the one that rises from conversation between Mrs. Thorkildsen and our guest.

Mrs. Thorkildsen waxes enthusiastic to the Librarian about her hero Lindstrøm as she arranges the meat on the plates and I almost drown in my own saliva. I don't bark, nowhere near it, but I think a couple of choice words wouldn't be out of place.

"Steak!" I shout, and nearly add: "For fuck's sake!" To hell with manners. This is serious business. And what do you know, for a second the two cackling hens actually pause to pay attention to the fact that yours truly is actually present and in the process of going insane from hunger.

"You'll get yours, too, Tassen," Mrs. Thorkildsen says. "Relax."

Then she keeps on blabbering about this, that, and the other, and they raise their glasses to toast again. But finally, finally the moment has arrived, and there comes the food bowl, filled to the brim. Meat! Juicy, bloody meat, as if I had torn it from the polar bear's bone myself. Satan Snarl tears the chunks of meat off his victim and greedily swallows them whole. Without sauce. Satan Snarl is happy.

"Well, an old mind has to occupy itself somehow," Mrs. Thorkildsen says as I return to the ladies in the living room, fully satiated. I've missed something. Maybe the Librarian has asked a question, something about why an old widow and her dog devour every book they can find about something that happened on an iceberg on the other side of the planet long, long ago.

"The famous South Pole journey is the kind of story you think you know, right?" Mrs. Thorkildsen asks, without waiting for an answer. "Brave men and brave dogs plodding through ice and snow to the South Pole and returning in triumph, while Captain Scott loses everything he has because he doesn't think to use dogs to pull his sleds. The foolish Englishman who'd rather tire himself out in the harness than risk harming a hair on a dog's head."

"I've mostly heard about Scott, actually," the Librarian says. "The moral victor, in a sense. I remember I saw a movie about him on TV. *The Great Son of the Empire.* That kind of thing. There's something so hopelessly Lord Byron romantic about scrawling out your final pompous reflections before you die for king and country. It's unbelievable that he even made it to the South Pole at all. Can you imagine dragging heavy sleds across a glacier up to a height of ten thousand feet? It's got to completely break a man.

"Why didn't the British use dogs?" the Librarian asks. Good question!

"Because they had no idea what they were doing. They probably eventually realized that they should have gone with sled dogs, but they hid behind the argument that it was undignified for civilized people to be pulled along by dogs. Horses, on the other hand, were perfectly fine. But the ponies Scott brought with him froze to death, as any Norwegian farmer would have expected. So it became all about human muscle power. Scott and his men exhausted themselves and got gangrene and scurvy and I don't know what else. Had they brought a dog or two for provisions, at least they would have avoided the scurvy. Terrible disease. You get back all the little cuts and wounds you've ever had, all at once. Subjecting your men to the most painful ailments because of a disease that could have been avoided by slaughtering a dog—I don't see the moral victory in that."

"A British honor code?"

"Unfortunately I don't think it's a particularly British phenomenon, though the Brits are former world champions in two-faced hypocrisy. I think it's about vanity. Male vanity. Any defeat, even if it means death, is preferable to a tainted victory, as long as the defeat looks good. I remember thinking that in connection with that Norwegian girl who won the New York Marathon many times."

"Grete Waitz?"

"That's it, Grete Waitz! She once had stomach issues during the race, but that didn't stop Grete Waitz. She scooped the worst of it out of her shorts using her hand and ran onward to victory with shit running down her legs. When she was asked why she didn't quit the race, she said it was for practical reasons. Before the race, she'd already sold the car that came with the winnings, and it would be very clumsy to have to reverse the sale. A man like Robert Scott would rather have died than subject himself to something like that. But to drown in terrible and unnecessary diseases, that was okay. You're still a polar hero!"

"So what is it that drives someone like Amundsen, then?" the Librarian asks.

"The same things that drive all men: honor, glory, fame, wealth, and women. In that order. And he won and lost it all—alone. Amundsen never formed a close bond with anyone. He saw women as a threat to his dreams and ambitions. He became the way certain men do when they don't get the necessary corrections from a woman. Combine that with a cynicism that set him up to step over the corpses of dogs to reach his goals, and you have a winner."

"And what do you think a 'Mrs. Amundsen' might have done for him, then?"

"That depends on when she comes into the story. Had she really been the right one for him, he probably wouldn't have left her to spend years of their lives in order to maybe be the first to get to a place where no one had any business being. Plodding along on the ice for months and years while your children grow up. By the way, Amundsen was also the first one in the country to get his pilot's license. If he'd had a wife, they could have discussed this idea of going to the South Pole on the porch over a glass of white wine, and perhaps he would have had the brains to say, 'Let's wait a few years, dear, and go there for a long weekend. Then we won't have to kill all those beautiful dogs in order to get there.'"

"When was this?"

"They arrived at the South Pole on the fourteenth of December, 1911."

Mrs. Thorkildsen gets contemplative; I can sense that before she opens her mouth after a slight pause:

"When I was growing up, the South Pole expedition was like something that had happened in prehistoric times. The pictures might have been taken a hundred, five hundred years earlier, and the motives would be the same. Men, dogs, and sleds, and otherwise pure white. But it turned out it wasn't from prehistoric times after all, it was less than twenty years before I was born.

"The way I read the story now, it's about the end of an era. It was the world that belonged to my mother and her generation kind of writing a period. Or a semicolon. Those of us who survived the war can easily forget that there was a world and a life before it. It overshadows older memories. All the urgings not to forget the war, they may have succeeded in keeping the memory alive, but they may also have suppressed the subsequent history, and not least the prehistory. Do you have any kind of relationship to the war?"

"Well, our family didn't have any kind of relationship to that war, but we had a clear connection to another war, of course. I've managed to keep both wars out of my life. Seeing the Vietnam War through the eyes of a Norwegian, and the occupation of Norway through the eyes of a Vietnamese. I don't feel anything special when I hear the national anthem. I don't like skiing."

"Bad Norwegian!" Mrs. Thorkildsen says, audibly tipsy now. "No respect for our culture."

"I know! I'm a terrible person." The Librarian chuckles. "A goddamn alien, that's what I am."

What do you think two librarians talk about when they're chatting over the dinner table? That's right, they talk about books they've both read, and books only one of them has read and the other simply must read. Long books, good books. But slowly and surely, Mrs. Thorkildsen and the Librarian begin to close in on their prey: bad books.

"Crime fiction is a symptom of societal decline," Mrs. Thorkildsen says in a somber voice, and I sense what's coming. "The crime trend has infected a whole generation of readers. A generation that has seen the world change like never before, who have all the filth and injustice in the world available at the tap of a keyboard, who have war in their living rooms. The most challenged generation of all time, you might say, so they seek refuge in a static literary universe where nothing ever really changes, and the law always wins. And that's not the worst part . . ."

Mrs. Thorkildsen catches herself and calms down a bit before she continues:

". . . the worst part is that the world of crime is disguised as the real world, that's one of the stock phrases in the newspapers' panegyrics, that it's so real. So realistic! And ideally it's supposed to be nauseatingly brutal. The fun part is how the reviewers use precisely this brutality to declare that the work is realistic, as if they'd all survived the most maca-bre forms of torture themselves! What on earth is this need that's being fulfilled by these detailed descriptions of human degradation, whether you're writing or reading them? If you really need crime to come so close up against your life, why don't you expose yourself to a crime, or, better, commit one!"

"But, as you say, people read it," the Librarian says in her soothing voice. "And what needs does crime fiction fulfill? I'd say it's pretty ob-vious that it's excitement, wouldn't you? Excitement and escapism. Isn't that what good writers provide?"

"Sure. But why isn't *Crime and Punishment* regular fare for all those people who devour the crime fiction of the week? Capote? Genet? Mailer? Fucking Edgar Allan Poe!"

"Nevermore!" the Librarian adds. They toast. They get quiet, and it's a good quiet, until the Librarian asks:

"But they ate dogs?"

Is that a tiny sigh I hear out of Mrs. Thorkildsen? And what, in that case, could it mean?

"They did," she starts. "Both dogs and men ate dogs. The part about the diet is a side of the polar history I never before considered, but really I should have, since I've played the role of steward myself. Calculating purchases and preparations for number of people times physical activity times time. On budget. Ideally under. And this was before vitamins were discovered, so the first challenge was simply not to get sick or die from bad food. The British were bothered to death by scurvy, but none of Amundsen's people. Why? Roald Amundsen's forte in Antarctica was the food. And the dogs. Which turned out to be partly the same thing. The dogs were listed under both the debit and credit columns of the provisions plan. You're going to move five men and fifty-two dogs twenty miles a day for a certain number of days. Then you're going to slaughter dogs as obstacles are overcome, sleds get lighter, and the daily distance is covered. The only requirement for completion, apart from the conquest of the South Pole, is that the men survive. The dogs can be sacrificed. Not only can they be sacrificed, they're calculated sacrifices, estimated to make up fifty-five pounds of provisions per capita. Of the fifty-two dogs who set out for the South Pole, only eleven made it back to the winter quarters."

"They shot forty dogs?"

"Or beat them to death. Well, actually, some of the dogs did escape."

Mrs. Thorkildsen slowly gets to her feet and walks over to the coffee table to retrieve, perhaps unsurprisingly, a book.

"You'll have to read for yourself," she says as she strides across the room. "It's the closest you get to the human being Roald Amundsen throughout his whole story about the South Pole expedition."

The Librarian takes the book, almost obscenely caresses it between her fingers as she pulls it toward her, acknowledges its purely technical quality with a complimentary remark, and then reads aloud from a spot Mrs. Thorkildsen has marked with one of her little flags:

What went quicker that evening than before was the lighting of the Primus stove, and pumping it up to high pressure. I thus hoped to create as much noise as possible, to avoid hearing the many shots that would soon be fired. Twenty-four of our brave companions and faithful helpers had the bitter wage—death.

It was hard to bear, but it must be so. We had agreed to stop at nothing to reach our goal.

"At least he's honest, for once." Mrs. Thorkildsen holds her glass close to her chest.

"You can say that again," the Librarian says. "To stop at nothing."

"I tried to keep count, but I've given up trying to figure out exactly how many dogs were sacrificed, all in all. With bitches who were born on board the *Fram*, at the South Pole, and later additions included, it must have been as many as two hundred. Maybe more. Some of the dogs ended up meeting the sorry fate of being skinned and taxidermied. Tassen and I met a few of them at the Fram Museum. What do you say, are you shocked?"

"Not shocked," the Librarian says, pausing. "Maybe a little surprised at the extent of it. I knew they used and killed dogs, but I was under the impression that it was a matter of just a few, perhaps for medical reasons. Two hundred is pretty extreme."

"Right? On the other hand, it's just a number, isn't it. Two or two hundred, does it really matter?"

"You mean: How many deaths does it take to declare something a war?"

"That question also has to do with who's dying. Did you know that some places in America, it's now illegal to eat horse meat? Illegal! It's created a huge industry for those in charge of handling horse cadavers. There are horse funerals where the giant animal is put six feet under with the help of an excavator and a crane. Can you imagine?"

"I read something about some people who had their deceased dog taxidermied; apparently it's become quite common. That's probably why I reacted when you told me about the dog waste on the South Pole expedition. But you mean to say they really loved the animals?"

"You can see for yourself what the Chief says about it, I've flagged the passage—I thought it was noteworthy."

Mrs. Thorkildsen hands the book back over to the Librarian, who reads with a clear, young voice that marks a sharper and sharper contrast against the content the longer she reads:

> I loved my dogs under normal circumstances, and apparently
> the feeling was mutual. But the circumstances in question were
> not normal. Or perhaps it was me, that I wasn't normal? I've
> later thought that might be the case . . . the goal I refused to
> give up on made me brutal. I was too brutal when I forced these
> creatures to haul the heavy burdens on those sleds.

"And why do we care about these dogs at all?" Mrs. Thorkildsen asks. "The animals we should really feel sorry for here are the native inhabitants. Tons of seals and penguins killed and devoured by creatures that didn't belong on the continent. The seals down there weren't accustomed to people, and they didn't try to run when they were hunted, just lay there waiting to be clubbed. Even better, with a fish in hand, it was easy for the hunter to lure the seal all the way over to the ship before killing it, so he wouldn't have to drag his massive prey across the ice. God knows how many animals they killed."

"Well, if you start thinking that way it'll never end," the Librarian says. "How many ants did I kill off when I walked from the gate to your front door? We're daily mass murderers, all of us."

They laugh.

The room grows quiet, the way it does when good food is digested. Everything feels fat. Then Mrs. Thorkildsen, apropos of nothing, pulls out an old classic of hers:

"Getting old is a drag."

I've lost count of how many times I've heard Mrs. Thorkildsen utter these words, and after all, I can only count to four. But the Librarian does what I never do. She asks the right question:

"In what way?"

Mrs. Thorkildsen thinks carefully before answering. This is new:

"There are so many ways getting old is shit, but since you asked, I'd say that first and foremost, it's the fact that you don't."

"Get old?" The Librarian seems alert.

"If only I could have all of me age at the same tempo—well, that might not be so easy either, but I might not constantly forget how old I am, only to have it brutally thrown in my face every time I see my own reflection. If the mind aged at the same rate as the skin, to put it that way. But the soul doesn't wrinkle. Not in that way. On the inside, I'm not getting any older. My body, my brain, everything about me is getting old, but I'm not getting old. In my dreams I'm still sixteen years old, and I don't think the soul gets any older. Not mine, anyway. But there it is, trapped in the prison that is me, while the building slowly crumbles around me thanks to wear and tear and lack of maintenance. I see a handsome man on the street, and I think and feel what I might think and feel, and he might do as I hope and throw a glance my way, but I feel it going right through me. I've become invisible to that glance. The impulse to run across a field and roll into the summer night doesn't go anywhere, but I can't run anymore, and God knows what would happen if a young Adonis took me in his arms and fulfilled my innermost desires. He'd probably break every bone in my body. Or maybe it would simply catch fire, dry as it all is."

More laughter. More dragon water. More Mrs. Thorkildsen:

"One can hope to get wiser as the years go by, but that very 'one' remains the same. The joys and the fears remain the same, so that you shall truly realize how many of your joys depend on the body's power, while fear is driven by its own renewable energy. Am I boring you now?"

"Not at all. I'm just glad you're telling me this. That you can be bothered to have an honest conversation about something real. Something serious. One big difference I see between Mom and Dad's homeland and my own is that the connection between older and younger people is so much weaker here, and that death is totally absent from our lives."

"It's not death that's the problem—it's life," says Mrs. Thorkildsen. "One of the old Greeks said that the gods envy people because people know they're going to die, they just don't know when. The fact that life won't last forever, that it could be over at any minute, is what gives life to life, the way the Greek gods see it. Isn't the world much more exciting when you know it could be gone in the next moment? But what the gods forget to imagine is how it feels to sit and wait for the moment to come, when you've had your fill of life long ago. When you've done all you plan to do and you don't have much use for life anymore, but you still don't know when your time will come."

"Is that what you're doing?" the Librarian asks quietly. "Waiting impatiently to die?"

"On the contrary, I'm being very patient. If I were impatient, I'd certainly find an escape hatch. I just want to live without the death denial that's become a scourge for so many in our time, which hits us old folks the hardest. They talk to us as if death is the enemy. They have us exercise and diet and stimulate us so you'd think death was defused. Past its expiration date. But that's not our fear of death. That's our children's, those who are still at an age when death makes its mark unfairly and randomly, those who still think death can be conquered if you only exercise and live a life of moderation, preferably with a diet full of vegetables."

"I think I know what you mean," the Librarian says. "When I see the joggers in the park where I live, I always think: Why? What's driving you to do this? I think: A better body? Okay, have at it. Higher self-esteem? Meh. Is there any reason to have higher self-esteem just because from time to time you switch from a walk to a gallop?"

"And they all have those wires coming out of their ears." Mrs. Thorkildsen points to her ears.

"Guilty as charged! I don't run, but I like to listen to music when I'm walking or biking. Come to think of it, that's the only time I have to listen to the music I want to hear. Are you worried about the future?"

Mrs. Thorkildsen answers without thinking:

"Yes."

Then she takes a long pause, before adding:

"Well. Hmmm. Or maybe not. As you can tell, I don't plan to spend a big part of my life in the future, but when I do think about it, I am worried. I don't know what it is that worries me, exactly. Financially I'm just fine, I can safely live here as long as I want, whatever they might come up with. I have my health. What's left of it, anyway. Getting old is a drag, but it only gets worse if you start whining about it, and since old age paints everyone with the same brush, at least it feels . . . fair."

"You spend a lot of time alone," the Librarian says. I don't know whether that's a question or a statement.

"Yes," says Mrs. Thorkildsen, "and sometimes I worry about what it does to me, spending so much time alone. On the other hand, I'm just happy my family isn't pounding down the door more than they already do. I thought it would make me happy when they told me they were thinking of moving home, but instead it made me feel unsettled. Now they're talking about moving away again, and I'm just as happy. I know that somewhere in their thought process they're considering that the little one should be able to see his grandmother, or that the grandmother should be able to see her grandchild. But when I really think about it, all I see is myself babysitting a boy who knows how to take care of himself. Truth be told, my own grandchild is a stranger to me, and I don't feel any sadness about that. On the contrary. Is this sounding cold?"

"I don't think so," the Librarian says. "Would I feel differently if I had kids of my own? Maybe. But seen from the sidelines, the fourth commandment is the worst of them all. If there's one verse in the Bible that reveals it was written by men rather than God, it's this one: Honor thy father and mother, that it may be well with thee, and thou mayest live long on the Earth. I mean, it's the only one of the Ten Commandments that empowers people, and nowhere near all people, but exclusively parents," the Librarian continues, growing excited now. "Notice that it's the only commandment that uses a concrete reward to entice people into following it. It's strange in many ways. 'Honor thy father and mother.' Okay. So when your mother and father die, you're suddenly free from one of the Ten Commandments? The nine others are permanent and eternal, but this fourth commandment is apparently the only one that's circumstantial. Dependent on family circumstances, even. You can almost hear Moses going: 'Maybe we should just add a few lines to keep those bratty teenagers in line? It's not like someone's going to notice.'"

34

THEY NEVER DID FINISH TALKING, but eventually it becomes time for the Librarian to leave us after all. As she stands in the hallway lacing up her boots, Mrs. Thorkildsen comes trudging out of the kitchen with a book in her hand and a secretive smile on her face.

"As long as you're here," she says, "could you do me a favor and bring back this book I forgot to return?"

Mrs. Thorkildsen is lying! For once it's not my nose that catches her, but my eyes. For there, in Mrs. Thorkildsen's outstretched hand, is the book about Adolf Lindstrøm, the one on which she spilled red wine. And if there's one book Mrs. Thorkildsen hasn't forgotten about, it's that one. Like a red-hot ball of guilt it's been sitting there on the shelf, day in and day out, and now she just gives it away with a smile, just like that. Perhaps that was her plan all along? To get the Librarian so liquored up that she just accepts the tarnished book without noticing Mrs. Thorkildsen has dunked it in dragon water? Either that, or there's something I've missed, which would be a shame.

I can barely wait until the Librarian, after an eternity of giggles and hugs (and a few scratches, I have to confess), is out the door:

"You're shameless in your shamefulness," I say. Laconic, I hope. I'd like to be a little laconic now.

"What are you babbling on about now?" Mrs. Thorkildsen says. Alcoholic.

"This whole charade," I say. "It was all so you could return a library book?"

"Nonsense, I could have returned that long ago."

"But it was damaged. What happened?"

"I saved it," Mrs. Thorkildsen says with a secretive, mocking smile.

Behind my back, God knows when she's found the time, Mrs. Thorkildsen has sought out the black market. She's visited a rare bookshop, she admits. That would not have happened on my watch.

"You could have been killed!" I say.

If you've never set foot in a rare bookshop, be glad. Consider yourself warned. Rare bookshops, you see, are built on the premise of taking full advantage of sick people. There might be a fine line between being a *bibliophile* and a *bibliomaniac*, but it's a very important line. Bibliophiles can typically make do with the Library, but bibliomaniacs *have to have it*!

Mrs. Thorkildsen is in no way a bibliomaniac—on the contrary, she stays on the right side of the line. Still, I don't think the rare-book pusher has any problems recognizing a person walking into the store with a desperate need for precisely *that* book. And Mrs. Thorkildsen had that need. The book hawker probably only had to take one look at her to see the desperation and anticipation. God knows how much he cheated her out of before she could grab the book with her arthritic hands and stuff it into her wheelie bag.

"But what about the smell code?"

"Can you imagine, there was a code on it already. Isn't that what you'd call a stroke of good luck? All it took from there was a pair of scissors, some contact paper, and the old stamp I grabbed before I left the job."

I'm tempted to tell Mrs. Thorkildsen that she's becoming more and more like the Chief with each day that goes by; on the other hand, it's probably unwise to give her any ideas.

The Librarian has gone home, or wherever it is young librarians spend the night, and Mrs. Thorkildsen sits in her chair with her glass and a newspaper clipping that she reads over and over again. The Librarian gave it to her, one last thing she remembered while attempting to wedge the Lindstrøm book into her overstuffed handbag. Maybe to make space, she pulled a newspaper clipping out of the bag and handed it to Mrs. Thorkildsen.

"You should read this," the Librarian said. "It was in the paper yesterday."

And that's what Mrs. Thorkildsen has done. Over and over again. It's not easy to sniff out exactly what it is the little piece of text has done—and is doing—to little Mrs. Thorkildsen, who's already full and tired and drunk.

"Are you sad?" I ask. "Do you want to cuddle?"

"No, I'm not sad. And, yes, I'd love to cuddle."

"What did she give you?"

"A letter to the editor. Let me read it to you."

And then she read it to me.

> When I think back on my childhood, I realize now that I took
> you for granted. I didn't know how lucky I was to go to a school
> with its own library, and a librarian who knew me and always led
> me to new reading experiences.

Mrs. Thorkildsen sounds like she has a bit of a cold, I think.

> Through the books you showed me, I traveled all over the world,
> and lived many lives. I now have an idea about what it's like to
> be adopted or to be a gypsy girl during the Second World War.
> I was there when Pompeii was buried in volcanic ash and I have
> memories of being plundered by Vikings.
>   The library gave me a safe place to read while I waited for
> rehearsal or when I got to school early, and sometimes I was
> lucky enough to be able to meet a real author.
>   All kids should have a librarian in their lives.

And that seems to be the end of it. At least, there's nothing more to
say. The heart beats and the breath goes on, and Mrs. Thorkildsen is sad
and content. I'm full and content.

"Is it about you?" I have to ask. "Are you the librarian?"

"I'm not that librarian," Mrs. Thorkildsen says. "But it is about me."

35

As she begins the next leg of her story, Mrs. Thorkildsen is wearing her green dress for the occasion and is standing by the fireplace, where again it's now magically tighter quarters than it used to be. She's been drinking, but only enough to get the required flush in her face. Mrs. Thorkildsen's interest in "The Big Pissing Contest in Antarctica" is located somewhere within a condition defined at both ends by a glass of dragon water. Without dragon water in her body, Mrs. Thorkildsen has no interest in telling stories. With too much dragon water on board she's incapable of telling them. She has to hit a certain window of light and chatty tipsiness, which is right where she is now.

"There are thirty-nine dogs here, Tassen," she says. And maybe it's the way she says my name, but suddenly the mood seems a bit conspiratorial. "This according to Thorvald Nilsen."

"You're not going to trick me into asking who Thorvald Nilsen is."

"Was. Thorvald Nilsen was the Chief's second-in-command."

"A beta," I say with ice-cold irony, but it goes straight over her head.

"Nilsen sailed around the world two and a half times over the course of the South Pole expedition. Can you imagine!"

"So that makes him a good man?" I ask, possibly a bit curtly, but I am trying to be a good dog, believe me. I could have said something about Mrs. Thorkildsen's relationship to men generally, be they fathers, sons, or lovers. Not to mention if they're naval captains in distant seas. But I let it go, a choice I don't regret. I don't get an answer to my question, though. Everyone is entitled to their opinion, right?

They are going home with seventy-seven fewer dogs than when they first arrived in Antarctica, Mrs. Thorkildsen says, less than a quarter of all the dogs on the expedition, including the fish food. All eleven South Pole dogs are among the thirty-nine on board.

"So they set sail, away from the giant block of ice where the British men are still fumbling their way toward death without the help of a single dog. But great stories are just like great deeds: they're all about coming first. And given the choice of coming first with the deed or with the story," Mrs. Thorkildsen explains, "always choose the story."

"I'll try to remember that," I say.

The Chief sits in the ship's cabin, writing the story of his victory and feeling his old creeping anxiety about coming last, the one he thought he'd left behind in that little tent he pitched on the South Pole. What the Chief really thinks about the loser in the race, as he sits there carving his legacy into something he thinks is stone, but really is ice, nobody knows.

Mrs. Darling gives birth to eight puppies, four of each. Half of them get to live, two of each sex. *Splash! Splash! Splash! Splash!* But now it's the boys' turn to drown and the girls' turn to live. And that's that. Mrs. Thorkildsen moves four new dogs to the floor.

"Forty-three," she says, and it sounds just fine to me. And she places four new figures on the mantel.

The Chief ran ashore and telegraphed his feat to the whole world as soon as the *Fram*, after a long rough sail, arrived in Tasmania. The expedition got rid of a whole new batch of dogs at that point. These dogs weren't murdered, but sold as slaves to some crazy local imperialist with Antarctic ambitions. He probably wasn't hard to find.

All eleven South Pole dogs stayed with the *Fram* as it wearily wobbled its way through the Pacific toward Buenos Aires without the Chief on board: he's now traveling separately aboard a passenger ship, under an alias to be safe—and with a fake beard!

"You see, he doesn't give up!" Mrs. Thorkildsen says. She can't help herself. "Lies his way to the South Pole and, God help me, he lies his way right back."

"If you all didn't have such a ridiculously bad sense of smell, it would be impossible to fool someone with a fake beard," I allow myself to point out.

There, in the hot, humid harbor city of Buenos Aires, Argentina, the Chief's team falls apart. He has already sailed off on his own, he's wrapped in the arms of fame now, the embrace that will slowly suffocate him throughout the rest of his life.

The lie is fading, but it still has a pulse. The *Fram* is still on course for the North Pole. That assurance is the only thing protecting the Chief from being branded as a liar in official circles. But the truth is that the *Fram* isn't really headed anywhere other than the ocean floor, at least over the long haul. The polar ship should have kept going long ago, but she's still docked in the harbor, stinking as the provisions for the North Pole expedition sit rotting on board.

The South Pole dogs are still alive. One of them is already on his way to Norway; the rest are starting to become a problem. And what do people do about problems? Stuff them away where they can't be seen. Lock them in if they can. That was exactly what happened to the polar dogs.

The dogs get stuffed away in Buenos Aires's hot and humid, stuffy zoo. An establishment that apparently had a certain degree of experience taking care of polar dogs as long as there was money to be had. So that's the way it went.

"And that's where the journey ends," Mrs. Thorkildsen says.

"In a zoo?"

"They die," Mrs. Thorkildsen says. "Of various illnesses."

"What kind of illness?"

"I don't know, Tassen. Some kind of canine flu the other polar dogs brought with them, they think."

"And that was that?"

"Apparently that was that."

"After traveling around the world, after being the first to set paw on the Last Place on Earth, they die of illness in a dirty zoo?"

"Well, we don't know that it was dirty, but yes," Mrs. Thorkildsen says. "All but one. The only one of the dogs from the South Pole to survive and make it back to Norway. The Colonel."

The Colonel stood out from the crowd as early as that day two years before outside Kristiansand, when the happy, well-fed dogs stood lined up to board the *Fram* for the first time. Unaware that the big party they'd been enjoying was about to come to an end, most of them simply let themselves be transported out to the ship via rowboat, a couple of them at a time—some more willingly than others, though. It was time-consuming, but the most efficient way to get it done. The crew had time to position and tie up the dogs as they arrived on board, and the men in the rowboat got a personal first impression of their four-legged traveling companions.

Lindstrøm was one of the men in the rowboat. The other was Oscar Wisting, the dog wrangler himself. None of the Chief's men had a better grasp of Greenland dogs than Oscar Wisting. The dogs did what Wisting wanted, down to the last reddish brown renegade who decided he wasn't getting in a rowboat that day, no sir. Had he not been wearing a muzzle, he might have attacked, but the way things stood, he would have to try to escape instead. The dog jumped overboard and started to swim, the first recorded escape attempt of the South Pole expedition. Oscar Wisting jumped after him.

And that's how they found each other. Or that's how Oscar found the Colonel. He knew what he was looking for. The animal was one of the largest ones in the pack. Born to lead. That is, if the beast also could be forced into being led.

"Suppression techniques." I mumble it almost under my breath, but Mrs. Thorkildsen, the same Mrs. Thorkildsen who can't hear me when I shout that the food bowl is empty, picks up on it anyway.

"What the hell do you mean?" she asks with a strange mix of genuine surprise and light irritation.

"That's exactly how you make the whole dog-and-pony show run," I say, trying to match her light irritation. "Precisely by mucking up and obscuring the whole relationship. The master designates a slave to lord it over his fellow slaves ever so slightly, and that's how the dirty work is done. It's the oldest trick in the book. I mean, if it were me going to the South Pole, with humans pulling the sled, I'd certainly get them to slaughter one another when the time came. All it would take would be giving some of them the slightest advantage, and they'd instantly think they were better than the rest of them, yes, simply superior to their fellow specimens. They'd believe it enough to kill their brothers without thinking twice or getting mad about it. Do you know what people like that are called?"

"No, Tassen, I don't know," Mrs. Thorkildsen says with affected patience.

"They're called most people."

"Well, well," Mrs. Thorkildsen says, and pours herself another glass. "But let me tell you how it all turned out with the one dog who made it home," she continues, glass filled.

"The Colonel and a couple of other dogs who were born during the trip were sent back to Norway. It might have been luck. Or it might have been the Chief realizing that without having a single living South Pole dog to show for himself, the criticism of the dog slaughter would have been relentless. So the Colonel came home to Norway as the sole survivor. At least that's something."

"Back to Norway? The guy had barely set paw here his whole life!" I naturally object.

"The Colonel became the most famous dog in the history of Norway. A dog superstar, plain and simple. The newspapers reported on everything he did, and the *Fram* sponsors lined up to borrow him and show the Colonel off."

"It might have been better if he'd died in the zoo, rather than ending up as a circus attraction."

I mean that.

"Well, he doesn't, you see, and the Chief is precisely the one who prevents that from happening. He's suddenly become a dog lover now that there's only a single dog left. You might call it a conscience. The Chief, with his two hundred beautiful dogs lying dead in his tracks, has suddenly become concerned with the Colonel getting a good life in peace and quiet. He splurges on an expensive operation for the animal, for an illness that would have been treated with a bullet through the skull in Antarctica. The Chief wants to personally take care of the Colonel when he at some point returns from his world speaking tour about the conquest of the South Pole, he telegraphs. The Colonel is promptly moved to the Chief's gloomy, secluded home on the Bunnefjord outside Kristiania. Here, in pastoral surroundings, the four-legged polar hero would be able to live out his days."

It's possible the Colonel was happy. But to his surroundings, meanwhile, the Greenland beast was a source of fear and alarm. At night he sat behind the Chief's house and howled at the moon. Other than the howling, the neighborhood was upset because some of its own dogs had started mysteriously vanishing after they were last seen with the Colonel on their heels. Amundsen's caretaker wrote to the Chief in America that the Colonel had most likely killed them and stored them as provisions somewhere in the woods.

"A depot," I point out.

"And the whole time, he continues to make life a living hell for anyone who comes near him," Mrs. Thorkildsen adds. "If the Colonel had been any other dog, he would have been banished to the north or gotten a bullet through his skull, but he was a national treasure now. A snapping, uncontrollable national treasure; a natural disaster waiting to happen. In a saga in which dogs' lives are cheap, in which dogs have had to pay with their lives whether they created problems or not, the last remaining survivor has become untouchable."

The end is almost too sweet. The Colonel is sent to Oscar Wisting in his hometown of Horten, where he becomes the big hero and a regular feature of the streetscape. The Colonel roams freely and can usually be found outside one of the town's two butcher shops. He gets to mate all the time; there's a long line of breeders begging to pay admission to join the polar hero's family tree. The Colonel is still a leader by nature. Just as there was in Antarctica, in his old age in Norway there's always a small following of dogs that respectfully flock to him.

And then, after a good dog's life, the last of the dogs to make it to the end of the world dies with little fanfare, full of tasty meat at the end of his days.

One of Mrs. Thorkildsen's old friends, most likely a library colleague, I'd imagine, once put it this way:

To be or not to be—that is the question.

Sure, sure. If you're going to be that black and white about it, it might look like that's the question: to be or not to be. So black. So white. Black as fur, white as snow.

But usually life looks more like brown slush in late winter.

One trip out of the cage. That's another way you might look at it. You lie curled up in your nest, safe and sound. All your needs are satiated and you're at peace. Then one day the cage door opens, and without understanding why, or really having any desire to, you leave life in the cage and wander out into another life. Maybe it's a good life, with adequate portions of love, food, and exercise. Maybe it's a sad life, with loneliness. Maybe it's short, maybe it's long, but whether you're ordered there or escape there, you'll eventually find yourself back in the cage, safe and sound in your nest.

A bullet through the skull after a deed well done at the end of a tiring day, or years of illness and decline? More brown slush. Still, what do I gain by fearing, even thinking about death—I who, unlike Mrs. Thorkildsen, can't say that the world has changed much since I was young? I'm not talking about all the daily death traps that must be summarily avoided, from atomic bombs to the mailman. I think of the fear that grows so strong it becomes a hunger. I think that may be what happened to Mrs. Thorkildsen.

If a dog and not a librarian were to make that statement, it wouldn't be *to be or not to be*, but *to be alone or not alone*. It's not about many or few. It's about somebody or nobody.

It's about not having to be alone when you die, just like it was about not being alone while you lived. A death-defying pack to flank you on the battlefield, or a frightened, arthritic old hand holding your paw while the vet's IV enters your vein, it doesn't really matter. But not alone.

That's what matters.

Everyone remembers—or should remember—the space dog Laika for her groundbreaking efforts in the next stage of the human conquest of the universe, after Earth had finally been fully discovered, with the help of dogs, and the ensuing two wars had ended. Laika, too, was the first to make tracks where dogs, not to mention most people, had no business being. Out in the great unknown.

But that's where the similarities end. While the Chief's pack went into the unknown with a clear mission and a plan for how to get back with their hides intact, there was no going back for Laika. Unlike her fellow canines the Greenland dogs, also unable to turn back, this had nothing to do with her race. Laika was a stray from Moscow, of indeterminate origin.

Laika died weightless and panicked from overheating after a few hours aboard *Sputnik 2*, but her job was already done at that point. She had involuntarily proven that a person could survive being shot into nothingness with a rocket launcher, and humanity hasn't stopped doing it since. A wolf and a human meet one day along the road, and soon they're both weightlessly floating in the Great Nothingness. From Nowhere to Nothing: I suppose that's the logical next step. But again, one might ask Mrs. Thorkildsen:

What are they doing up there?

The official story is that Laika was put to sleep after a few comfortable days in space, in a humane and dignified way, of course, but that's the thing about the truth—it tends to come to light once it reaches a certain age. It took its time. And not only that. A scientist who had joined the Laika project and later penned the masterpiece *Animals in Space*, Oleg Gazenko, later said:

"*I'm sorry about that. We shouldn't have done it . . . we didn't learn enough from that project to justify the dog's death.*"

Determining whether the average human being might have a future in space wasn't a good enough reason to kill a single shabby street dog, according to wise old Oleg. What I don't know, unfortunately, is how he felt about wiping out a couple hundred Greenland dogs to reach the South Pole fifteen minutes before the British men. That's all guesswork.

36

IT'S AN ELABORATE PROCESS WHEN Mrs. Thorkildsen sets out to transform herself from tired, disheveled troll with fire breath and papyrus skin to perfumed society lady. I don't even know which of the two smells worse. Regardless, it can take years for Mrs. Thorkildsen to primp, an ocean of time. At least. Many oceans.

First she has to take off the clothes she for one reason or another slept in, and spend some time wading around in her faded, old, and increasingly wrinkly skin where the blue bruises bloom. There's less and less of Mrs. Thorkildsen, but her skin seems to be growing. Then she has to shower. I'm not a big fan of all that, I avoid the bathroom while this is happening, so I don't know exactly what she does in there, but I can smell the chemicals. She emerges wearing the oversized bathrobe with a towel on her head. Coffee break. After a selection process that takes its time, she puts on one garment after another, until the weekday edition of Mrs. Thorkildsen is firmly in place, the Mrs. Thorkildsen I think of as Mrs. Thorkildsen when Mrs. Thorkildsen isn't here.

At this stage in the process Mrs. Thorkildsen sensibly enough takes a break for some food, and it would be natural for me to try to sneak a treat, but since Mrs. Thorkildsen doesn't let me out because we're going for a walk later, I'm starting to feel the urge to pee, and then—and *only* then—the hunger for a treat isn't quite as strong.

I didn't comment on it, but when Mrs. Thorkildsen had finished her traditional daily crispbread with cheese and her silly little glass of cow's milk, Mrs. Thorkildsen downed a considerable portion of dragon water.

The strolling tempo is decent today. The wheel on the wheelie bag squeaks as usual, and we have a relatively pleasant walk as we plod along down the roads of suburbia, Mrs. Thorkildsen and me.

I don't know what comes over me, but I hear myself ask Mrs. Thorkildsen whether she'd ever seen that Jesus Our Lord and Savior guy that the two anxious women came by to inquire about. Mrs. Thorkildsen stops dead in her tracks, suddenly very serious.

"Why do you ask?"

"Maybe because you said you don't like him. You don't say that about anyone else."

"There are lots of people I don't like," Mrs. Thorkildsen says, sounding a little offended.

"Like who?"

"Hmmm . . . like Paulo Coelho, for example, or Dag Solstad. For example."

"Who are they?"

"Miserable celebrity authors."

"I meant people you can touch and smell."

"Like who?"

"I'm thinking, for example, about how you might not like your son's bitch. Just feels like I get a whiff of it whenever they come by."

"Well, do I *like* her . . ." Mrs. Thorkildsen says. "I wouldn't say I *dislike* her. We're just not very . . . compatible."

"My goodness," I say.

"That's just the way it is, some people are better together than others," Mrs. Thorkildsen says on a concluding note, but I keep pushing.

"She seems very focused on getting you to notice her?"

"I can't imagine that."

"Maybe this is the kind of thing you can't imagine, but only sense? If you had a trace of a sense of smell, I wouldn't have had to tell you this. Or maybe I would've had to anyway. Even though your eyes and ears work *perfectly* according to you, you don't look at her, and you don't hear what she says."

"Of course I do!" Mrs. Thorkildsen snaps.

I can't be bothered to answer. I mean, what in the world can I say? If you're the least bit wise, or *experienced*, as it's called, you sometimes know better than to say anything at all. I stay silent, though Mrs. Thorkildsen is wide open now, like George Foreman against Muhammad Ali in Zaire. "The Rumble in the Jungle." But I'm not Muhammad Ali. Even in the most dire circumstances, I'm not what you might call a *fighter*. "The Hysteria in Suburbia" is officially canceled. I'm nonconfrontational and proud of it.

"Nonconfrontational." What a terrible word. What a terrible thing to be. But lucky for me, that's how we solve conflicts in these parts. We avoid them. Should a conflict suddenly appear and block the road, you simply step to the side and keep strolling along as if nothing happened.

That's all there is to it.

An ancient day. The Humanoid and the Wolf-Dog.

On our way from the dragon watering hole to the Library, in the deserted alley behind the movie theater, Mrs. Thorkildsen halts our march, opens the wheelie bag, pulls out a small bottle, opens it, and looks around before taking a giant swig. She shoves the bottle back in her bag and suddenly seems very pleased with herself.

"I've never understood people who say they only drink aquavit with fatty foods," Mrs. Thorkildsen says. "Aquavit *is* a fatty food."

The wheelie bag has grown too heavy. Mrs. Thorkildsen realizes that as soon she begins dragging it up the steps to the Library. I knew the day would come when that stupid bag would get us in trouble, and I've tried in my subtle ways to suggest as much, without being heard, but today was a reality check for Mrs. Thorkildsen.

"This isn't going to work, Tassen," she says.

"I think you're right about that," I say.

"So what do we do now? I can't leave the wheelie bag outside the Tavern, either, with every broke panhandler in town pouring in and out of these doors."

"What would the Chief do?" I ask.

"What?" Mrs. Thorkildsen asks. I don't know if she doesn't understand what I mean, or simply doesn't hear what I say.

"What would Roald Amundsen do in this situation?" I repeat.

"Hmmm. Fortify himself with a dog tenderloin?"

Mrs. Thorkildsen laughs. Alone. Dog-eating humor is just so passé.

"The Chief would split us into two teams," I interrupt coolly. "Team A tackles the ascent to the next plane to get help for transporting the rest of the equipment, and team B stays by the wheelie bag and keeps a lookout so no bad drunkards come and help themselves to the dragon water therein. So the question we really need to ask ourselves is: Who is team A, and who is team B?"

Mrs. Thorkildsen has to pause to consider this. A long while, I'd say. But this may be hindsight playing tricks on me.

"You know, Tassen," Mrs. Thorkildsen finally says quietly, "sometimes I worry about you."

"Thanks," I say. "I worry about you, too."

Sadly, we don't have to execute my brilliant plan for the stair climb. A white knight, a drunkard in the prime of his youth, stinking of perfume and dragon water, lifts Mrs. Thorkildsen's wheelie bag up the stairs with tattooed arms and a cheerful disposition that, from one second to the next, puts Mrs. Thorkildsen in a considerably better mood. The youngster slips into the Tavern, and for a moment I am afraid Mrs. Thorkildsen is going to let all her inhibitions go and run after him.

So here we are, at the gates of the Kingdom, ready for wisdom and scratches, but the gates are closed, and a small sign hangs from them. Unfortunately it isn't a pictogram, so I have to wait patiently for Mrs. Thorkildsen to put on her glasses and read the message. The fatal message.

This branch is closed as of November 1. Borrowed books may be returned to the red box on the left. Looking for a book? Help yourself from the green shelf on the right. We thank our patrons for 43 wonderful years!

After some consideration, Mrs. Thorkildsen, without taking her eyes off the note, says:

"Well, that's shit."

Since Mrs. Thorkildsen had given the book she had to return directly to the Librarian after the famous dinner, she is now completely purposeless in front of the Library's shuttered doors. That must be why she begins sniffing around the shelf with the books looking for a new home, I think. And what does she find there on the shelf of discarded library books, can you guess?

"*A Life on the Ice: The Polar Chef Adolf Lindstrøm*," Mrs. Thorkildsen says.

Then she says no more. Just stands there with the book in her hand and shows no sign of moving.

"Well, I suppose there's no point in going to the Tavern now that the Library is closed?" I say, referring to Mrs. Thorkildsen's "food for the belly and food for the soul" doctrine. The Tavern visits were connected to the Library visits, and without the Library, the Tavern loses all meaning. I think.

Mrs. Thorkildsen considers this, and sets Lindstrøm back on the shelf. He'd have to find himself a new home.

Mrs. Thorkildsen just stands there, staring at the letters on the sign hanging on the Library door, as if she is hoping they'd change. Switch positions and alter their message. The same letters that warned of the Library's closure could simply rearrange to instead announce the Library was more open than ever, but this wasn't meant to be. So Mrs. Thorkildsen and the wheelie bag go to the Tavern. Not fair.

37

AFTER AN ETERNITY, MAYBE TWO, Mrs. Thorkildsen is still sitting in there, feasting on the most luscious patty melts and washing them down with one beer after another, apparently without giving a thought to me as I sit tied up, lonely and forgotten out here in the hallway. Sure, there was an elkhound bastard here when I arrived, but we chose to ignore each other completely, which worked out just fine, then his owner came and took him away and everyone was happy. His name was Growl, and his owner made it very clear that Growl was a good boy, without specifying why. Good at chasing elk, I guess, but beyond that I'm not quite sure exactly what Growl has to offer.

The door opens and, God help me, here comes Mrs. Thorkildsen! She's moving slowly but somewhat steadily, although the wheelie bag seems to have grown even heavier.

I get so irrationally happy I don't quite understand it myself. It's a joy that takes hold of body and soul and shakes me up and down until I'm dizzy, and I would have loved to throw myself in Mrs. Thorkildsen's arms, but I stay on the green Astroturf mat while Mrs. Thorkildsen drags the wheelie bag over the threshold. And continues. Before I realize what's happening, Mrs. Thorkildsen takes the first step down the stairs, and before I can say anything, she's on to the next. Moment of truth. The wheelie bag is on its way down the first step, and Mrs. Thorkildsen still hasn't noticed me. I should bark to alert her, but I'm dumbstruck with anticipation, afraid I'll scare Mrs. Thorkildsen, who's obviously in trouble.

Right behind her, you see, comes an ugly little gnome. The gnome reeks of old cooking fat, but that's pretty much the only good thing I can say about him. His voice is angry and sharp.

"Hey!" he yells so loudly that Mrs. Thorkildsen jumps and sways momentarily, until she grabs the banister.

"You ran out on the check!"

Mrs. Thorkildsen is filled with shame on the spot. Like a broad brush-stroke by a master's hand, it colors the moment sad and scary and piti-ful. Mrs. Thorkildsen is afraid now, so afraid I could have nuzzled my nose against her knee, maybe shot her the handsome look she loves, tilted head, broad smile, but it's impossible. Mrs. Thorkildsen, standing there on the stairs, accused as a thief and a swindler in her old age, has one witness against her. And that witness is me. Because I'm not there on the stairs with her, I'm still here tied up by the door.

Mrs. Thorkildsen has forgotten me!

The surprise between us is palpable. It's a deeply humiliating mo-ment. I simply don't know what to say. This might change the whole game. We'll see.

"Have I forgotten?" she asks.

"Yes, you've forgotten," I say. Say it like it is. I'm about to offer some words of consolation, add that it's not a big deal in the grand scheme of things, let's just get home so I can get some food in my stomach, but I don't have time before Mrs. Thorkildsen breaks out in a warm smile, wherever that came from.

"Oh, of course!"

Her admission/acknowledgment floods me with relief, but then it's not my turn anyway, not this time either. She's not talking to me but to the gnome in the stinky apron, the one I would have bitten and chased away if I weren't helplessly bound.

"It seems I've forgotten to pay," Mrs. Thorkildsen stutters, and the shame drives both her voice and her hand as it frantically digs around in her purse as if it were a newly planted flower bed where a juicy bone lies buried.

"Come and pay!" barks the gnome.

"I can't find my wallet . . . it was just here . . ." stutters Mrs. Thorkildsen.

"Don't have money?"

It's not a question, it's an accusation.

Mrs. Thorkildsen's hands and voice shake.

"Someone . . . maybe it's up there, did I leave it?"

Mrs. Thorkildsen turns around to reattempt the stairs she had just begun precariously descending, and only then—*then!*—does she look at me with her perplexed eyes, and my instinctive elation over being seen vanishes quicker than a biscuit on a dog's snout. Because she doesn't, to tell you the truth. Mrs. Thorkildsen sees a dog, but she doesn't see *me* until it's been so long that there simply is no comfortable explanation.

"I'm calling the cops!" the gnome shouts.

"Thank you, would you be so kind?" Mrs. Thorkildsen smiles a forlorn version of her sweetest smile.

"I mean I'm calling the cops on you!"

"Oh, thank you. I'm sure it's best to report these things right away. Perhaps they can find the thief? And if there is no thief, I suppose one has to report it anyway, the insurance company probably requires it, I'm sure."

"Shit, you drunk or what? I'm calling the cops to come and get you. For fuck's sake, trying to run away!"

What a rude dude! I'm furious, but I'm tied up. And I can instinctively sense the stinky gnome is a kicker, a demon who with power and gusto and great satisfaction would plant his boot in the belly of any defenseless creature who happens not to be human. He probably even kicks humans, too. That's normally how it goes: from animal abuse to human abuse.

Mrs. Thorkildsen sees me and Mrs. Thorkildsen trips. Trips so slowly that for a moment it looks like she's floating, as if she's had enough of this bizarre situation and has decided to leave it behind. Fly up to the sky like a soaring spirit. But the soaring is short before it becomes a fall, and Mrs. Thorkildsen stumbles backward on the stairs. It all happens without a sound, takes forever, and ends with a short, awful thud. And afterward, when Mrs. Thorkildsen is done falling, it gets even quieter.

"Fuck," the gnome says.

Maybe he thinks it's his fault. It's not. It's my fault.

Fuck.

Last Bite

Imprisoned

Me

In Prison

—FROM TASSEN THORKILDSEN'S
POEM CYCLE *Primal Barks from the Depths
of an Okay Kennel in Outer Enebakk*

38

FROM ONE MOMENT TO THE NEXT, I went from being a relatively free creature to being a relatively unfree creature. I say "relatively," because it's such a convenient word on these occasions, relatively speaking. It puts whatever precision a statement may have out of commission with a mocking sneer, and I can use that now, in my captivity. Relatively unfree. Oh, yes. On the other hand, I can see now how relative my freedom was.

Gassestranda Dog Home. Don't let the welcoming name fool you like it fooled me. Gassestranda Dog Home is a good old-fashioned dog prison of the medium-security variety. Yard time during the day. Locked cell door at night. No probation. No education with a focus on rehabilitation. Death Row. I know as little about how long I have left here as I know about how long I've been here. Time works differently in prison. Chases its own tail. Life mostly consists of sleeping and moping around. In one way, everything is as it should be. I get the food I need, though it's nowhere near as varied or beautifully arranged as it was at home. Far too much kibble. (I have a conspiracy theory about kibble, that kibble is a plot hatched by a greedy veterinary industry that profits grossly from removing the plaque dogs inevitably get from eating this crap, but we can talk about that another time.)

If Amnesty International, which Mrs. Thorkildsen has single-handedly funded for years, did a raid on Gassestranda Dog Home, they'd find a whole range of poor conditions, including indefensible lack of gravy, dog snacks, and other goodies. I've always said that you never know when there might be a treat in store, but at Gassestranda Dog Home, this rule doesn't hold sway. In here, you know there's *never* a treat in store, and that realization does something to a dog. I must admit that the Gassestranda Diet is probably better for me in the long run than the Thorkildsen Diet. I'm in better shape than ever but, as I said, I fear the plaque.

The terrain around Gassestranda Dog Home is, well, it's terrain. Hard to take it seriously when none of the young people who work here can be bothered to bring weapons when we go out in the woods, despite the fact that the moss *reeks* of game. On the whole, life, despite the lack of gravy, smells more interesting here than it does at home. With my eternal romantic dreams of being part of a pack, I suppose I've never philosophized much about what it might entail, aromatically speaking. Well, it stinks, to put it that way. Being locked up at night in a room with sad dogs of all sizes and ages is like trying to sleep in a hurricane of senseless, more or less desperate information. Smells crisscross one another at an exhausting pace, even when the whole pack is asleep. Pink clouds and green gas everywhere. The snoring. The whimpering. The horrors.

The yard is, well, a yard. The gangs are in charge out here. First and foremost Rusty and Rover, bird dog hybrids who are brothers and can never agree about which one is boss, but instantly lay all strife aside when they encounter the rest of the prison population. Those two jerks win over all the easily swayed dogs, many of them yesterday's or tomorrow's bullying victims, and they terrorize whomever they please. Everyone's afraid of them. Everyone, except Ruffen Rasmussen.

Unlike all the other inmates and staff at Gassestranda, Ruffen Rasmussen, a light brown furball of a teddy bear, is always in a good mood. A lighthearted spirit for the simple reason that he feels sure he's going to get out of here. Ruffen Rasmussen is not a *believer*, Ruffen Rasmussen is a *knower*.

"The Lord shall return!" Ruffen Rasmussen exclaims, sure in his convictions. He's done this before, you see, or so he claims. He appeals to patience and loyalty, then once again tells the story of his family vacationing in a land where dogs were forbidden and they parked him at Gassestranda Dog Home for a while.

"Just like you, brother," Ruffen Rasmussen says, to one dog after the other, "I was a lost soul when I first got here. When the Lord said: 'You just stay here, Ruffen, and we'll be back to get you!' and then left me, I thought my heart was going to break into a million pieces. Everything went black as a Labrador. I became a listless shadow of myself. Instead of bringing joy to others, which I was born to do, I brought misery on myself. I started shitting on the floor again! And why did I do that, Tassen?"

I know the routine by now, I know what's coming, I deliver my line: "Because you doubted, Ruffen. Because you doubted."

"Because I *doubted*!" Ruffen is triumphant. "I doubted that the Lord would come back. And when you doubt the Lord, how can you ever trust yourself?"

Doubt is the root of all evil, according to Ruffen Rasmussen, and he might just be right. "You must trust your Lord blindly," he lectures, "and you'll be rewarded and live a long life in the house."

"What if you don't have a lord?" I asked him one day when we—or he, really—were discussing this in the yard. "Or if the Lord has fallen down the stairs and disappeared, for instance?"

"The Lord will *always* come back!" Ruffen Rasmussen said empathically, with a little snort. "The question is: Will *you* be here when *he* comes back?"

"*She*. My lord is a lady. I doubt she'll be back to get me anytime soon," I said.

"You see!" Ruffen Rasmussen said. "You are a doubter!"

Otherwise, the clientele is like any other prison: Half of those who are here should never have been here. The other half should never have been anywhere else. That is, some of them should maybe be somewhere else entirely. I mean, what are Romanian street dogs doing in Outer Enebakk? I'm not a racist, far from it, but I have my own thoughts about the prison population's background. There isn't a surplus of Norwegian elkhounds here, to put it that way.

"There's a meaning behind it," Mrs. Thorkildsen would say when life didn't go the way she thought it should. It was, as far as I could tell, her mother who at some point had first discovered this phenomenon. I hold tight to those words in here, but it's not easy to get a whiff of meaning behind these locked doors. I'm safe here in my cage, might even go so far as to say that I like my cage—I'd love to have one at home—but I'm not too stupid to realize that I'm captive. But, like I said, I'm getting food and exercise, and were it not for Ringo's snoring below me, I wouldn't have much to complain about.

Ringo, on the other hand—he has a great deal to complain about. Still, he has only himself to blame. Ringo, you see, has bitten a child. You might say he was acting on behalf of many, and that there was probably a very good reason for doing what he did, but it doesn't matter. Ringo's been a bad dog, and he knows it. He regrets it so much it haunts his sleep, he sounds like an anxious poodle when he dreams, but it doesn't matter. Ringo's been here a long time, since before I got here, and to tell you the truth, I don't think he should get his hopes up about getting out, which I won't mention to him, of course. I'm worried Ringo's not going to make it. And Ringo isn't a dog suited for just anyone. I'd like to see Mrs. Thorkildsen handle a dog like that, who weighs more than her to top it all off. But who knows, maybe Mrs. Thorkildsen is a born dog-subduer. Maybe she would simply beat Ringo until the whip handle snapped and he became her obedient servant. Mrs. Thorkildsen zooms through the woods on a sled made of skin and bones, pulled by Ringo with ice in his mustache and a steely gaze. Who knows?

I hope and pray that's not the case but, as far as I know humans and especially Mrs. Thorkildsen, her absence might be explained by the fact that she's withdrawn in order to make good on her threat to write a book about the Chief and his dogs. It's a bad idea I unfortunately may have nourished simply by listening to her attentively. Asking a question now and then. But I've learned my lesson now. If you listen to people, you're only giving them something to say.

"Don't do it, Mrs. Thorkildsen," I'd say if she were here. "We can just go to town and buy a book, you don't need to write it yourself. On the contrary. You need to read."

Mrs. Thorkildsen might sneer in disgust at these warnings. Might look at me askance with her serious, mocking eyes.

For my part, I can't honestly say that I see a deeper meaning in my existence the way it looks these days, but I'm not blind to the fact that a cage may be the most appropriate frame for the last chapters in the story about the dogs who went around the world to Nowhere.

It would be wrong to claim that I eventually tired of the story about the dogs who went to the South Pole. On the other hand, the damn dramaturgy of the story was such that any feelings of pride or victory were tainted with blood long before they reached their destination.

But what happens if we try to break the performance in *Le Théâtre Antarctique* into a classical three-act structure? That is:

1. Chase a man up a tree.

2. Threaten him with a stick.

3. Get the man safely down from the tree.

Let's give it a try:

1. Chase a dog up a tree.

2. Whip the poor bastard.

3. Get the dog down from the tree with a well-aimed shot.

As you can see: total narrative collapse. No need to wonder whether there will be a happy ending. You won't get Hollywood to make that movie. Not until they've made *Lassie Goes down the Well* and *101 Dead Dalmatians*.

39

STRICTLY SPEAKING, I DON'T HAVE much to complain about in prison—almost nothing at all, from a dog's point of view. But some of the problem, perhaps *the* problem, is that my needs have long since exceeded a dog's natural needs, and there's no going back. For me either. I simply miss the sound of human voices, the sweet hum. And gravy, of course. There isn't a drop of gravy in here, did I mention that?

Human voices make mornings the best time of the day. There are usually two guards on duty, and I feel a sense of inner calm as I listen to their voices chatting away, weaving in and out of each other when they're not barking orders to the inmates, who bark back whether they're being spoken to or not.

• • •

"Tassen," I hear a voice say one sweet morning. Life behind bars has taught me to be careful with spontaneous reactions of joy, it's so easy to be misunderstood, so all I do is perk up my ears and raise my head. But I am curious and realize I haven't felt this way in far too long.

Two pairs of feet in front of the cage. A familiar smell. Or to be specific, several familiar smells with the same origin. Home! The smell of Mrs. Thorkildsen doesn't seem to belong here at Gassestranda Dog Home, and it brings me more joy and despair than the place can handle.

I am in no way in the process of forgetting her, far from it, but it is a longing that is so hard to bear, I've tried to hide it away as much as I can, a little bit like Mrs. Thorkildsen did after the Major wandered off unarmed to the eternal hunting grounds.

It is the Puppy who is here! The Puppy! The Puppy himself, the Puppy, hi, hi! I never thought I'd be so happy to see him, but when the cage is opened, I howl like an idiot, and my whole body, from snout to tail tip, just wants to sing and dance. I howl for peace and freedom. I howl for good old Mrs. Thorkildsen back home.

Like a dog, I immediately forget everything I don't need in the moment, and so I leave my prison friends without saying goodbye, without giving them a second thought. I should have asked the Puppy to take them all with us. Mrs. Thorkildsen has plenty of space and food for them all: Ernie. Ruffen Rasmussen. Posie. Gunda. Pan. Ringo. Leo. Rusty. Beula. Mary Jane. Rover. Good dogs. Even the Romanian street dogs. They're good dogs too. May their food bowls always be filled and may their walks be long.

The Puppy actually seems happy to see me, too. Really. I'd love to know how he found me, which strings he pulled to get me out. I may have underestimated him. It might be the case that Mrs. Thorkildsen underestimated him as well, I'm not sure. But I'd like to point out that I didn't throw up in the car. The Puppy repays me by not hitting me.

Mrs. Thorkildsen is not at home. And home isn't home, for that matter. Home has become a completely different place. It looks the same from the outside, but as soon as I bound happily through the front door, I am lost in a strange new world. Mrs. Thorkildsen isn't home, I can ascertain that with one simple sniff of the nostrils. The Bitch, however, is home. Very much so. The Bitch is sitting on a monstrously giant white couch between walls that have lost their nutty brown, warm sheen and have mysteriously also turned white.

"Nooooo!" Of course I don't know what the woman means and continue unfettered into the living room, but she screams again, and this time she shouts:

"Sit!"

Sit I know, and happily obey the command. The least I can do. I sit right on cue. But instead of recognizing my obedience in the form of maybe a nice pat on the head, not to mention a treat, the Bitch brutally yanks me by the collar and before I know it, I am just as brutally hauled out across the same threshold I had stepped across on my way in. All the way out to the front porch, where the Puppy finally comes walking up.

"That dog is not going in the house, I said!" the Bitch shouts, and thus begins a meaningless exchange of words with gradually rising levels of aggression and noise. The crazy lady is trying to deny me admission to my own home. I don't need to listen to the arguments behind the madness, all I have to do is glance at the Puppy's body language. Alpha gets what she wants. The Puppy might have prevailed in a larger pack of random individuals, but in his tiny little family pack, he is helpless and he knows it. Nature would have it that way.

"But he has to go *somewhere*!"

The Puppy comes to my defense and grows a few inches in my regard.

"So give him to Jack, then!"

The suggestion makes the Puppy go quiet for a moment. The Bitch seizes the silence:

"Your mother did say that Tassen liked him so much when she went to Copenhagen."

"And how would she know?"

The Puppy throws his arms open and stands still for a moment or two before angrily answering his own question:

"That's right, because Tassen *told* her! So why don't we just ask Tassen what he thinks?"

"I think . . ." I begin, but the Puppy interrupts me:

"And what are we supposed to tell Mom? Hi, Mom, we gave your dog away?"

"As if it matters what you tell her. This is not up for discussion, anyway. This conversation is over."

And it was. The Puppy retreats under a black cloud and takes off in the car with a roar. I am tied up and locked out of my own home. The Bitch goes back inside. I lie down in the freshly cut grass, trying to preserve the tiny bit of dignity I still possess. I take deep breaths through wide-open nostrils. No matter how closed the door is and how white the walls are behind it, I am home, after all. I can smell my own piss on the hedges. What I can't smell, however, is Mrs. Thorkildsen's shadow. Her absence is a mystery, perhaps the biggest mystery ever, a mystery that fills every living moment in the universe with turmoil, like a strange smell you've never smelled before, but it still scares you.

It's getting dark, and the Puppy returns from wherever he had gone. He pulls up in the same car he'd used to retrieve me from prison, the same car we went hunting in so long ago, him and I. Imagine that. I jump for joy when the car turns into the driveway. Maybe I can learn to love this life, too. I mean, what else am I supposed to do if Mrs. Thorkildsen is gone? Sit down and wait for death like she did, or go on until it's over, go on although my body is tired, my feet are sore, and I'd rather be done with it all?

The Puppy doesn't want to play. The Puppy wants to go into the house with the white walls. He slips inside and slams the front door behind him without so much as acknowledging me with a simple "Good dog!" That's how quickly things can change. I'd forgotten that. Now I smell the trace of him, too, and there's something new about it, something that wasn't there when he left. It's the smell of another woman, not the Bitch. She's pregnant, too. God knows where the Puppy has picked up this smell.

The Puppy comes out again as quickly as he went in. He takes quick, decisive steps toward the car, rummages around in the trunk, and comes back over. Without saying a word, the Puppy lets me off the stupid rope, and suddenly I'm no longer bound and confused, but free and confused. It's probably safest to follow the Puppy, now that he's finally started acting like a leader. His ability to ignore me is impressive and growing. Maybe the Puppy has come of age. At last, Mrs. Thorkildsen would say, but of course she's not here now. She's somewhere else.

40

HE STOPS THE CAR OUTSIDE a tallish brick building that looks like any other brick building, but the smell is unmistakable after the first whiff through the nostrils. We are back, way back then. Why? you might ask, but I don't. I'm just glad to be here. Glad to be anywhere, really, but right now, since this is where we are, this is where I'm glad to be.

The house where the Major died. A long time ago now, half an eternity ago, maybe more, but the smell is the same bittersweet one, the kind of smell that changes the air it travels. The smell of death, I think. I never thought that before.

The Puppy puts me on the leash, and that makes me feel safer. Now it is his turn to lead. I make sure not to pull on the leash, generally put my best foot forward, and it doesn't feel so bad. I think I could get used to walking the Puppy.

The home is as warm as last time, and the light from the ceiling is as grim and the old people are as old as ever, sitting still in the same chairs as they wait their turn. Two frankly quite stinky old ladies sit there sleeping as the TV alludes to the passing of time. Old people don't like it when time passes, but they hate it even more when it doesn't. TV helps a lot with that.

It is a room that looked so much like the room the Major died in that I think for a moment it is him half sitting, half lying in the giant bed-machine under the dim light of the bedside lamp.

"Hi, Mom," the Puppy says in the half darkness. "Look who came to visit you."

Mom?

Mom!

It really *is* Mrs. Thorkildsen there in the bed! I feel a little ashamed that I hadn't recognized her at once (though she did smell different now), but no less ecstatic. What a wonderful day! As my tail lives a life of its own back there, I get on my hind legs up against the bed, and the Puppy understands. He loosens the leash and nudges me up into Mrs. Thorkildsen's flea box.

"Look, Mom, Tassen came to see how you're doing!" he says way too loudly, as if he is still standing in the doorway.

Mrs. Thorkildsen doesn't dignify the Puppy's lies with as much as a sigh. I step across the comforter to give her a big warm kiss, a good old-fashioned tongue bath, while trying my best not to place my paws wrong, not to step on her little body, which is now smaller than ever.

I lick her face, but Mrs. Thorkildsen seems not to notice that I am there, though her eyes flicker and her eyelids flutter. She glances around the room but sees nothing. I go from ecstasy to frustration in a moment, so who could object to me letting out a little bark?

The Puppy could.

"No! For fuck's sake, Tassen!" he says.

I lie down on the comforter and stare at Mrs. Thorkildsen as hard as I can. I feel her breathing and I can sense the smells that come with the air she exhales. I can hear her loyal little heart beating. But, beyond that, nothing.

"Stay!" the Puppy yells as he slips out the door. He doesn't have to worry. I'm certainly not planning on going anywhere, now that I am reunited with Mrs. Thorkildsen at last. We are finally alone. I bury my snout in her elbow crease, as close to a safe haven as you can find in this world.

"Tell me one thing," I say: "You're not planning to die, too, are you?"

Mrs. Thorkildsen clears her throat and says:

"I'm already dead, Tassen. Finished. History. Deceased. An ex–Mrs. Thorkildsen. Call it what you want, Tassen. Call it bingo, if you want."

She says it without pathos or melodrama, with the same quiet assurance she used to declare that it was time to go for a walk or time for food. And when Mrs. Thorkildsen says she's dead, I have no reason to doubt her honesty. I take her at her word most seriously. Dead seriously.

"But what happens to me," I have to ask, "if you're dead?"

"You'll be fine," Mrs. Thorkildsen says. "You'll get to live with the young ones. I've made sure of it. They'll take good care of you."

Given the situation, I have no choice but to swallow all my objections to white pillows and white walls and the Bitch's black rage. Mrs. Thorkildsen knows best, anyway.

"So," I say, mostly to break the silence, "what's it like being dead?"

Mrs. Thorkildsen laughs, and it makes my tail wag.

"You're the same as always," I say to encourage her. "With a sense of humor over the river Styx."

All in all, it doesn't sound very encouraging at all. On the other hand, who knows what use encouragement is to dead people. Like giving a hungry dog a gummy bone.

"It's just this body I don't need anymore," Mrs. Thorkildsen says. "You can see what's going on. I don't see how it's possible."

"So can't you get rid of it somehow?"

"That has proven quite difficult."

"Can't you just get someone to shoot it?"

"Like the Chief's dogs?"

"Something like that. But I'd rather not have to eat you afterward."

"I don't think there's much meat left on me, Tassen. And what's left is probably pretty tough. You might be able to make a good stock if you're patient and let it simmer for a few days. But remember to drain it carefully, Tassen. Promise me that, and let it rest in the fridge overnight. Rest in a cold place."

"We've been there."

"Yes, we have."

"Thank you for telling me that story. It was . . . thought provoking."

"Really? What kinds of thoughts did it provoke?"

"Well, what can I say? What can I compare it to? I must admit I have a hard time seeing the point of it all."

"You're not the only one," Mrs. Thorkildsen smiles.

"No one really had to die, neither the dogs nor the men. But the equation is there, with how many dead dogs?"

"I know math isn't your strong suit, Tassen, but almost two hundred dogs fell victim on the journey."

"That's a lot! I know that for sure. Almost."

"That's twice as many as the first pack of paper wolves we made. Do you remember them?"

She says "we."

"Of course I remember them. And even if I don't understand numbers, I understand twice as many. Two hundred percent. That's easy."

"The point is it's way too many."

"Would it really make a difference if just one single dog had been slaughtered? On the other hand, far more dogs die a far uglier death after a far worse life, every day. Don't you think about that?" I add.

"I know, but I think about it anyway, even though I'm dead. I can't separate it from what happened afterward, when they came home and claimed the flag was planted in the Last Place on Earth, and now there were no more places that could be declared *mine*!"

"And then there was war?"

"I can promise you that."

"The war that the Major was in?"

"I don't know if there's any point in separating one war from another. It's all the same mess. Men fighting over status and power. And honor. Honor! Ugh, I hate that word! Has it ever been about anything other than honor?"

"Well," I say. "Maybe it was about food?"

"You know me well enough to know that I'm no vegetarian, Tassen. No good cooks are vegetarians. Humans eat animals and that's just the way it is, but it should be done with intention and dignity. You don't throw a puppy overboard because it doesn't fit into the pack in front of the sled you could have pulled on your own."

Mrs. Thorkildsen is true to herself even in death, but I'll admit that her new condition lends a certain gravitas to her words.

"It's mostly the *precision* of the dog killings that makes me so sad. Maybe because I know what's to come in the years that follow, that millions of people will be murdered in the most efficient and cost-effective way possible. Bitches, male dogs, puppies are reduced to factors in an equation where X equals death, and the solution is honor."

"Equation?" I say, but Mrs. Thorkildsen lets that one go. Instead, she says:

"There are a couple more things I need to tell you about 'the big journey to the middle of Nowhere.' When the Chief returned from the South Pole, he was welcomed everywhere. Even where he wasn't welcome. You can understand that the British men were a little mad at the South Pole's celebrated conqueror, and that was *before* they found the stiff-frozen remnants of Scott's expedition. In the spirit of British sportsmanship the Chief, half-heartedly, was invited to a victor's banquet in London. Lord Curzon was president of the Royal Geographical Society, and it was his duty to propose a toast to the guest of honor. In his speech, Lord Curzon unsurprisingly emphasized the Norwegians' use of dogs."

"Naturally," I pipe in.

"'So I will let myself suggest a triple hurrah—to the dogs!' Lord Curzon exclaims."

"Hah! Did he *really* say that?"

"He did. And the dogs got their hurrahs. The Chief didn't."

"Was he mad?"

"It bothered him for the rest of his life. A few years before he died, the Chief published an autobiography that was so mean and bitter, it robbed him of all his dignity and the few friends he had left. In the book, he tells the story of the insulting speech in London with a pen dripping with resentment. He never forgot it."

"Serves him right. It should sting a little. You can't just stand at the back of the sled. Nothing is that simple."

"That wasn't the only sting the Chief ever felt. The whole time they were in Antarctica, he had pains in his anal opening."

"Oof! It's impossible to reach back there, no matter how hard you try. He wouldn't have been able to lick himself."

"I don't think so, no."

"So all the way to the South Pole and back, his butt hurt?"

"He had some creams to put on, but I don't know how much they helped. The difference between a *little* pain in your butt and a *lot* of pain in your butt may not be so big, after all."

"Maybe that's what drove him onward? The fact that his rear end hurt so badly?"

"Now you're making Roald Amundsen sound like a cat running for the hills after somebody's smeared mustard under its tail."

"Might not be a bad comparison."

"The journey to the South Pole as a symptom of anal irritation?"

"Mental anal irritation. And *from* is the key word, anyway, not *to*. The Chief was the first one to come *from* the South Pole."

"Your bum is behind you whichever way you aim."

"True."

Captain Scott stands at the South Pole, exhausted and defeated. An honorable expedition diminished to a humiliated retreat in a moment, and he's still only halfway. Life doesn't seem so big anymore. But death? Death is huge.

Captain Scott wants to die, and he gets his wish. The four men on his team have to die for his wish to be granted, one more miserably than the next. They die the way free animals die, the way vegetarians think animals should die, of terrible diseases that torment the body to its last breath.

So there's the equation, you who can do math:

The Chief, with his decisions, takes the lives of an unknown number of local animals of prey and a giant pack of dogs, while Captain Scott, beyond the animals of prey, takes the lives of a dozen horses, his teammates, and not least himself.

So, who's worse?

Either way, the solution to the equation is a story. Or, strictly speaking, two stories, about going to the same non-place, only to turn around and crawl back home. One is written in human blood, the other in dog blood.

Imagine if the participants, including the Chief, had been sworn to secrecy. You're more than welcome to be first to the southernmost point in the world, you just can't tell anyone about it afterward. All scientific data will be published, of course, and the Norwegian flag on the South Pole will still be the basis of territorial claims no one will ever recognize. The only difference is that *you* don't get to tell the story. Everyone will know someone was there, but no one will know it was you. Who wants to be first? Anyone?

When it comes down to it, that's what all the fuss was about, wasn't it? Placing yet another story on the Library's shelves. I personally think Mrs. Thorkildsen is undervaluing this particular reward of the Big Journey. When I suggest it to her, she dismisses me:

"So we should be happy about the war, because there have been so many books written about it?"

As always when she plays the war card, there's nothing I can say.

Of course Captain Scott was frightened as he struggled in front of the sled. Fear that the trip to the South Pole was in vain, and then, after that fear had turned to certainty, fear of pain, cold, shame, hunger, sickness, and death. Had he used (and eaten!) dogs, maybe the British men would all have survived. One single dog tenderloin, maybe with a side of liver, and who knows? They were so close to making it to the South Pole and back without dogs, but the moral of the story remains:

Bring a dog!

But as long as you're wandering around out there in the frozen tundra, when it dawns on you that you're not going to survive this, you might as well make the most of it, provided you have pen and paper. With pen and paper, you can tell the story after you're dead. Mrs. Thorkildsen, for example, would hardly have survived a trip to the South Pole, but if I know her, she definitely would've brought a pen and paper, so her dramatic story would have survived even if she perished. No stories ring truer than those of the dead.

History is written by the victors, they say. The race to the South Pole is the exception that proves the rule. The Chief's two-volume work with its scientific measurements and descriptions of the weather became a bestseller, but it was Scott's death chronicle that became *the story*. The

Norwegians came first, but the British men won. Won the story. British schoolchildren were taught that Scott was the first one to the South Pole, he was just unlucky enough to die a heroic death on his way home, and that's a much nicer story, even if the bodies in it are just as cold.

There were a lot of gala dinners held in the Chief's honor, but eventually they all began to taste like dog tenderloin. In the end it all went completely wrong. Unnecessarily so.

Mrs. Thorkildsen once showed me a picture that was taken an hour before the Chief vanished from the world in a flying machine. He's sitting alone, older than his fifty-five years, and he looks like he's lost something. But what? A soccer game? A friendship? A life? It's impossible to tell where his thoughts are. Maybe they're on the other side of the world, seventeen years ago, with a man out there in the middle of a howling inferno, waiting for death to bring eternal life? The Chief knows he's going to die himself in the next few hours, and I think he's accepted it. He's already lived too long. He's done. Death is freedom. In that respect they're not so different, the Chief and Mrs. Thorkildsen.

Or maybe he's just sitting there in his seaplane, annoyed that his ass is itching like hell.

In the end, on Judgment Day, of course the Chief must also be judged by his personal choice of dog. The South Pole expedition was business, and the dogs were both workforce and provisions, but what kind of a dog did he keep at home? This is a kind of Rorschach test.

"Show me your dog, and I'll tell you who you are."

It's a pity that the Colonel was sent to live with Oscar Wisting before the Chief came home from his tour. I would have really liked for the Chief to lie awake at night, listening to the howling from the last surviving South Pole dog in the backyard. Fifty-five pounds of food, many tons of guilty conscience.

So, what kind of dog do you think the polar hero chooses to have around him?

The answer is . . . a St. Bernard!

I'm not kidding. You know, those sluggish beasts who mostly resemble bears who have sniffed glue. The Chief probably rationalized his choice by saying the breed has a certain reputation as guard dogs, if I know him, but seriously:

What do *you* associate with a St. Bernard?

Salvation.

Right?

With a barrel of dragon water around his neck, this good-natured teddy bear of a dog finds his way to the victim hopelessly trapped in the snow and rescues him. Rescues him from the cold, carrying civilization in its most liquid form. I know a lot of dogs will disagree with me on this, but what we're dealing with here is a dog as diametrically opposed to the Greenland dog as it's possible to get, at least as far as concerns the breeds' roles in human lives. The polar dog expanded the domain of man by pulling him farther and farther into the cold, the St. Bernard pulls him back out again. The latter is apparently wonderful with human children. The Chief has no children.

What does a man clad in wolf's skin want with a St. Bernard?

In the end, only one question remains. It's the kind of question you hesitate to ask, because the answer will resonate in the chambers of your heart for the rest of your life. A positive answer is a sun that will shine through all your days. A "no" is a small dark cloud with eternal rain.

A third option would of course be to shut your mouth and keep living with doubt, but you know me. So here we go:

"Am I a good dog?"

Mrs. Thorkildsen smiles. I can smell it.

"Yes, Tassen," she says. "You're a good dog."

41

OF COURSE I HAVE REGRETS. I regret not spontaneously asking Mrs. Thorkildsen whether she might have a little treat in store, but there isn't time once the Puppy suddenly reemerges from wherever he's been, and he is in a hurry.

If I knew him better, I'd say he has changed. The Puppy puts on the coat he'd left behind in the chair, the chair that was just like the one Mrs. Thorkildsen sat and dozed off in while the Major was dying, and he does it with a weightiness that is unlike him, at least not the way I knew him. Or am I the one who's changed, now that Mrs. Thorkildsen has posthumously declared her son the leader of the pack? Am I simply seeing him with new eyes, now that he's numero uno? Maybe the Puppy has always been this decisive in his movements, maybe he's always passed over me with his gaze.

"Come on!" the Puppy says. I hesitate. It feels wrong to leave Mrs. Thorkildsen, no matter how dead. If only she could have helped me a little, but Mrs. Thorkildsen says nothing.

"Come on, Tassen!" the Puppy says again, and I can tell from his tone there is no more room for hesitation, unless I really, really want a smack on the nose.

So it's thanks to Mrs. Thorkildsen. Thanks for all the food. Thanks for the walks. Thanks for the good scratches. Thanks for what you understood and didn't understand. Thanks for loving me. Thanks for the cinnamon rolls. And the stuffed pancakes with meat and brown gravy. I was sad you stopped making them after the Major passed away, but that's how it is. Too late now. Thanks for taking care of the Major. Thanks for bringing me to the Fram Museum. Thanks for not beating me to death and stuffing me with sawdust. Thanks for letting me sleep wherever I wanted. Thanks for the nice green ball that says *peep-peep!* Thanks for the paper wolves. Thanks for being kind.

Did I forget anything?

Probably. But that's how it is. A dog's memory has roughly the same shape as the universe, and there's not much we can do about it.

I know what Mrs. Thorkildsen would boil all her life wisdom down to, if she had to express it in one simple piece of advice:

"Be kind!" she'd say. As she said to me. Many times. And I'm going to keep trying, though it's easier said than done. You often chew the shoe to pieces before you realize you've done anything wrong.

The Puppy has wires attached to his ears. The Puppy talks as he drives the car, and I'm starving.

"No change," he says into thin air. "She's there, but she's not there . . ."

"I agree with that, but . . ." I begin, but the Puppy interrupts right away:

"Impossible to say. Tassen, he went wild, but I don't know if she even knew he was there . . . no change . . . I've spoken to the police today . . ."

It's just impossible to get a word in edgewise here, as impossible as it is to understand what the Puppy is babbling about.

"They've finally decided they're not going to take any more measures . . . the weapon will be confiscated, that's it. No fine, nothing . . . on my way home now . . . see you soon . . . bye."

It gets quiet, but the Puppy starts fiddling with buttons and dials until, God help me, music starts coming out of the car. Luckily it's reggae. Reggae is music without fiddles.

The Puppy speaks again. Peppy and cheerful and he's talking to me!

"You didn't know that, did you, Tassen, that mommy dearest was carrying around a revolver in her purse!"

Mommy dearest? Who on earth is that? Instead of letting me answer the question, the Puppy says:

"We didn't know either . . ."

The reggae song ends and we go to a commercial. For anal cream! It's a sign.

"Mom was walking around with a goddamn piece in her purse! You could have been shot, Tassen! A bullet through the skull from a Smith & Wesson. That would have been quite a headline, wouldn't it: *Drunk Old Lady Shoots Dog!*"

I can't imagine Mrs. Thorkildsen would ever have done such a thing. She would have put the famous piece to her own head and pulled the trigger before she'd ever turn it on me. That's the difference between Margrethe Thorkildsen née Lie, and Roald Engelbregt Gravning Amundsen.

"I don't fear death," Mrs. Thorkildsen said. "And every time I forget that I don't fear death, and wake up small and afraid in the middle of the night, I remind myself that the worst that can happen to me right now is a long life."

• • •

I began this eventful day locked up in a cage. I'm ending it locked in a car. This might be progress, but it doesn't feel like it. I'm having a hard time believing it. Not that I can remember doing anything wrong, but here I sit, hungry and all alone in a car in the middle of the night.

"No!" the Puppy said when I naturally tried to follow him out of the car when we finally parked in the driveway.

"You stay here! Stay!" *Slam!*

It is a surprising and disappointing message to hear in itself, but never in my wildest dreams do I imagine it will be a life sentence. Which, truth be told, won't be that long. I'm only a short while away from becoming the next dog to end up in the newspaper after a hot, uncomfortable death in a car, I'm sure of that. When the sun comes up and heats up the interior the soup will be cooked, or more accurately: *I'll* be cooked. Hot dog. You need neither a revolver nor an axe to make short work of a dog, all you have to do is avoid rolling down your car window so the poor creature can get some air. All the windows here are hermetically sealed, and even with a dog's limited capacity for foresight and planning, I can see this is going to be hell. It's already hell.

Luckily there's always a solution when life is hell, with a method Mrs. Thorkildsen had mastered to her arthritic fingertips: you move over a bit, and the nail stops gnawing at your ass. You think about something else. That's why it's good to always have a little too much to think about.

There are no dogs in Antarctica.

Not anymore. With a stroke of the pen, our polar adventure to the south was suddenly over, after almost a hundred years. No dogs allowed. That's how it was. Perverse penguins and stupid seals suddenly needed the continent to themselves.

The dogs were put to sleep or sent away. Business as usual. And ever since, there have been no dogs in those parts, except for one. It's made of plastic and works as a piggy bank, collecting money for guide dogs in Australia. I don't think it would be appropriate to count that one. If a dog isn't filled with juicy entrails, but sawdust or loose change, you can't consider it a *real* dog anymore.

The law that forbids dogs from visiting (!) or living in Antarctica, as you may already have guessed, is not a law of nature but a specially designed man-made law. As if it weren't enough to rule over the top of the food chain without strength, claws, or sharp teeth, humans have also made themselves masters of who gets to live where on this Earth. Humans, out of all of us, drive creatures out of whole continents with the sole justification that they "don't belong" there. As if humans belong anywhere!

One can hope, humans say. I've always liked that expression. It's the human version of "you never know when there might be a treat in store," in a way. And the good thing about treats, and the good thing about hope, is that it doesn't take much.

Some escaped.

Two little words in the Chief's hand. The best ones he wrote, if you ask me. There were some dogs who just disappeared during the march to the South Pole. They wised up, I'm guessing, and ran away. "Enough of this." The wolf's motto. Nobody knows where the escaped dogs went. They probably died, of course they died, froze to death if they didn't starve to death first.

But as Mrs. Thorkildsen would say:

Can you be sure?

The Greenland dog thrives in Antarctic conditions, better than any animal on four legs who has attempted to live in such conditions. There's no lack of food, either. The perverse penguins could use a few more natural enemies, I'm sure. They need to pull themselves together, plain and simple, and you can say whatever you want about having a wolf on your heels, but it seems to wake you up.

The escaped dogs probably found a good life with a steady diet of penguins and seals, and they probably mated incessantly and grew into many packs who live scattered all over the South Pole, day after day, under the cover of winter darkness. Wasn't that something the scientists said? That they had no idea how rich the animal life might be, down there in the winter?

Lupus antarcticus howls at the aurora australis.

Let's say that.

42

ONE DAY WE WERE ON our way home after a successful raid at the Center, and Mrs. Thorkildsen accidentally stopped and read a sign someone had been thoughtless enough to hang on the lamppost by the bus stop. Since dogs famously can't read, I had to ask Mrs. Thorkildsen what the poster literally said.

"It's about a cat who's missing."

"I doubt that," I said, "it's probably just vanished."

"The cat's name is Tassen," Mrs. Thorkildsen said.

"Pardon me?" I said.

"It actually says that," Mrs. Thorkildsen said.

"There must be some mistake," I said. "Tassen isn't a cat's name. It must be a typo. Tassan, maybe. That sounds more like a cat's name, don't you think? A little more exotic."

"Tassen the Bengal cat," Mrs. Thorkildsen insisted.

It was only later that evening, as I was rolling around in a pile of clothing in the laundry room, that it hit me like a lightning bolt:

Maybe I'm a cat!

I realize it may sound silly, but in that moment, wrapped in the scent of Mrs. Thorkildsen's dirty clothes, it seemed like an acute existential crisis:

How do I know I'm not a cat? Mrs. Thorkildsen gives me dog food, talks to me like a dog, and treats me like a dog, but what if she's only part of a big conspiracy? These are the kinds of thoughts that can make a dog discouraged, depressed, and lethargic.

Still, I got back on my feet, literally and figuratively. It was night now, but I was wide awake. Normally it doesn't bother me if I can't sleep. I can sleep anytime. And the next best thing in the world, after sleeping in the laundry, is lying awake in the laundry. But that night I kept tossing and turning. Something told me I had to go out to the kitchen, but when I got there, all I could think about was needing to go into the hallway, and once I was there I was told to go into the bathroom again, and it went on like that for a few rounds until I forced myself out of the pattern and wandered into the living room.

On the floor in front of the fireplace was the last paper dog. The Colonel. All the others had migrated up to the heavenly mantel. Standing there on its own, it seemed neither threatening nor strong. Truth be told, it seemed a little feeble. Alone. I get scared when I'm alone, too. Mrs. Thorkildsen, too, I'd imagine. I don't know, since I've never seen what she's like when I'm not there, but I think she'd be scared.

We dogs may have our shortcomings when it comes to shoes and moral concepts, I don't deny that. What love really is, or what it's supposed to be good for, I'm not sure. I'll probably never learn to tell time or drive a car. I'll probably always leave behind a trail of dirt, and there isn't a dog that doesn't shed. Non-shedding dogs are an urban legend. But when there are no more sleds to pull, invaders to attack, prey to hunt, what do you do then? Who are you then?

The best thing you can aspire to in this world is company. Whether it's for pleasure or pain, a crowning or an execution: everything is better with company. You might say it all went to hell with Mrs. Thorkildsen, but you know what? It could have been worse, because Mrs. Thorkildsen had me to keep her company. And I had her. That's what we had in common, she and me, what bound us together. We were company.

• • •

There's someone behind the car!

I'm in a devil's bind now, locked inside the car. An alien being is rummaging around in the back of the car, scraping and rocking it up and down while I frantically try to come up with a reaction. I don't have time, I'm more and more paralyzed by fear until it all ends with the car door opening and I think it's all over, but it's only the Puppy—thank God it's the Puppy, I should have known it would be the Puppy, and I tell him exactly how deeply loved and missed he is.

He ignores me, so chills run down my spine. To the untrained eye he might seem unfriendly but, believe me, the Puppy isn't unfriendly, he's just the *boss*. He's just the kind of guy who doesn't need to yank the leash to make you do what he wants.

It's not so important that we talk. There aren't actually that many situations that require talking, are there? A dog and his master don't need anything in common beyond a shared goal, and it's enough if one of them knows it, as long as the two of them know to stick together. Traveling is often better in silence.

In my life with Mrs. Thorkildsen, there were endless decisions that had to be made, but in this new life I think I can leave it to the Puppy to make most of the decisions. Maybe we'll eventually get to a point where he can deal with the Bitch with my help, make her see me as "intelligent and eager to learn," too. Maybe there's a future for me on the couch, on the white couch.

I'm making that mistake again. Reflecting and planning for something other than what actually *is*. I have to learn to live in the here and now with my whole self and all that I am. I am a dog! I know that. But my instincts may have been slightly dulled by a life with an eternally full food bowl. The house dog's misfortune, but it wouldn't be to the dog's advantage if he knew about these dangers as he wagged and said yes to everything that appeared in the bowl. "If the dog is happy, everything is fine." Ignorance is bliss, they say. That's the animal's privilege. The human's privilege is called knowledge.

I can no longer trust my tired old snout, but I swear we're headed for the woods.

I don't know if we're on our way into the same hunting grounds as the last time we entered the woods, but as I said, it smells familiar, so the question is only of geographical interest, and geography is of no interest in a world where north is south and up is down.

My impulses and instincts beg me to jump, scurry, and run out into the bushes, dance and bark at the top of my lungs

We're back. The eternal, unbeatable symbiosis of man and dog. Our collective efforts, talents, and tools make us a formidable enemy for all the world's creatures. I have the instincts, the senses, the endurance, and the energy. He has opposable thumbs.

Awake and alert, but gentle as if I were walking in the park with Mrs. Thorkildsen, I slowly plod along the path. My best foot forward, my tail behind me.

Life is good.

ACKNOWLEDGMENTS

Thanks to:

Halfdan W. Freihow, Chandler Crawford,
Lasse Kolsrud, J. Basil Cowlishaw, Øyvind
Pharo, Lars Dahlin, and Ledig House/
Art Omi in Ghent, New York.

A NOTE FROM THE TRANSLATOR

The key to getting *Good Dogs Don't Make It to the South Pole* just right in English was finding the voice of its narrator. Having never translated a nonhuman speaker before, this took some time. Tassen is naive but skeptical, thoughtful but impulsive, frustrated but fascinated with the human world around him. I had to figure out how an overpowering sense of smell, a single whiff of wolf imbued with staggering primordial history, would translate into English diction, syntax, and figurative language.

Norwegian words are longer; the language is more prone to neologism in a way that is closer to German than English. In contemporary Norwegian literature, English has been increasingly entering the slang, so I had to figure out how to differentiate between younger characters, who speak more casually and use more Anglicisms, and Mrs. Thorkildsen, who never leaves a prim, buttoned-up register, even in moments of deep weakness, fear, and disorientation.

Hans-Olav Thyvold shows great attention and care to every vernacular detail. From polar fantasies to woodsy rambles to concentrated flavors of coffee, venison, and hard liquor. This is a deeply Norwegian novel with uber-Norwegian characters. And it is a universal story of aging, addiction, grief, and friendship. In it, human emotions are at first experienced obliquely through Tassen's eyes. Eventually, we gain an insight into the human psyche through his voice that we wouldn't have seen through a human narrator. The narrative self is simpler and more central, but dissolves faster, and it was fun trying to render those quick slides from solipsism into selflessness in English.

Hans-Olav, his agent Chandler Crawford, and I had several conversations about our hero's name. "Tassen" is an Everydog name in Norwegian, but "Fido" felt too cartoonish, so at first I tried "Buddy" to match his friendly, happy-go-lucky nature. Hans-Olav wanted to retain the double consonant of the Norwegian name but wished for something a bit more puny and forlorn, a little less confident. We tried "Toby" but it didn't feel quite right. The closest English translation of the onomatopoeic verb "tasse" might be "to plod," but the motion it implies is softer, sweeter than trudging or slogging. It is the movement of a truly faithful, if flawed, companion through the house—the kind of relationship we seek in our pets as they stand by us through short, tumultuous seasons of life. Ultimately, we decided that Tassen wanted us to leave his name as is. It seemed to me, in Emily Apter's words, "something stubbornly resistant to equivalency and substitution . . . a boundary line of the sacred, that issues the edict 'Do not translate here! Thou shalt not translate me!'"* (Tassen does have a flair for the dramatic.) His name marks both the piece of Norwegian-ness that this novel hopefully retains in translation, and the constantly intriguing mystery of what might be going on inside a dog's simple but fascinating mind.

—Marie Ostby

---

* Apter, Emily. "'Doing Things with Untranslatables': The Problem of Translation and Untranslatability in the Comparative Humanities." Transdisciplinarity and the Humanities: Problems, Methods, Histories, Concepts, 25 January 2012, Kingston University, London. Workshop 1.

Here ends Hans-Olav Thyvold's
Good Dogs Don't Make It to the South Pole.

The first edition of this book was printed and
bound at LSC Communications in
Harrisonburg, Virginia, June 2020.

A NOTE ON THE TYPE

The text of this novel was set in Adobe Garamond Pro, a typeface designed in 1989 by Robert Slimbach. It's based on two distinctive examples of the French Renaissance style, a Roman type by Claude Garamond (1499–1561) and an Italic type by Robert Granjon (1513–1590), and was developed after Slimbach studied the fifteenth-century equipment at the Plantin-Moretus Museum in Antwerp, Belgium. Adobe Garamond Pro is considered to faithfully capture the original Garamond's grace and clarity, and is used extensively in books for its elegance and readability.

HarperVia

An imprint dedicated to publishing international voices,
offering readers a chance to encounter other lives and other
points of view via the language of the imagination.